ZEGAS

MICHEL FIFFE

FANTAGRAPHICS BOOKS
SEATTLE, WASHINGTON

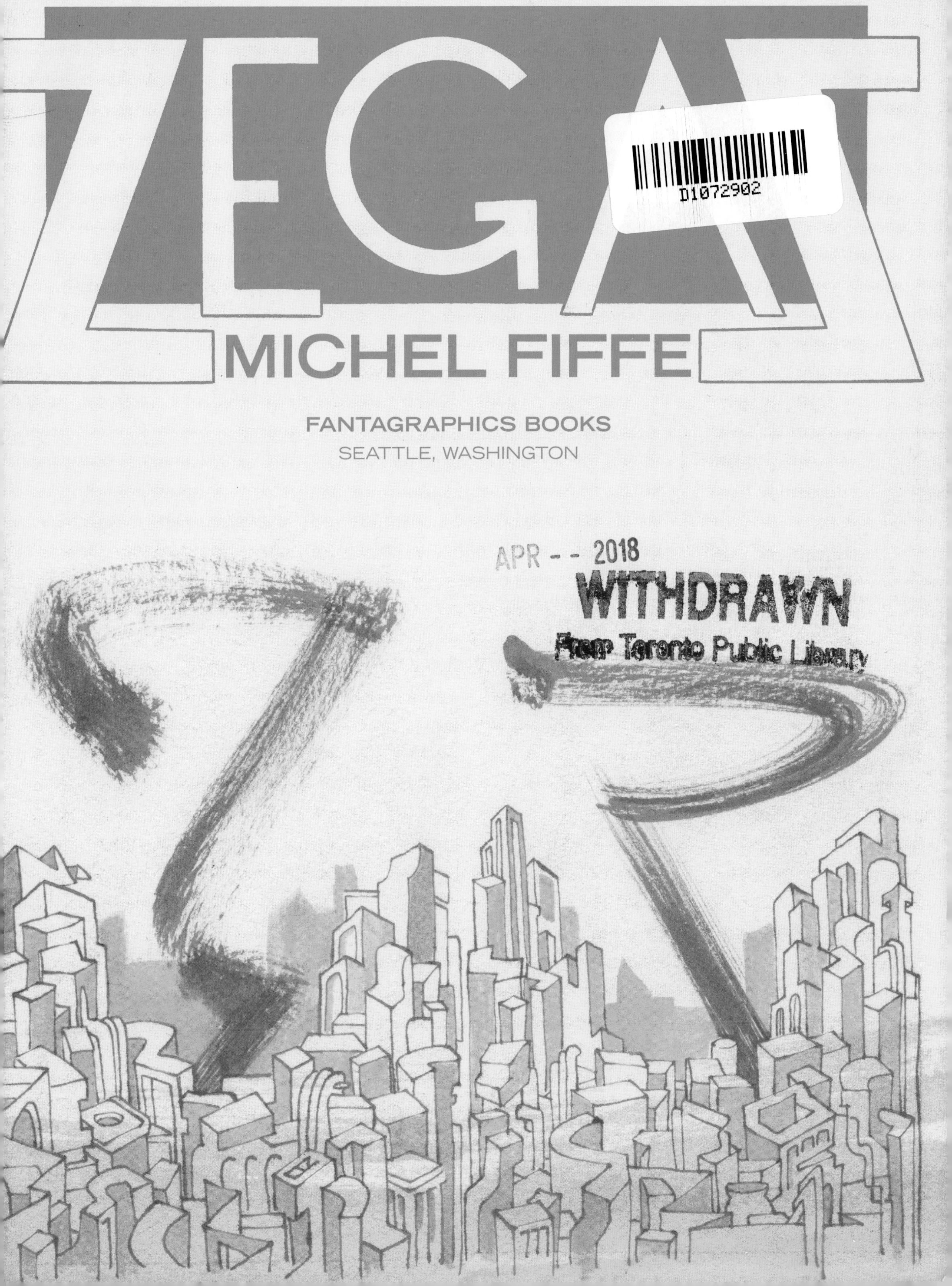

FOR KAT

FANTAGRAPHICS BOOKS
7563 LAKE CITY WAY NE
SEATTLE, WA 98115

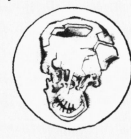

CONTAINS MATERIAL ORIGINALLY PUBLISHED
FROM 2009-2012 BY COPRA PRESS AS
ZEGAS #0-2. THANKS TO BRYAN GALATIS, GPMC.

EDITOR: JASON T. MILES
ASSOCIATE PUBLISHER: ERIC REYNOLDS
PUBLISHER: GARY GROTH

FIRST FANTAGRAPHICS BOOKS EDITION: NOVEMBER 2017
ISBN: 978-1-68396-065-2
LIBRARY OF CONGRESS
CONTROL #2017938240

PRINTED IN CHINA

ZEGAS

FEB - - 2018

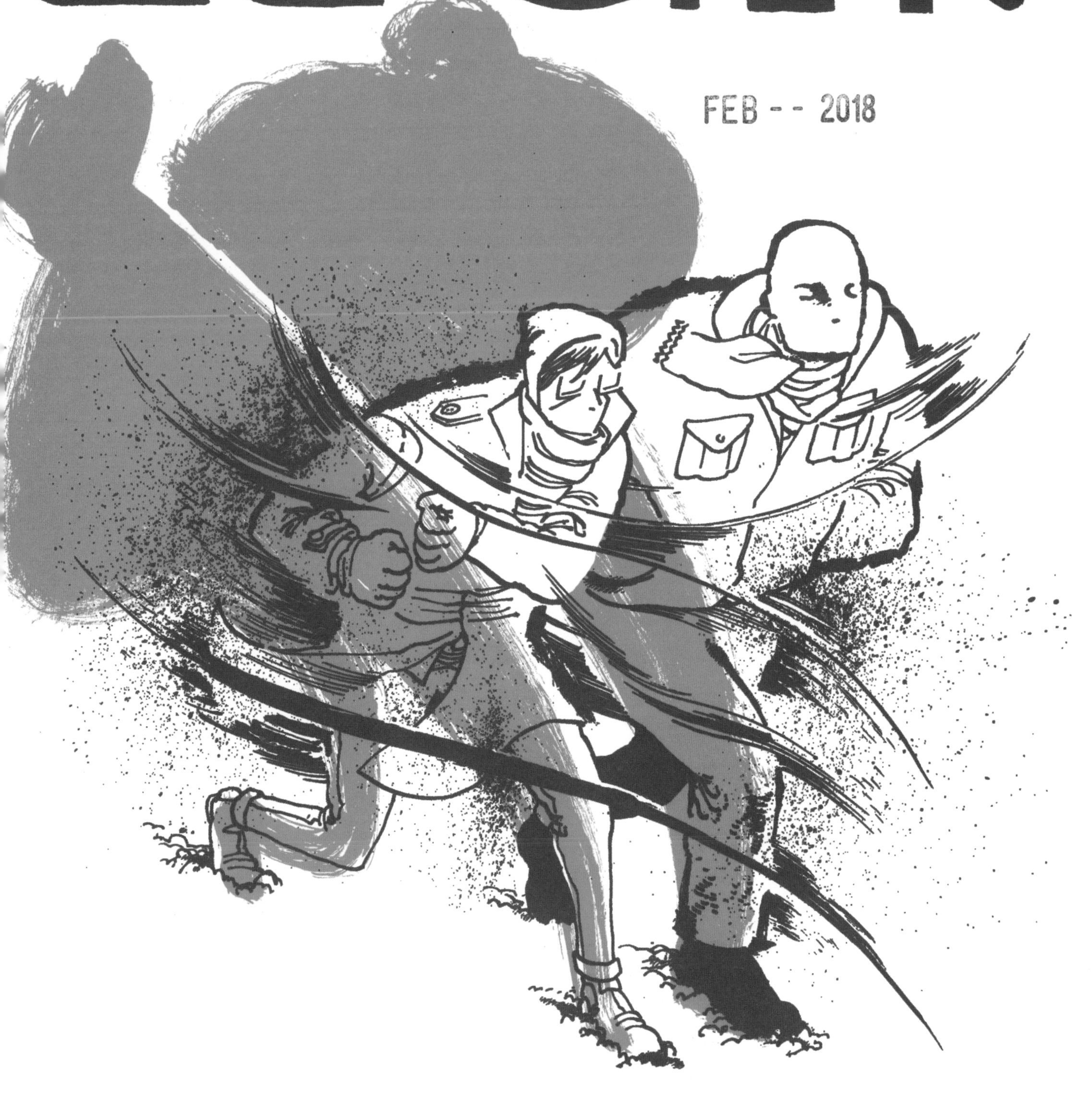

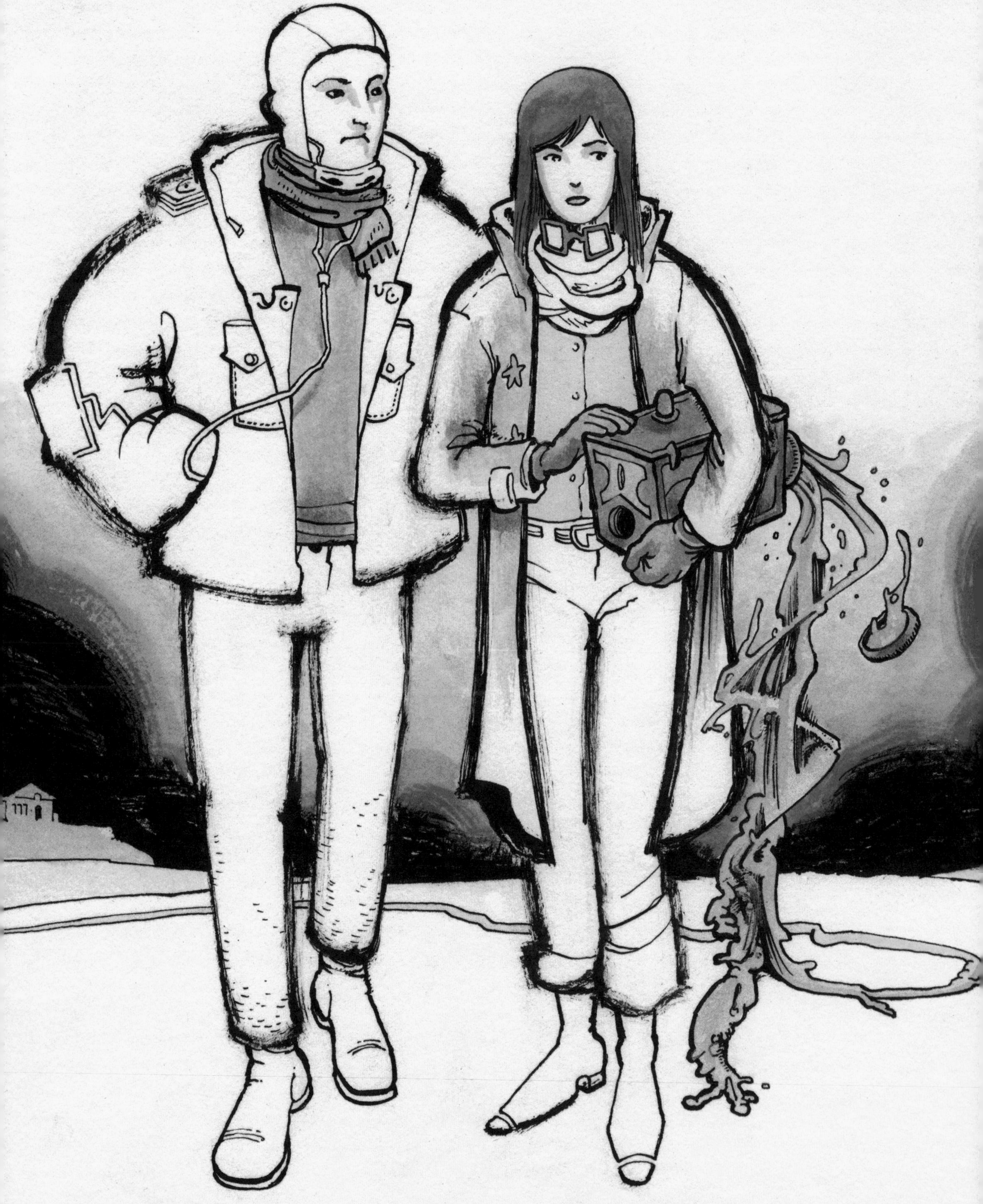

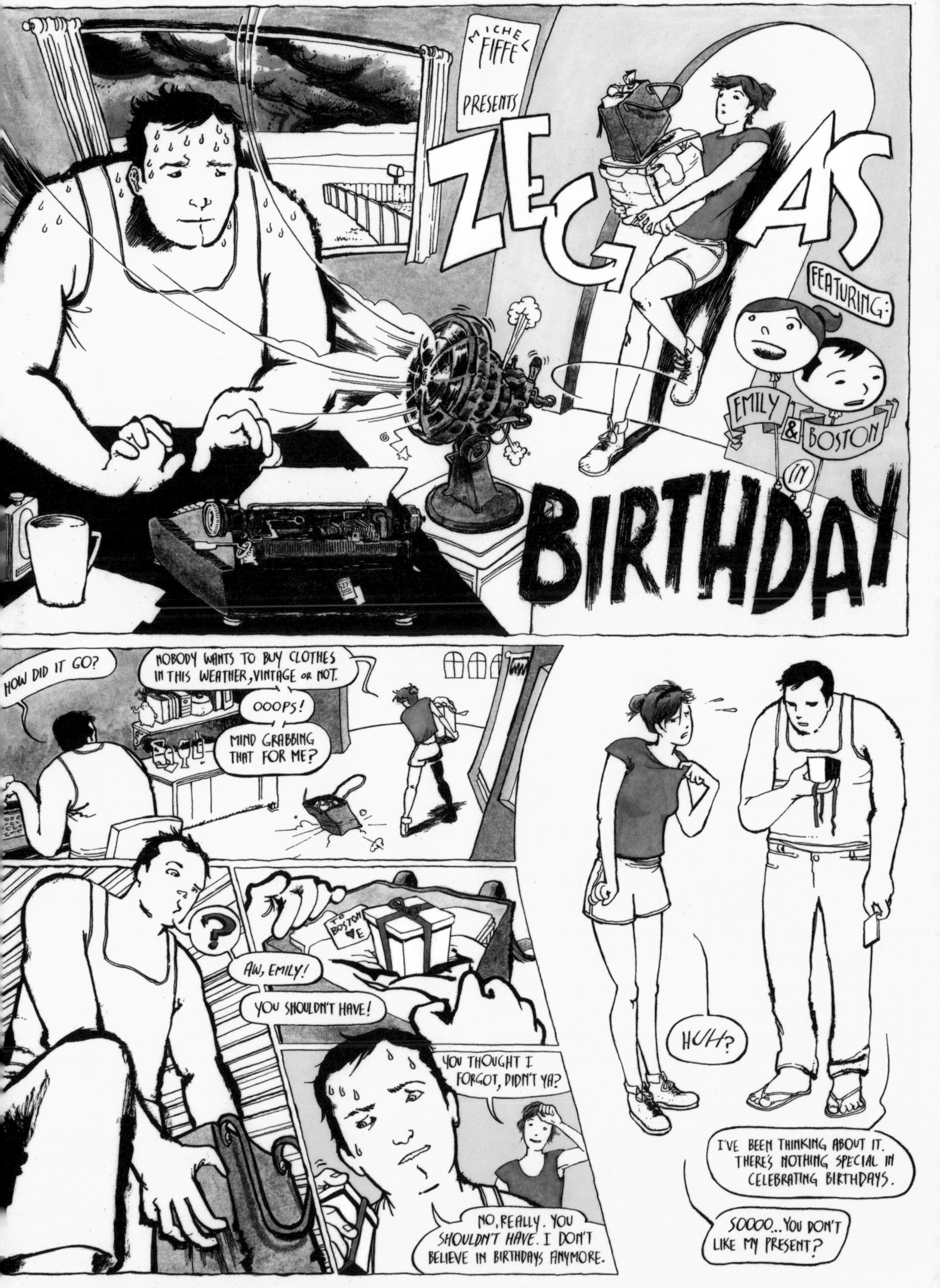
MICHEL FIFFE PRESENTS
ZEGAS
FEATURING:
EMILY & BOSTON
IN
BIRTHDAY
HOW DID IT GO?
NOBODY WANTS TO BUY CLOTHES IN THIS WEATHER, VINTAGE OR NOT.
OOOPS!
MIND GRABBING THAT FOR ME?
?
TO BOSTON ♥ E
AW, EMILY!
YOU SHOULDN'T HAVE!
YOU THOUGHT I FORGOT, DIDN'T YA?
NO, REALLY. YOU SHOULDN'T HAVE. I DON'T BELIEVE IN BIRTHDAYS ANYMORE.
HUH?
I'VE BEEN THINKING ABOUT IT. THERE'S NOTHING SPECIAL IN CELEBRATING BIRTHDAYS.
SOOOO... YOU DON'T LIKE MY PRESENT?

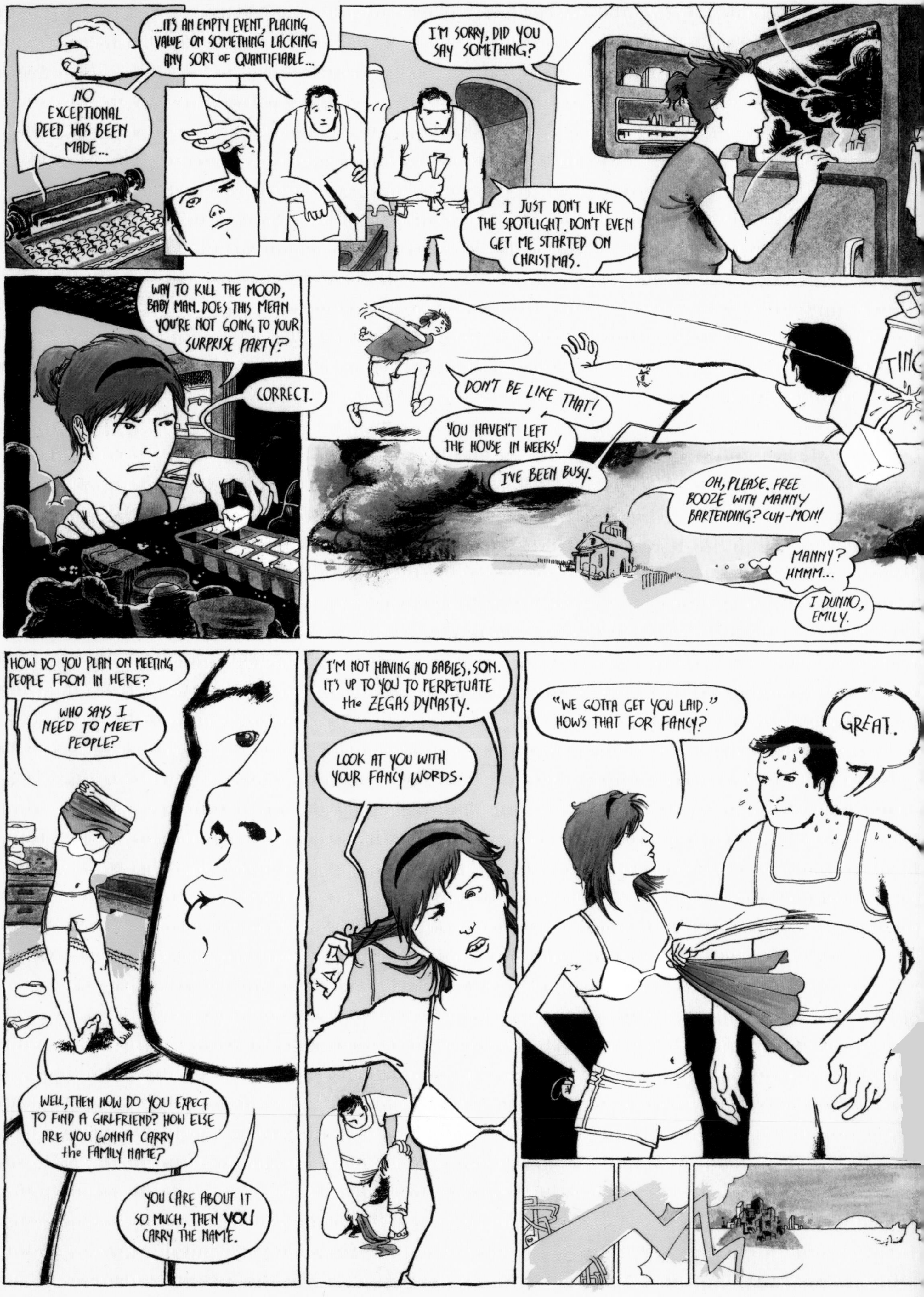

...IT'S AN EMPTY EVENT, PLACING VALUE ON SOMETHING LACKING ANY SORT OF QUANTIFIABLE...
NO EXCEPTIONAL DEED HAS BEEN MADE...
I'M SORRY, DID YOU SAY SOMETHING?
I JUST DON'T LIKE THE SPOTLIGHT. DON'T EVEN GET ME STARTED ON CHRISTMAS.
WAY TO KILL THE MOOD, BABY MAN. DOES THIS MEAN YOU'RE NOT GOING TO YOUR SURPRISE PARTY?
CORRECT.
DON'T BE LIKE THAT!
TING
YOU HAVEN'T LEFT THE HOUSE IN WEEKS!
I'VE BEEN BUSY.
OH, PLEASE. FREE BOOZE WITH MANNY BARTENDING? CUH-MON!
MANNY? HMMM...
I DUNNO, EMILY.
HOW DO YOU PLAN ON MEETING PEOPLE FROM IN HERE?
WHO SAYS I NEED TO MEET PEOPLE?
WELL, THEN HOW DO YOU EXPECT TO FIND A GIRLFRIEND? HOW ELSE ARE YOU GONNA CARRY the FAMILY NAME?
YOU CARE ABOUT IT SO MUCH, THEN YOU CARRY THE NAME.
I'M NOT HAVING NO BABIES, SON. IT'S UP TO YOU TO PERPETUATE the ZEGAS DYNASTY.
LOOK AT YOU WITH YOUR FANCY WORDS.
"WE GOTTA GET YOU LAID." HOW'S THAT FOR FANCY?
GREAT.

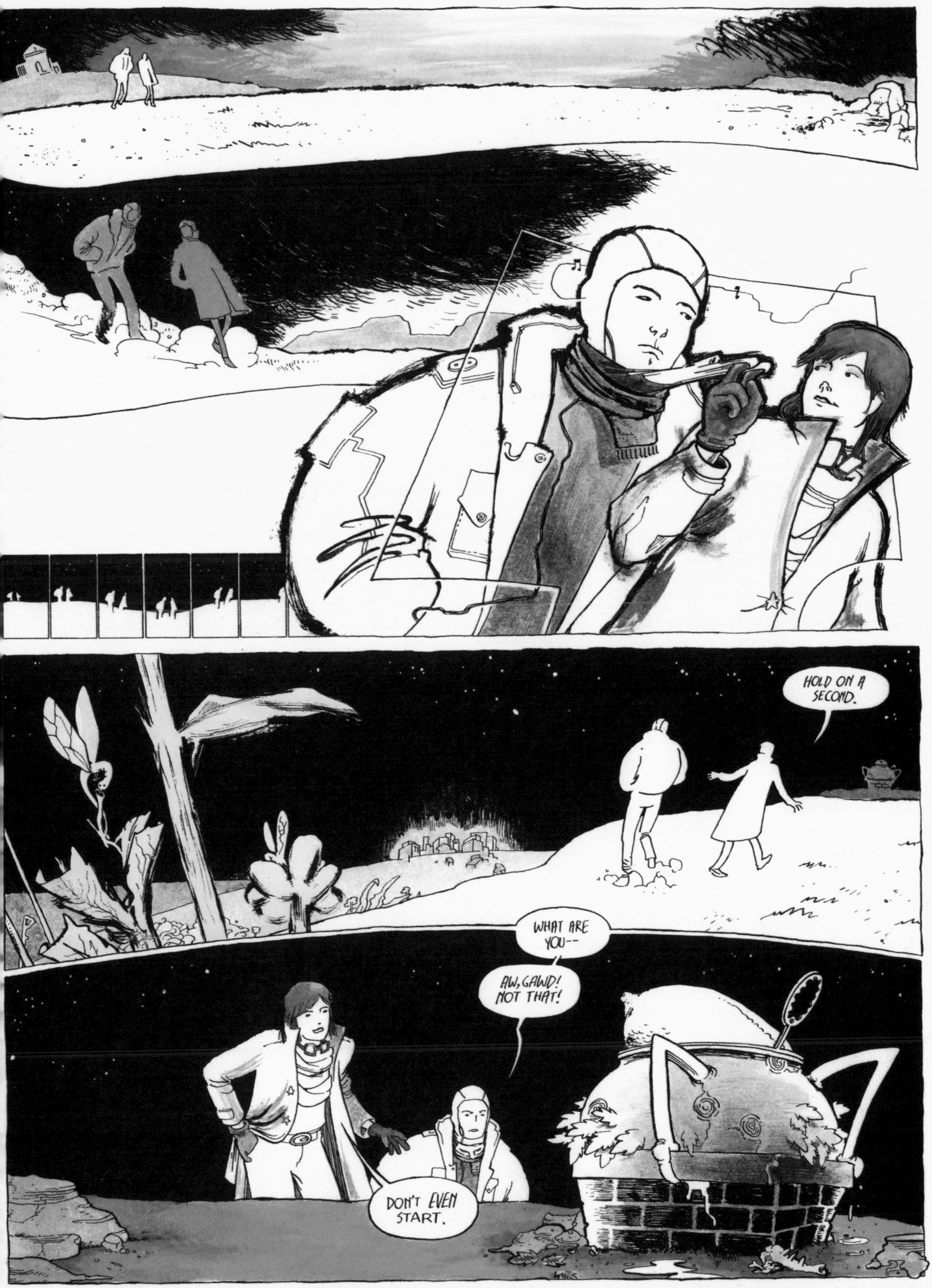
HOLD ON A SECOND.
WHAT ARE YOU--
AW, GAWD! NOT THAT!
DON'T EVEN START.

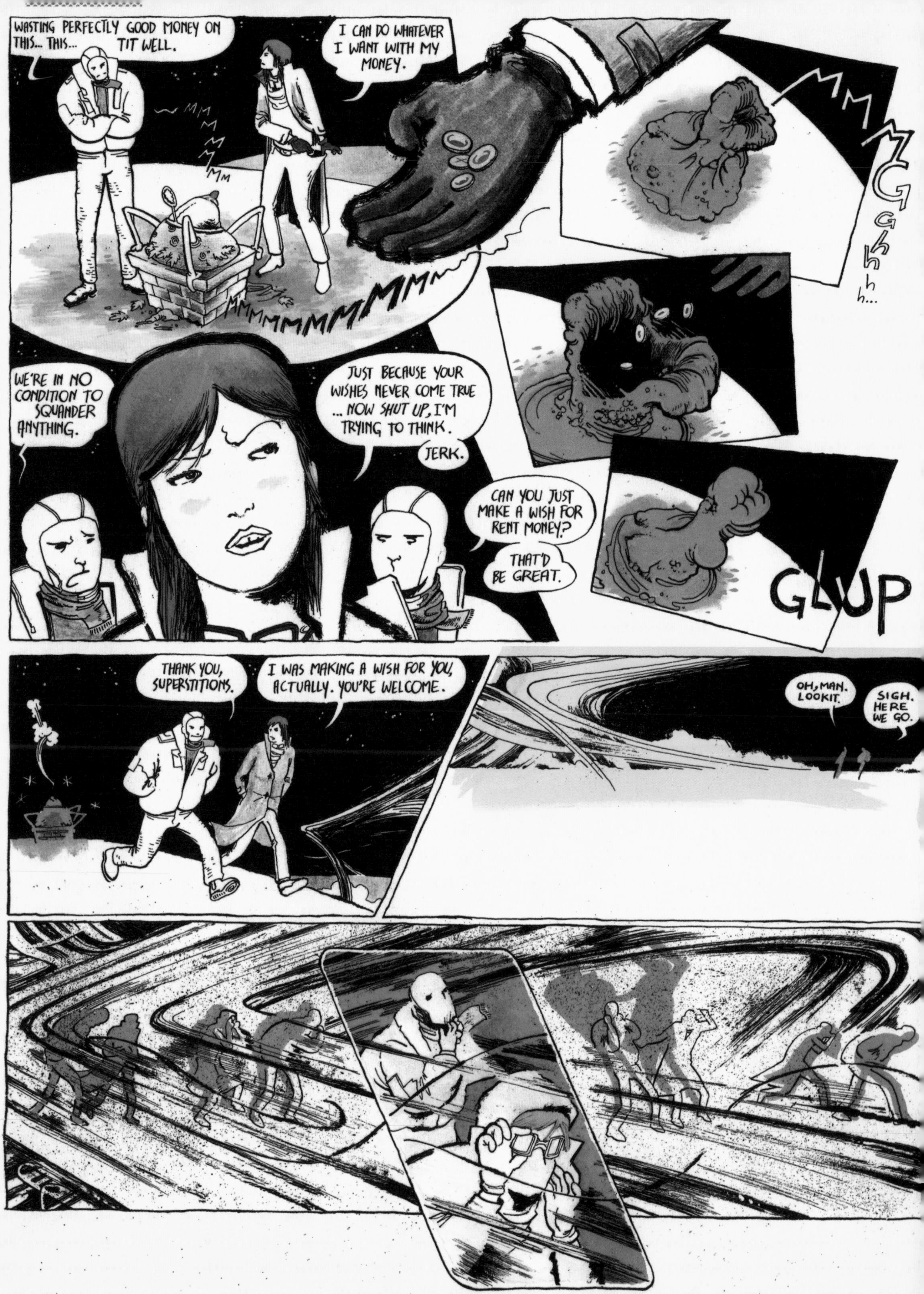

WASTING PERFECTLY GOOD MONEY ON THIS... THIS... TIT WELL.
I CAN DO WHATEVER I WANT WITH MY MONEY.
MMMMMMMMMMMMMMMMM
MMMGGhhhh...
WE'RE IN NO CONDITION TO SQUANDER ANYTHING.
JUST BECAUSE YOUR WISHES NEVER COME TRUE ... NOW SHUT UP, I'M TRYING TO THINK.
JERK.
CAN YOU JUST MAKE A WISH FOR RENT MONEY?
THAT'D BE GREAT.
GLUP
THANK YOU, SUPERSTITIONS.
I WAS MAKING A WISH FOR YOU, ACTUALLY. YOU'RE WELCOME.
OH, MAN. LOOKIT.
SIGH. HERE WE GO.

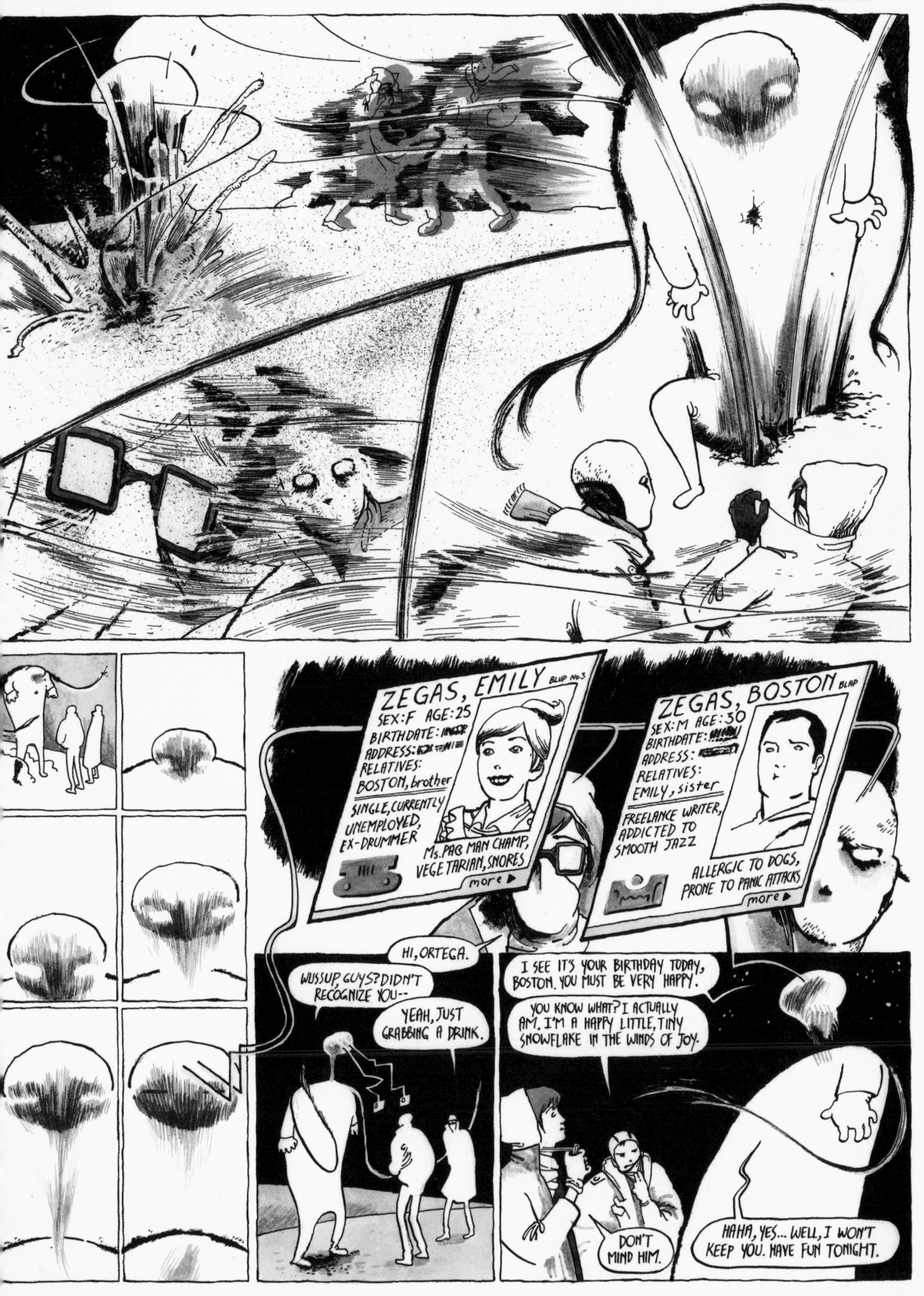
ZEGAS, EMILY
BLUP No.3
SEX: F AGE: 25
BIRTHDATE: [redacted]
ADDRESS: [redacted]
RELATIVES:
BOSTON, brother
SINGLE, CURRENTLY UNEMPLOYED, EX-DRUMMER
Ms. PAC MAN CHAMP, VEGETARIAN, SNORES
more ▶
ZEGAS, BOSTON
BLAP
SEX: M AGE: 30
BIRTHDATE: [redacted]
ADDRESS: [redacted]
RELATIVES:
EMILY, sister
FREELANCE WRITER, ADDICTED TO SMOOTH JAZZ
ALLERGIC TO DOGS, PRONE TO PANIC ATTACKS
more ▶
HI, ORTEGA.
WUSSUP, GUYS? DIDN'T RECOGNIZE YOU--
YEAH, JUST GRABBING A DRINK.
I SEE IT'S YOUR BIRTHDAY TODAY, BOSTON. YOU MUST BE VERY HAPPY.
YOU KNOW WHAT? I ACTUALLY AM. I'M A HAPPY LITTLE, TINY SNOWFLAKE IN THE WINDS OF JOY.
DON'T MIND HIM.
HAHA, YES... WELL, I WON'T KEEP YOU. HAVE FUN TONIGHT.

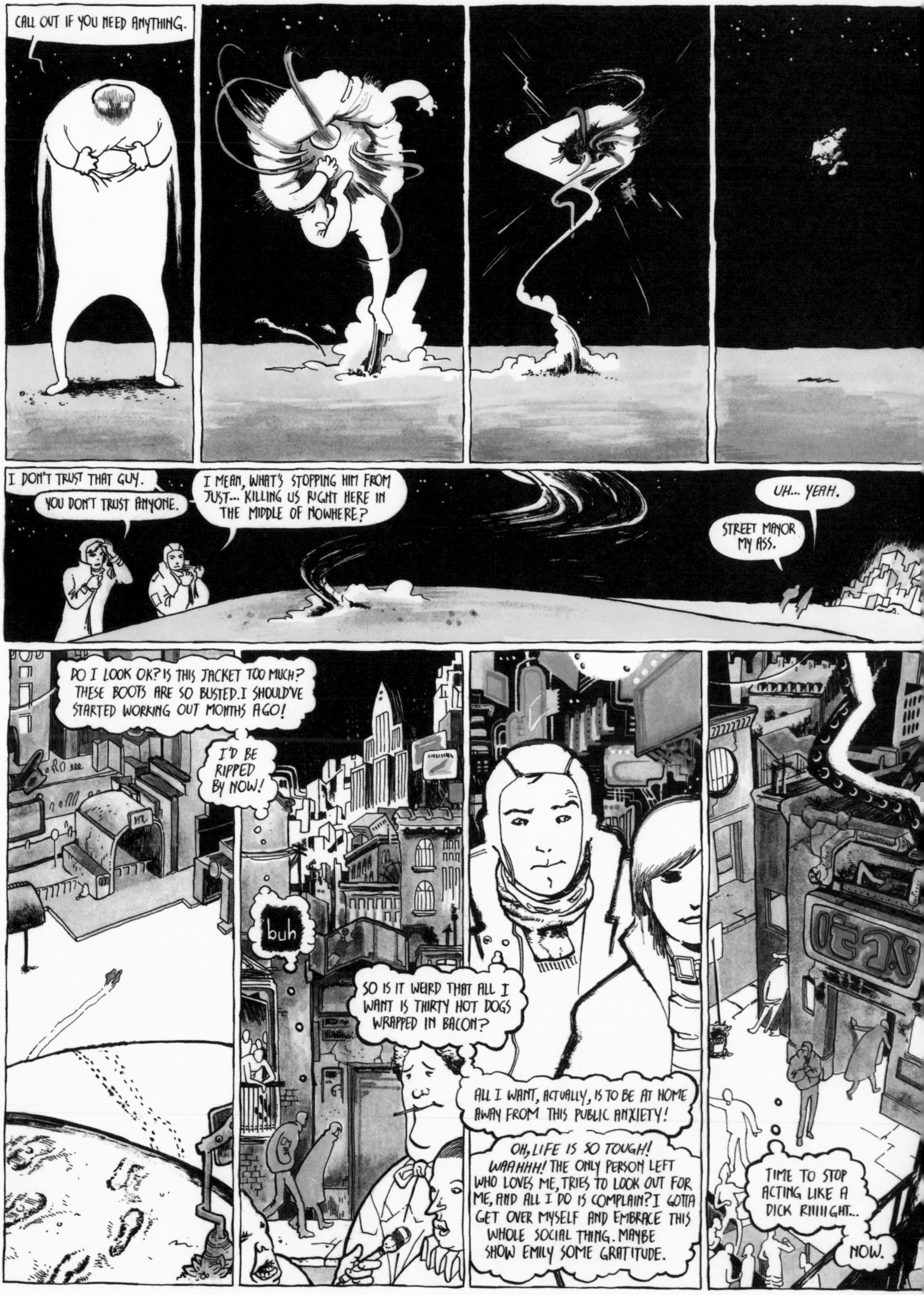

CALL OUT IF YOU NEED ANYTHING.
I DON'T TRUST THAT GUY.
YOU DON'T TRUST ANYONE.
I MEAN, WHAT'S STOPPING HIM FROM JUST... KILLING US RIGHT HERE IN THE MIDDLE OF NOWHERE?
UH... YEAH.
STREET MAYOR MY ASS.
DO I LOOK OK? IS THIS JACKET TOO MUCH? THESE BOOTS ARE SO BUSTED. I SHOULD'VE STARTED WORKING OUT MONTHS AGO!
I'D BE RIPPED BY NOW!
buh
SO IS IT WEIRD THAT ALL I WANT IS THIRTY HOT DOGS WRAPPED IN BACON?
ALL I WANT, ACTUALLY, IS TO BE AT HOME AWAY FROM THIS PUBLIC ANXIETY!
OH, LIFE IS SO TOUGH! WAAHHH! THE ONLY PERSON LEFT WHO LOVES ME, TRIES TO LOOK OUT FOR ME, AND ALL I DO IS COMPLAIN? I GOTTA GET OVER MYSELF AND EMBRACE THIS WHOLE SOCIAL THING. MAYBE SHOW EMILY SOME GRATITUDE.
TIME TO STOP ACTING LIKE A DICK RIIIIGHT...
NOW.

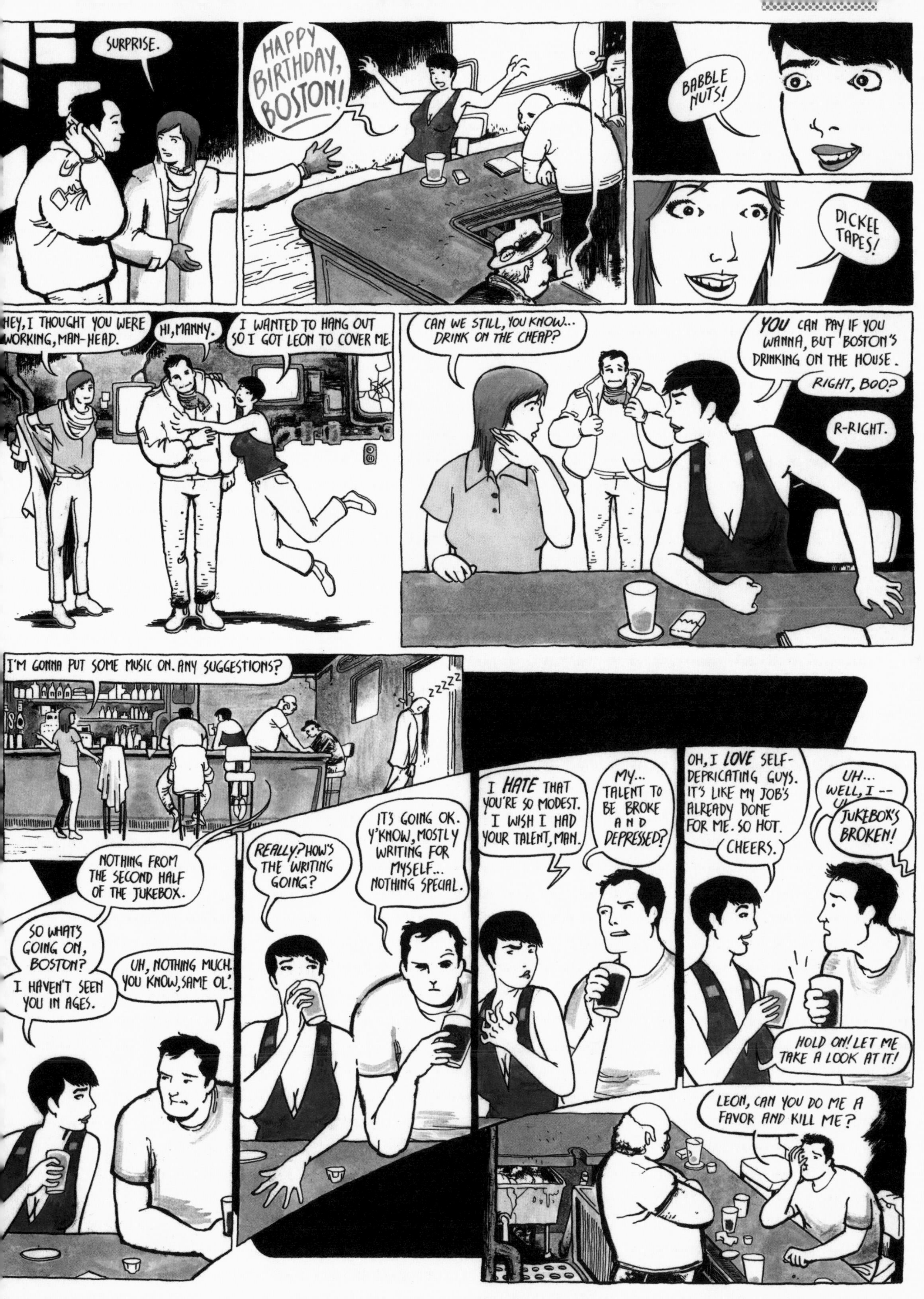
SURPRISE.
HAPPY BIRTHDAY, BOSTON!
BABBLE NUTS!
DICKEE TAPES!
HEY, I THOUGHT YOU WERE WORKING, MAN-HEAD.
HI, MANNY.
I WANTED TO HANG OUT SO I GOT LEON TO COVER ME.
CAN WE STILL, YOU KNOW... DRINK ON THE CHEAP?
YOU CAN PAY IF YOU WANNA, BUT BOSTON'S DRINKING ON THE HOUSE.
RIGHT, BOO?
R-RIGHT.
I'M GONNA PUT SOME MUSIC ON. ANY SUGGESTIONS?
ZZZZZ
NOTHING FROM THE SECOND HALF OF THE JUKEBOX.
SO WHAT'S GOING ON, BOSTON? I HAVEN'T SEEN YOU IN AGES.
UH, NOTHING MUCH. YOU KNOW, SAME OL'.
REALLY? HOW'S THE WRITING GOING?
IT'S GOING OK. Y'KNOW, MOSTLY WRITING FOR MYSELF... NOTHING SPECIAL.
I HATE THAT YOU'RE SO MODEST. I WISH I HAD YOUR TALENT, MAN.
MY... TALENT TO BE BROKE AND DEPRESSED?
OH, I LOVE SELF-DEPRICATING GUYS. IT'S LIKE MY JOB'S ALREADY DONE FOR ME. SO HOT.
CHEERS.
UH... WELL, I --
JUKEBOX'S BROKEN!
HOLD ON! LET ME TAKE A LOOK AT IT!
LEON, CAN YOU DO ME A FAVOR AND KILL ME?

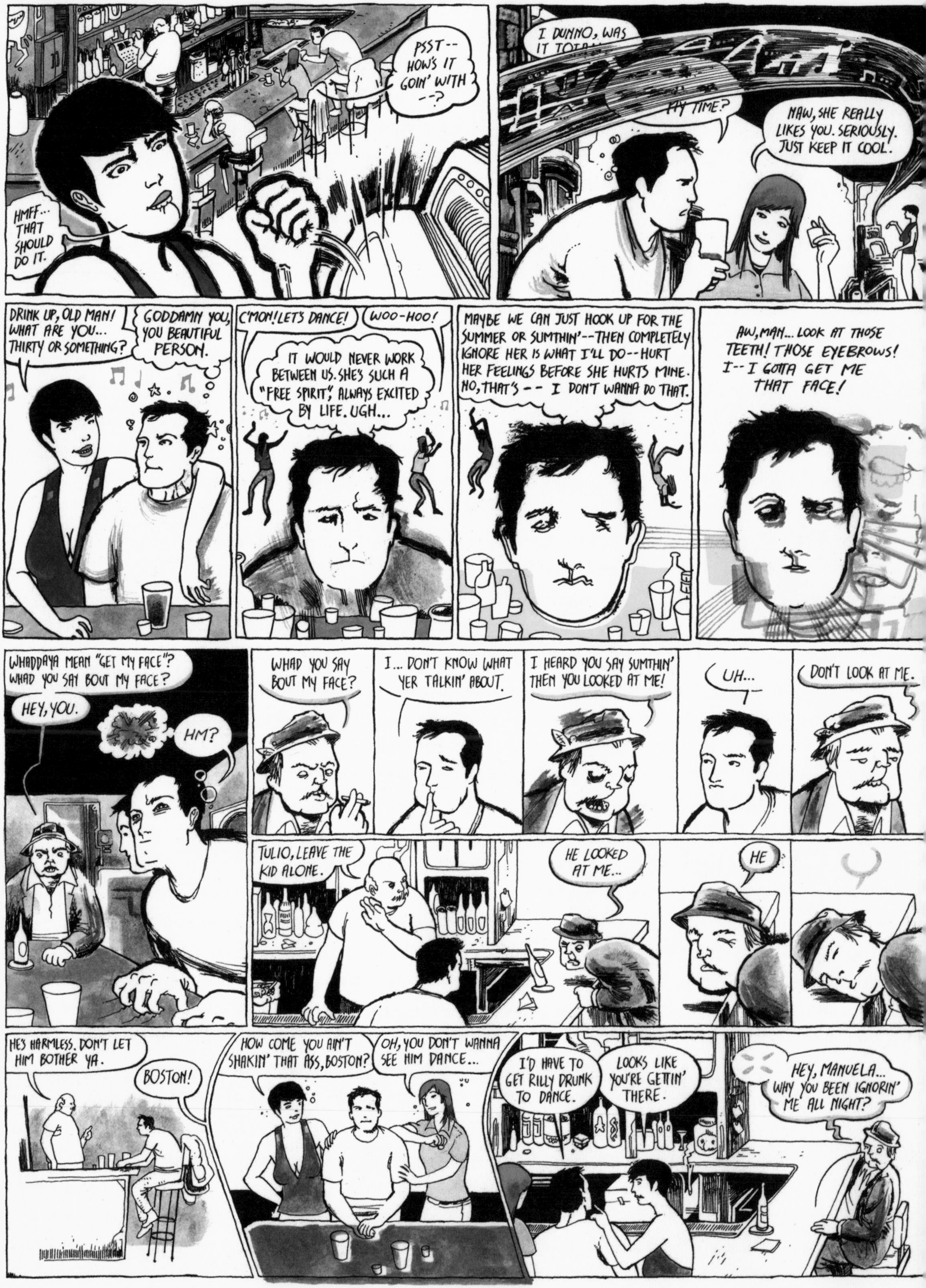
PSST -- HOW'S IT GOIN' WITH --?
HMFF... THAT SHOULD DO IT.
I DUNNO, WAS IT TOTA...
...Y TIME?
NAW, SHE REALLY LIKES YOU. SERIOUSLY. JUST KEEP IT COOL.
DRINK UP, OLD MAN! WHAT ARE YOU... THIRTY OR SOMETHING?
GODDAMN YOU, YOU BEAUTIFUL PERSON.
C'MON! LET'S DANCE!
WOO-HOO!
IT WOULD NEVER WORK BETWEEN US. SHE'S SUCH A "FREE SPIRIT," ALWAYS EXCITED BY LIFE. UGH...
MAYBE WE CAN JUST HOOK UP FOR THE SUMMER OR SUMTHIN'--THEN COMPLETELY IGNORE HER IS WHAT I'LL DO--HURT HER FEELINGS BEFORE SHE HURTS MINE. NO, THAT'S -- I DON'T WANNA DO THAT.
AW, MAN... LOOK AT THOSE TEETH! THOSE EYEBROWS! I-- I GOTTA GET ME THAT FACE!
WHADDAYA MEAN "GET MY FACE"? WHAD YOU SAY BOUT MY FACE?
HEY, YOU.
HM?
WHAD YOU SAY BOUT MY FACE?
I... DON'T KNOW WHAT YER TALKIN' ABOUT.
I HEARD YOU SAY SUMTHIN' THEN YOU LOOKED AT ME!
UH...
DON'T LOOK AT ME.
TULIO, LEAVE THE KID ALONE.
HE LOOKED AT ME...
HE
HE'S HARMLESS. DON'T LET HIM BOTHER YA.
BOSTON!
HOW COME YOU AIN'T SHAKIN' THAT ASS, BOSTON?
OH, YOU DON'T WANNA SEE HIM DANCE...
I'D HAVE TO GET RILLY DRUNK TO DANCE.
LOOKS LIKE YOU'RE GETTIN' THERE.
HEY, MANUELA... WHY YOU BEEN IGNORIN' ME ALL NIGHT?

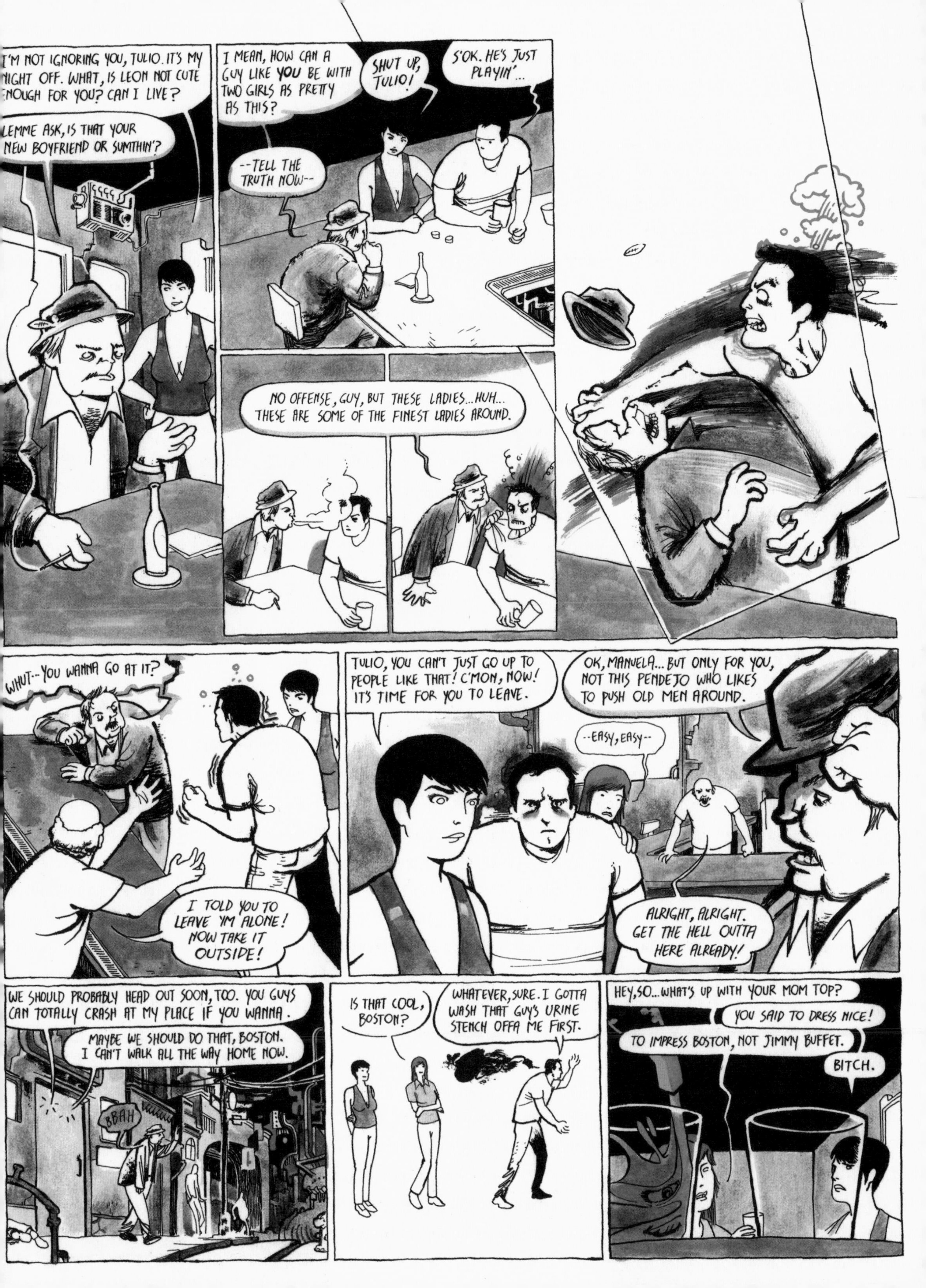
I'M NOT IGNORING YOU, TULIO. IT'S MY NIGHT OFF. WHAT, IS LEON NOT CUTE ENOUGH FOR YOU? CAN I LIVE?
LEMME ASK, IS THAT YOUR NEW BOYFRIEND OR SUMTHIN'?
I MEAN, HOW CAN A GUY LIKE YOU BE WITH TWO GIRLS AS PRETTY AS THIS?
--TELL THE TRUTH NOW--
SHUT UP, TULIO!
S'OK. HE'S JUST PLAYIN'...
NO OFFENSE, GUY, BUT THESE LADIES...HUH... THESE ARE SOME OF THE FINEST LADIES AROUND.
WHUT--YOU WANNA GO AT IT?
I TOLD YOU TO LEAVE 'YM ALONE! NOW TAKE IT OUTSIDE!
TULIO, YOU CAN'T JUST GO UP TO PEOPLE LIKE THAT! C'MON, NOW! IT'S TIME FOR YOU TO LEAVE.
OK, MANUELA... BUT ONLY FOR YOU, NOT THIS PENDEJO WHO LIKES TO PUSH OLD MEN AROUND.
--EASY, EASY--
ALRIGHT, ALRIGHT. GET THE HELL OUTTA HERE ALREADY!
WE SHOULD PROBABLY HEAD OUT SOON, TOO. YOU GUYS CAN TOTALLY CRASH AT MY PLACE IF YOU WANNA.
MAYBE WE SHOULD DO THAT, BOSTON. I CAN'T WALK ALL THE WAY HOME NOW.
BBAH
IS THAT COOL, BOSTON?
WHATEVER, SURE. I GOTTA WASH THAT GUY'S URINE STENCH OFFA ME FIRST.
HEY, SO...WHAT'S UP WITH YOUR MOM TOP?
YOU SAID TO DRESS NICE!
TO IMPRESS BOSTON, NOT JIMMY BUFFET.
BITCH.

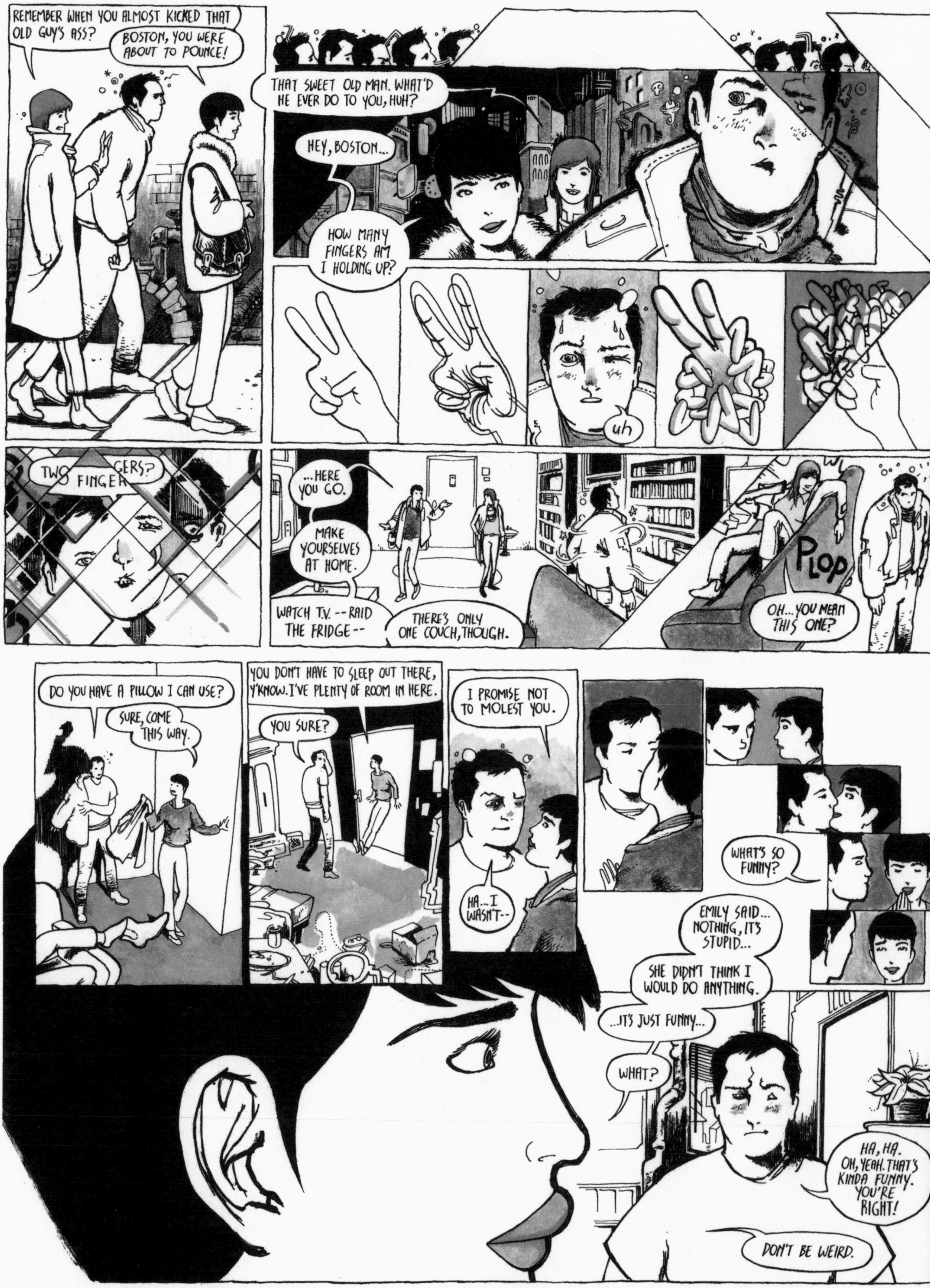
REMEMBER WHEN YOU ALMOST KICKED THAT OLD GUY'S ASS?
BOSTON, YOU WERE ABOUT TO POUNCE!
THAT SWEET OLD MAN. WHAT'D HE EVER DO TO YOU, HUH?
HEY, BOSTON...
HOW MANY FINGERS AM I HOLDING UP?
uh
TWO FINGERS?
...HERE YOU GO.
MAKE YOURSELVES AT HOME.
WATCH T.V. --RAID THE FRIDGE--
THERE'S ONLY ONE COUCH, THOUGH.
PLOP
OH... YOU MEAN THIS ONE?
DO YOU HAVE A PILLOW I CAN USE?
SURE, COME THIS WAY.
YOU DON'T HAVE TO SLEEP OUT THERE, Y'KNOW. I'VE PLENTY OF ROOM IN HERE.
YOU SURE?
I PROMISE NOT TO MOLEST YOU.
HA... I WASN'T--
WHAT'S SO FUNNY?
EMILY SAID... NOTHING, IT'S STUPID...
SHE DIDN'T THINK I WOULD DO ANYTHING.
...IT'S JUST FUNNY...
WHAT?
HA, HA. OH, YEAH. THAT'S KINDA FUNNY. YOU'RE RIGHT!
DON'T BE WEIRD.

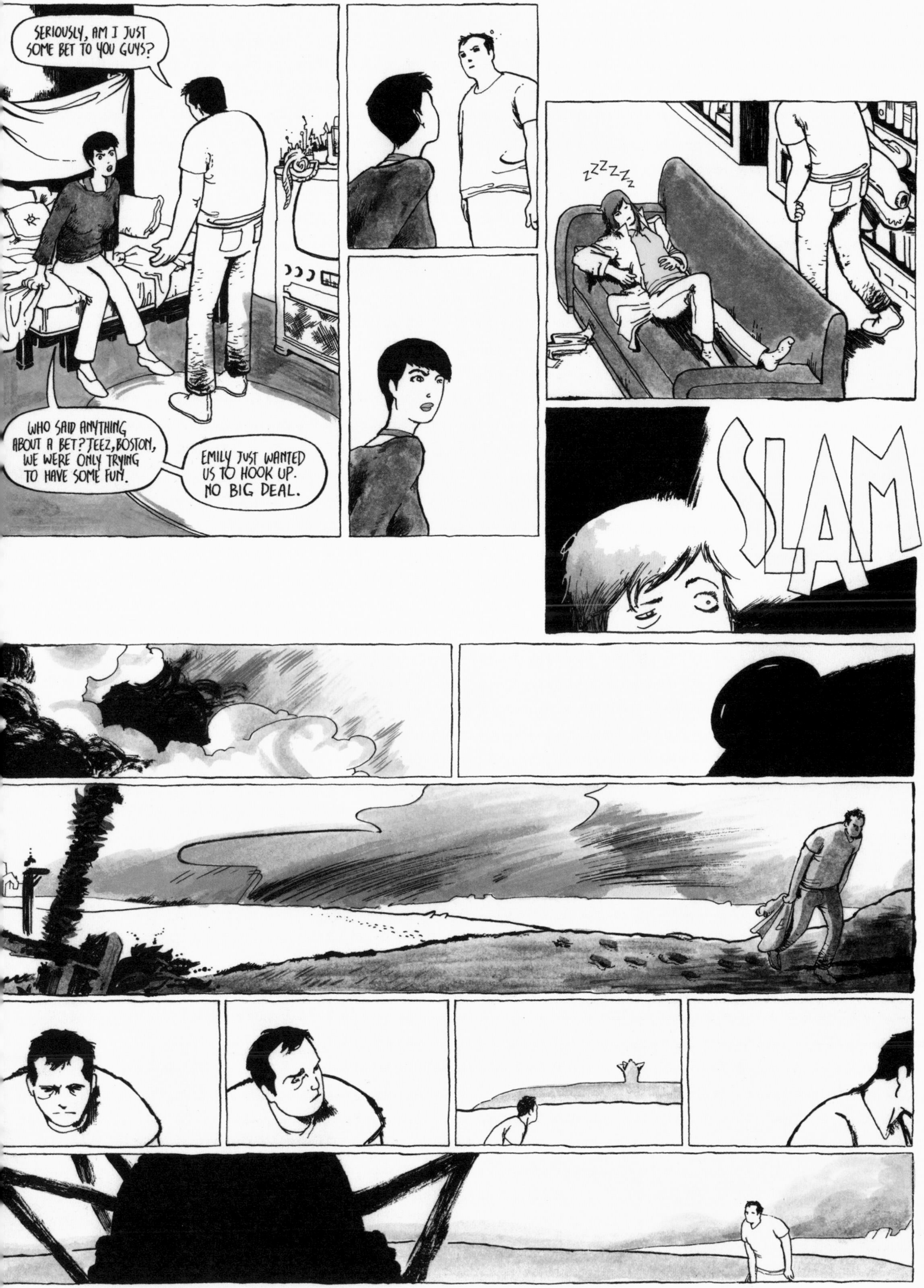
SERIOUSLY, AM I JUST SOME BET TO YOU GUYS?
WHO SAID ANYTHING ABOUT A BET? JEEZ, BOSTON, WE WERE ONLY TRYING TO HAVE SOME FUN.
EMILY JUST WANTED US TO HOOK UP. NO BIG DEAL.
ZZZZZZ
SLAM

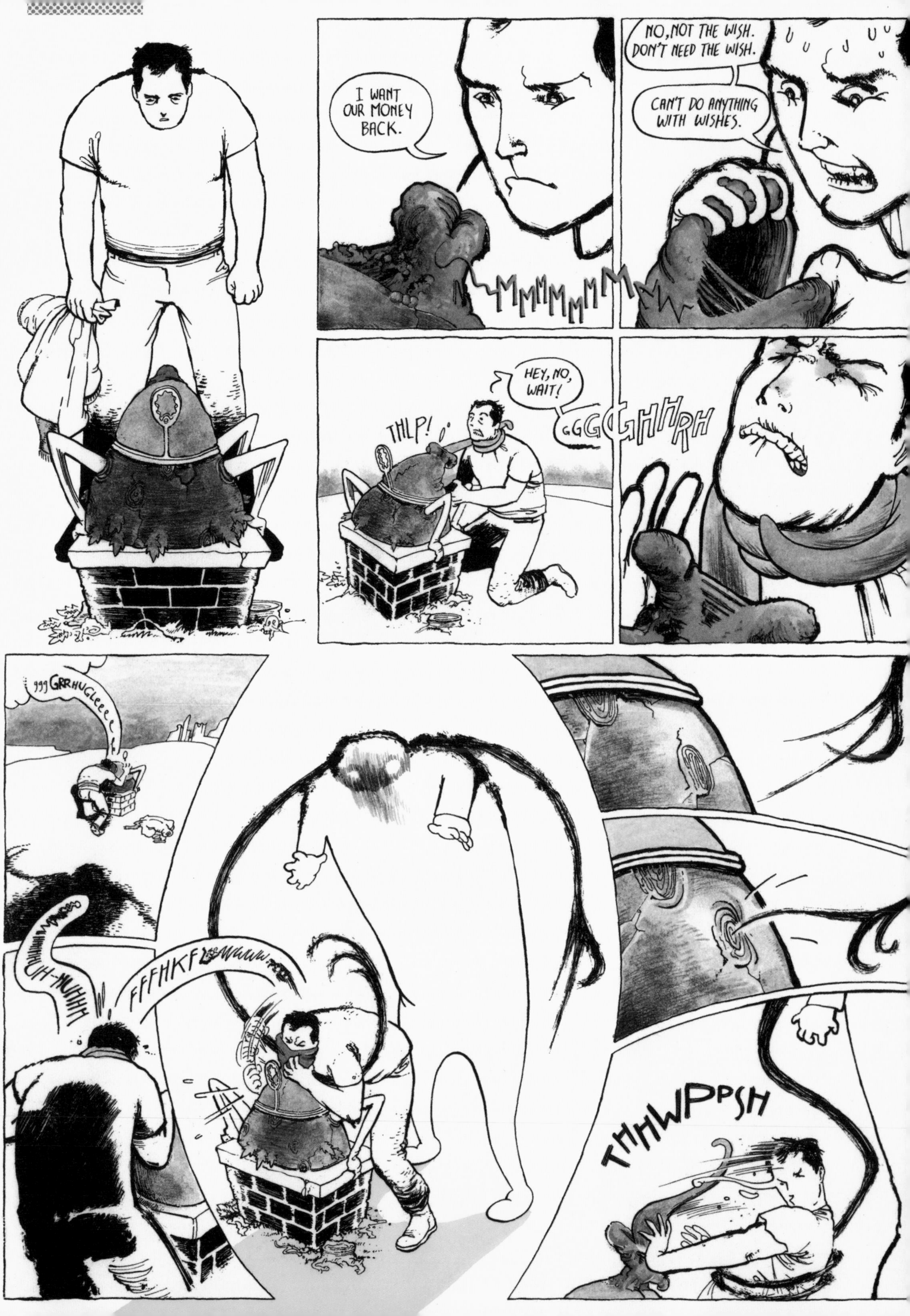
I WANT OUR MONEY BACK.
MMMMMMMM
NO, NOT THE WISH. DON'T NEED THE WISH.
CAN'T DO ANYTHING WITH WISHES.
HEY, NO, WAIT!
THLP!
GGGGHHRH
gggGRRHUGLeee
FFFHKF
UH-NUHH
THHWPPSH

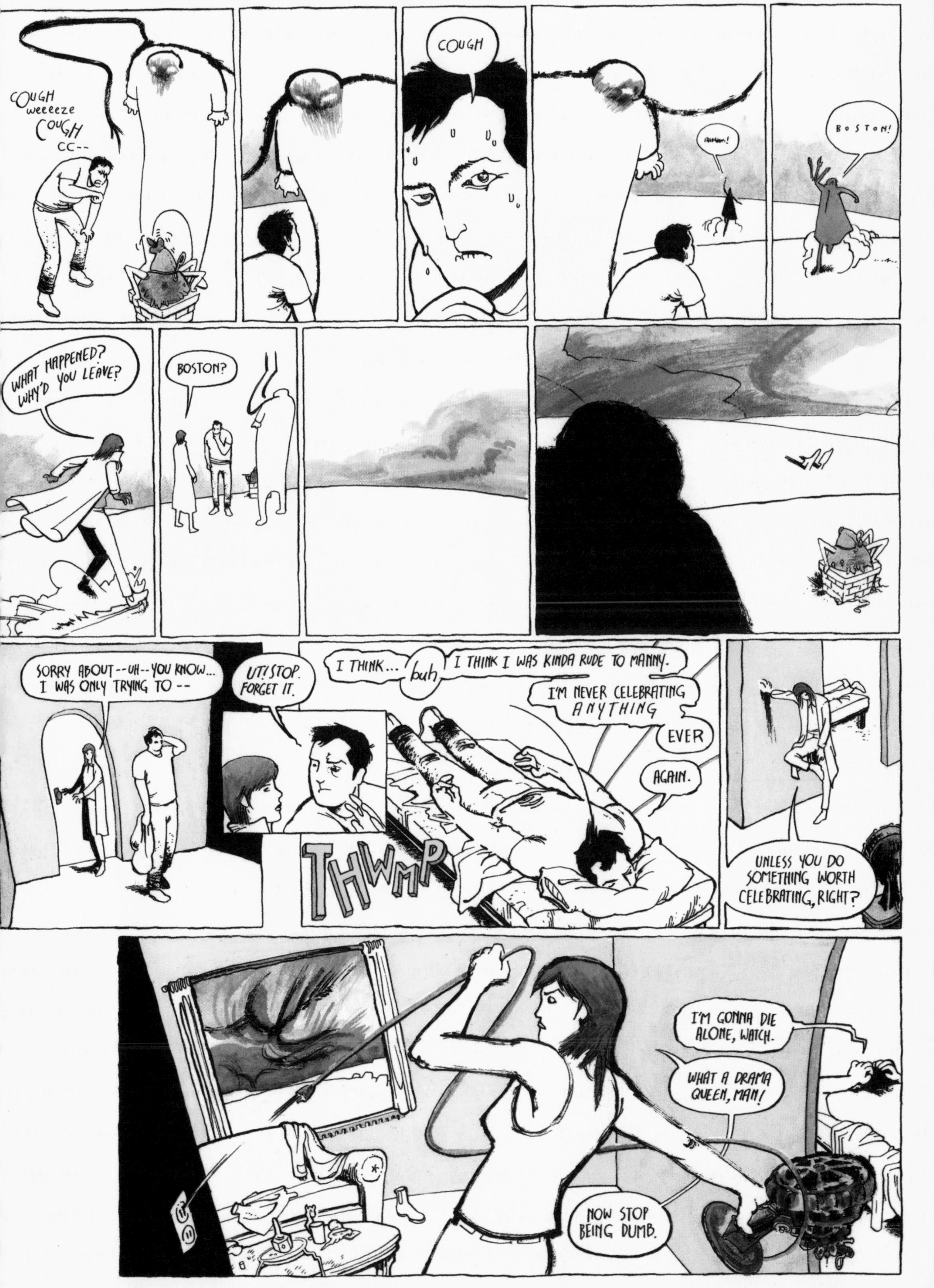
COUGH weeeeze COUGH CC--
COUGH
BOSTON!
WHAT HAPPENED? WHY'D YOU LEAVE?
BOSTON?
SORRY ABOUT--UH--YOU KNOW... I WAS ONLY TRYING TO --
UT! STOP. FORGET IT.
I THINK...
buh
I THINK I WAS KINDA RUDE TO MANNY.
I'M NEVER CELEBRATING ANYTHING
EVER
AGAIN.
THWMP
UNLESS YOU DO SOMETHING WORTH CELEBRATING, RIGHT?
I'M GONNA DIE ALONE, WATCH.
WHAT A DRAMA QUEEN, MAN!
NOW STOP BEING DUMB.

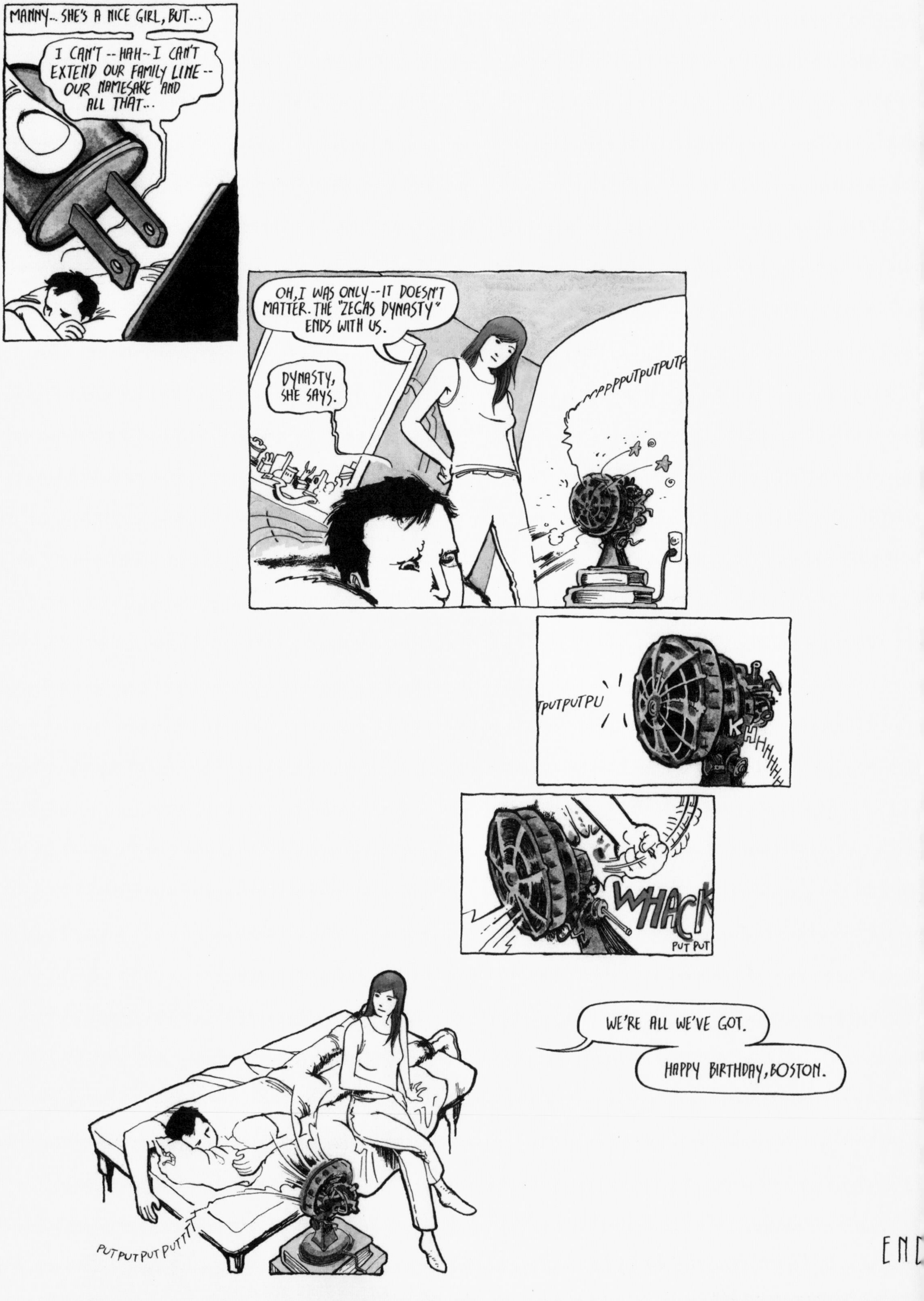
MANNY... SHE'S A NICE GIRL, BUT...
I CAN'T --HAH-- I CAN'T EXTEND OUR FAMILY LINE -- OUR NAMESAKE AND ALL THAT...
OH, I WAS ONLY --IT DOESN'T MATTER. THE "ZEGAS DYNASTY" ENDS WITH US.
DYNASTY, SHE SAYS.
PPPPUTPUTPUTP
TPUTPUTPU
KHHHHHH
WHACK
PUT PUT
WE'RE ALL WE'VE GOT.
HAPPY BIRTHDAY, BOSTON.
PUTPUTPUTPUTTT
END

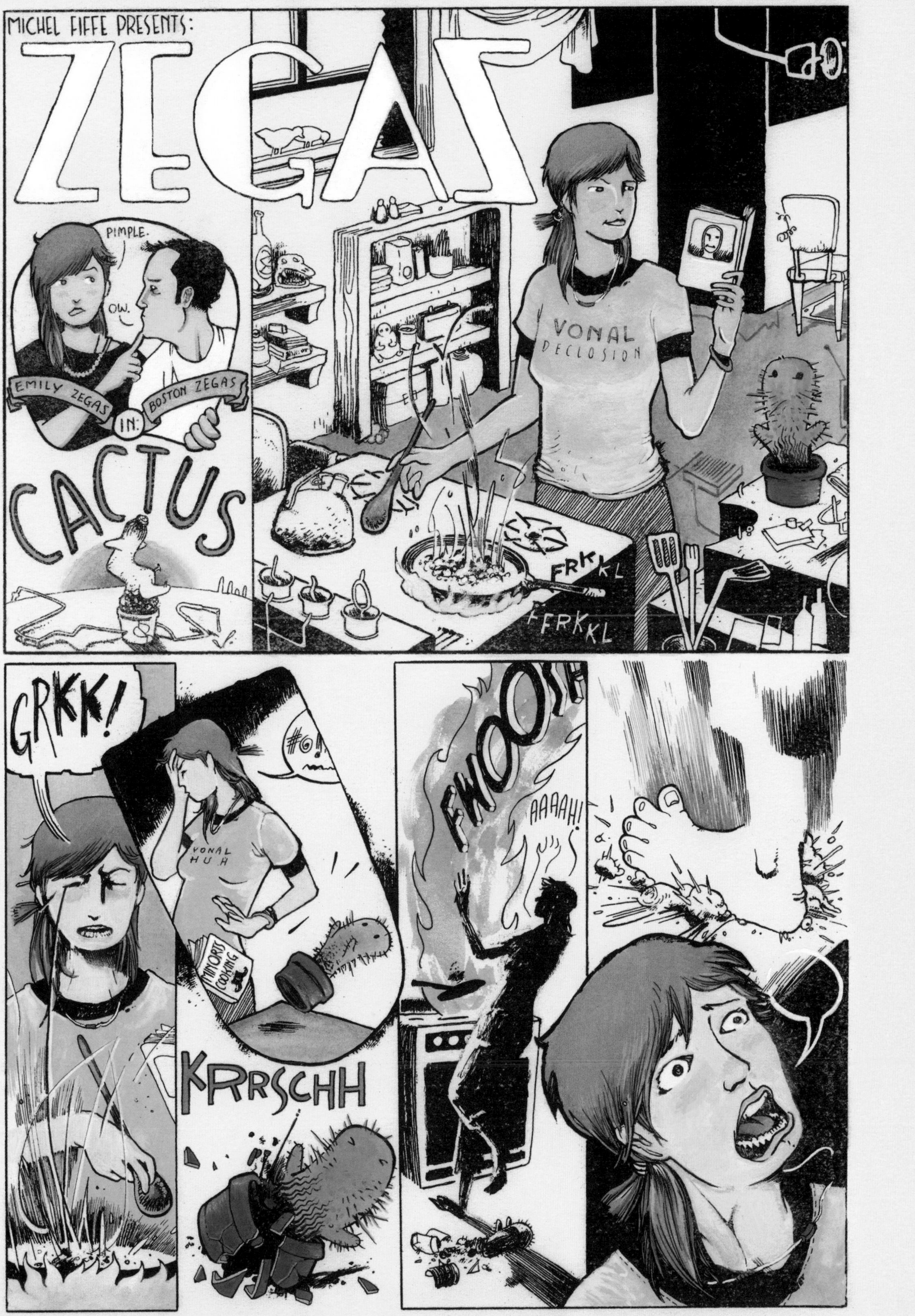
MICHEL FIFFE PRESENTS:
ZEGAS
PIMPLE.
OW.
EMILY ZEGAS
IN:
BOSTON ZEGAS
CACTUS
VONAL
DECLOSION
FRKKL
FFRKKL
GRKK!
VONAL
HUH
KRRSCHH
FWOOSH
AAAAH!

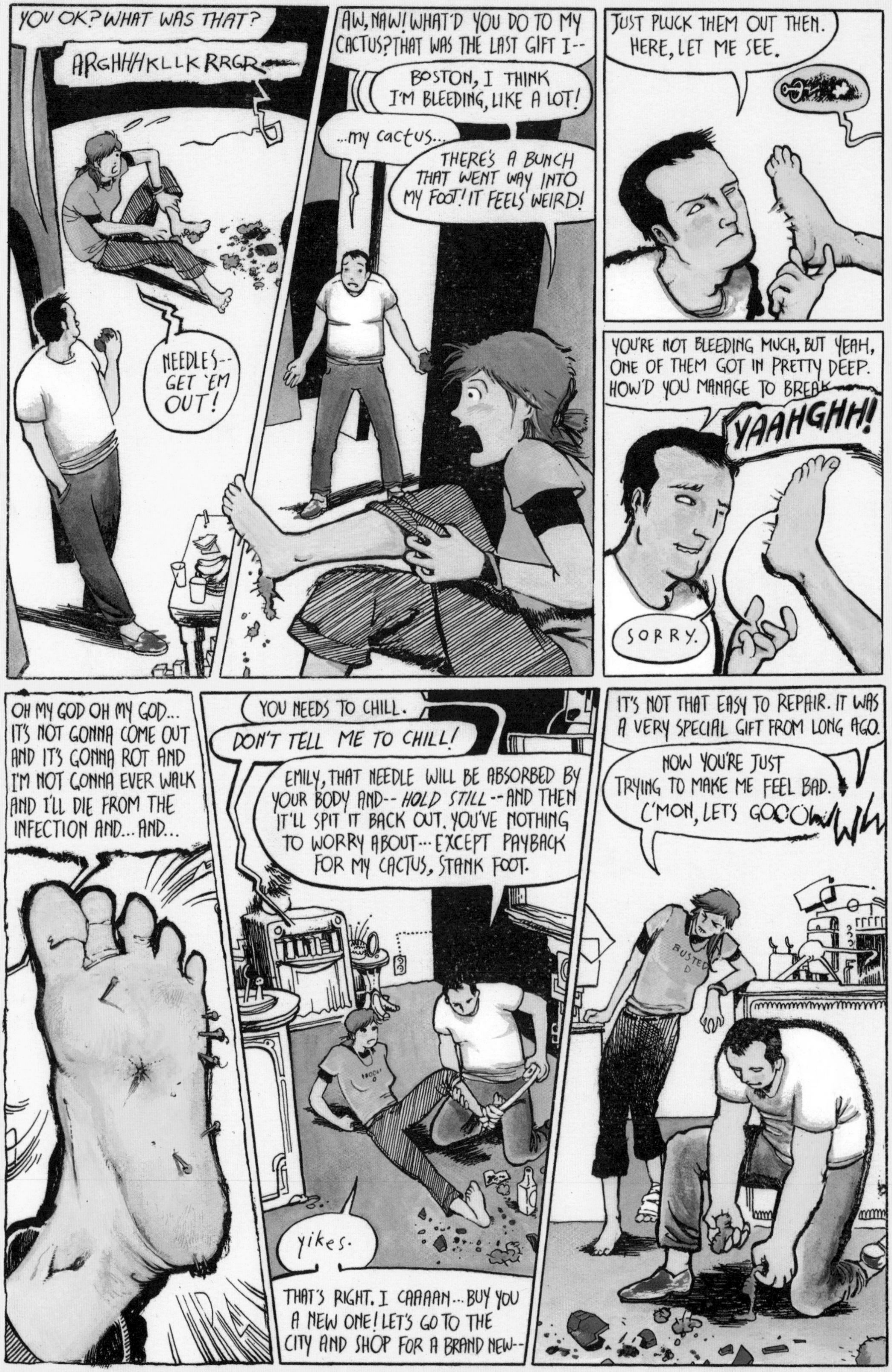
YOU OK? WHAT WAS THAT?
ARGHHHKLLKRRGR
NEEDLES--GET 'EM OUT!
AW, NAW! WHAT'D YOU DO TO MY CACTUS? THAT WAS THE LAST GIFT I--
BOSTON, I THINK I'M BLEEDING, LIKE A LOT!
...my cactus...
THERE'S A BUNCH THAT WENT WAY INTO MY FOOT! IT FEELS WEIRD!
JUST PLUCK THEM OUT THEN. HERE, LET ME SEE.
YOU'RE NOT BLEEDING MUCH, BUT YEAH, ONE OF THEM GOT IN PRETTY DEEP. HOW'D YOU MANAGE TO BREAK
YAAHGHH!
SORRY.
OH MY GOD OH MY GOD... IT'S NOT GONNA COME OUT AND IT'S GONNA ROT AND I'M NOT GONNA EVER WALK AND I'LL DIE FROM THE INFECTION AND... AND...
YOU NEEDS TO CHILL.
DON'T TELL ME TO CHILL!
EMILY, THAT NEEDLE WILL BE ABSORBED BY YOUR BODY AND-- HOLD STILL --AND THEN IT'LL SPIT IT BACK OUT. YOU'VE NOTHING TO WORRY ABOUT... EXCEPT PAYBACK FOR MY CACTUS, STANK FOOT.
yikes.
THAT'S RIGHT. I CAAAAN... BUY YOU A NEW ONE! LET'S GO TO THE CITY AND SHOP FOR A BRAND NEW--
IT'S NOT THAT EASY TO REPAIR. IT WAS A VERY SPECIAL GIFT FROM LONG AGO.
NOW YOU'RE JUST TRYING TO MAKE ME FEEL BAD. C'MON, LET'S GOOO
WW
BUSTED D

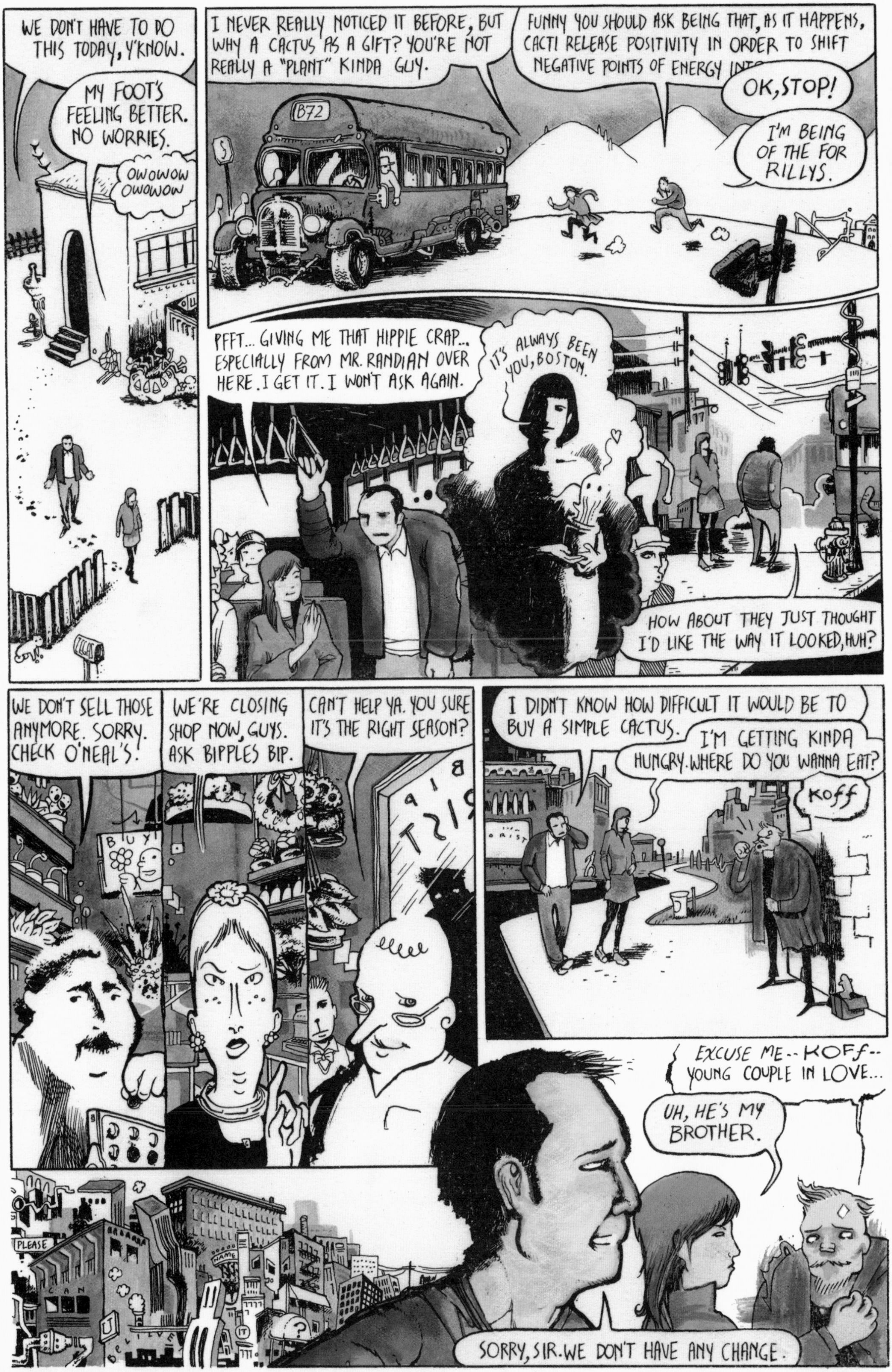
WE DON'T HAVE TO DO THIS TODAY, Y'KNOW.
MY FOOT'S FEELING BETTER. NO WORRIES.
OWOWOW OWOWOW
I NEVER REALLY NOTICED IT BEFORE, BUT WHY A CACTUS AS A GIFT? YOU'RE NOT REALLY A "PLANT" KINDA GUY.
FUNNY YOU SHOULD ASK BEING THAT, AS IT HAPPENS, CACTI RELEASE POSITIVITY IN ORDER TO SHIFT NEGATIVE POINTS OF ENERGY INT
OK, STOP!
I'M BEING OF THE FOR RILLYS.
PFFT... GIVING ME THAT HIPPIE CRAP... ESPECIALLY FROM MR. RANDIAN OVER HERE. I GET IT. I WON'T ASK AGAIN.
IT'S ALWAYS BEEN YOU, BOSTON.
HOW ABOUT THEY JUST THOUGHT I'D LIKE THE WAY IT LOOKED, HUH?
WE DON'T SELL THOSE ANYMORE. SORRY. CHECK O'NEAL'S.
BUY
WE'RE CLOSING SHOP NOW, GUYS. ASK BIPPLES BIP.
CAN'T HELP YA. YOU SURE IT'S THE RIGHT SEASON?
I DIDN'T KNOW HOW DIFFICULT IT WOULD BE TO BUY A SIMPLE CACTUS.
I'M GETTING KINDA HUNGRY. WHERE DO YOU WANNA EAT?
KOFF
EXCUSE ME -- KOFF -- YOUNG COUPLE IN LOVE...
UH, HE'S MY BROTHER.
PLEASE
SORRY, SIR. WE DON'T HAVE ANY CHANGE.

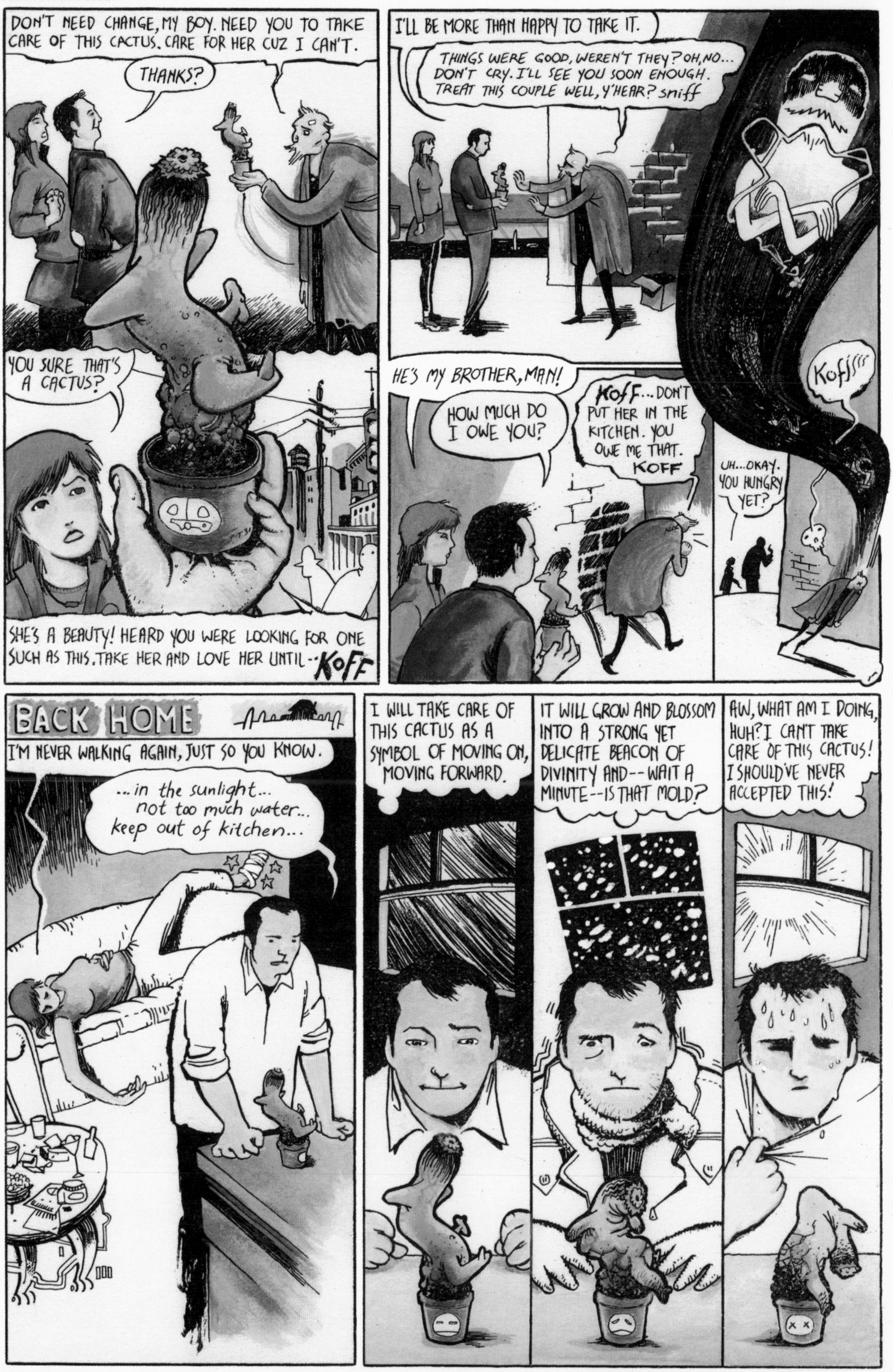
DON'T NEED CHANGE, MY BOY. NEED YOU TO TAKE CARE OF THIS CACTUS. CARE FOR HER CUZ I CAN'T.
THANKS?
YOU SURE THAT'S A CACTUS?
SHE'S A BEAUTY! HEARD YOU WERE LOOKING FOR ONE SUCH AS THIS. TAKE HER AND LOVE HER UNTIL-- KOFF
I'LL BE MORE THAN HAPPY TO TAKE IT.
THINGS WERE GOOD, WEREN'T THEY? OH, NO... DON'T CRY. I'LL SEE YOU SOON ENOUGH. TREAT THIS COUPLE WELL, Y'HEAR? sniff
HE'S MY BROTHER, MAN!
HOW MUCH DO I OWE YOU?
KOFF... DON'T PUT HER IN THE KITCHEN. YOU OWE ME THAT. KOFF
UH... OKAY. YOU HUNGRY YET?
KOFFSSSS
BACK HOME
I'M NEVER WALKING AGAIN, JUST SO YOU KNOW.
...in the sunlight... not too much water... keep out of kitchen...
I WILL TAKE CARE OF THIS CACTUS AS A SYMBOL OF MOVING ON, MOVING FORWARD.
IT WILL GROW AND BLOSSOM INTO A STRONG YET DELICATE BEACON OF DIVINITY AND-- WAIT A MINUTE-- IS THAT MOLD?
AW, WHAT AM I DOING, HUH? I CAN'T TAKE CARE OF THIS CACTUS! I SHOULD'VE NEVER ACCEPTED THIS!

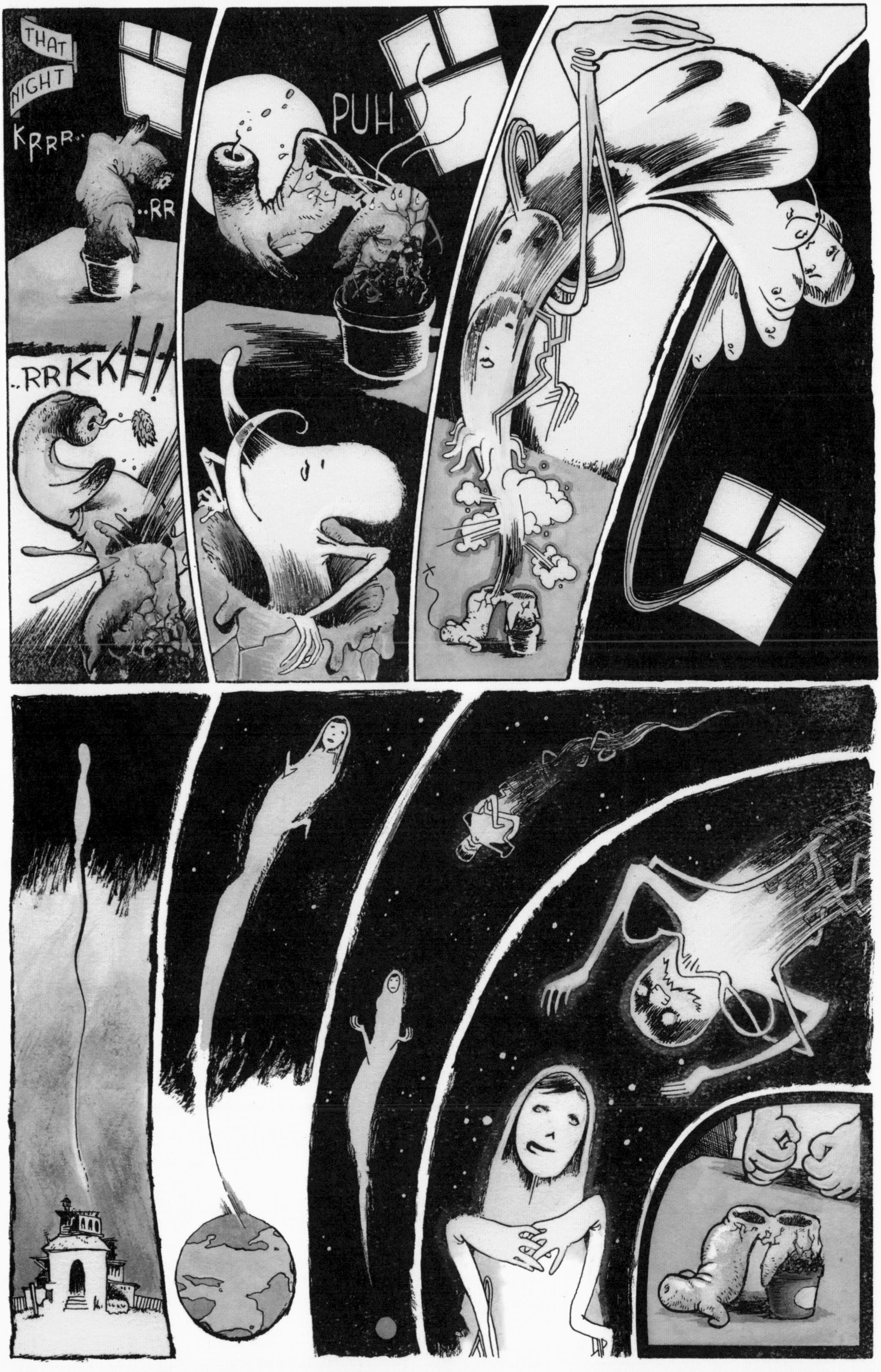
THAT NIGHT
KRRR..
..RR
..RRKKH!
PUH

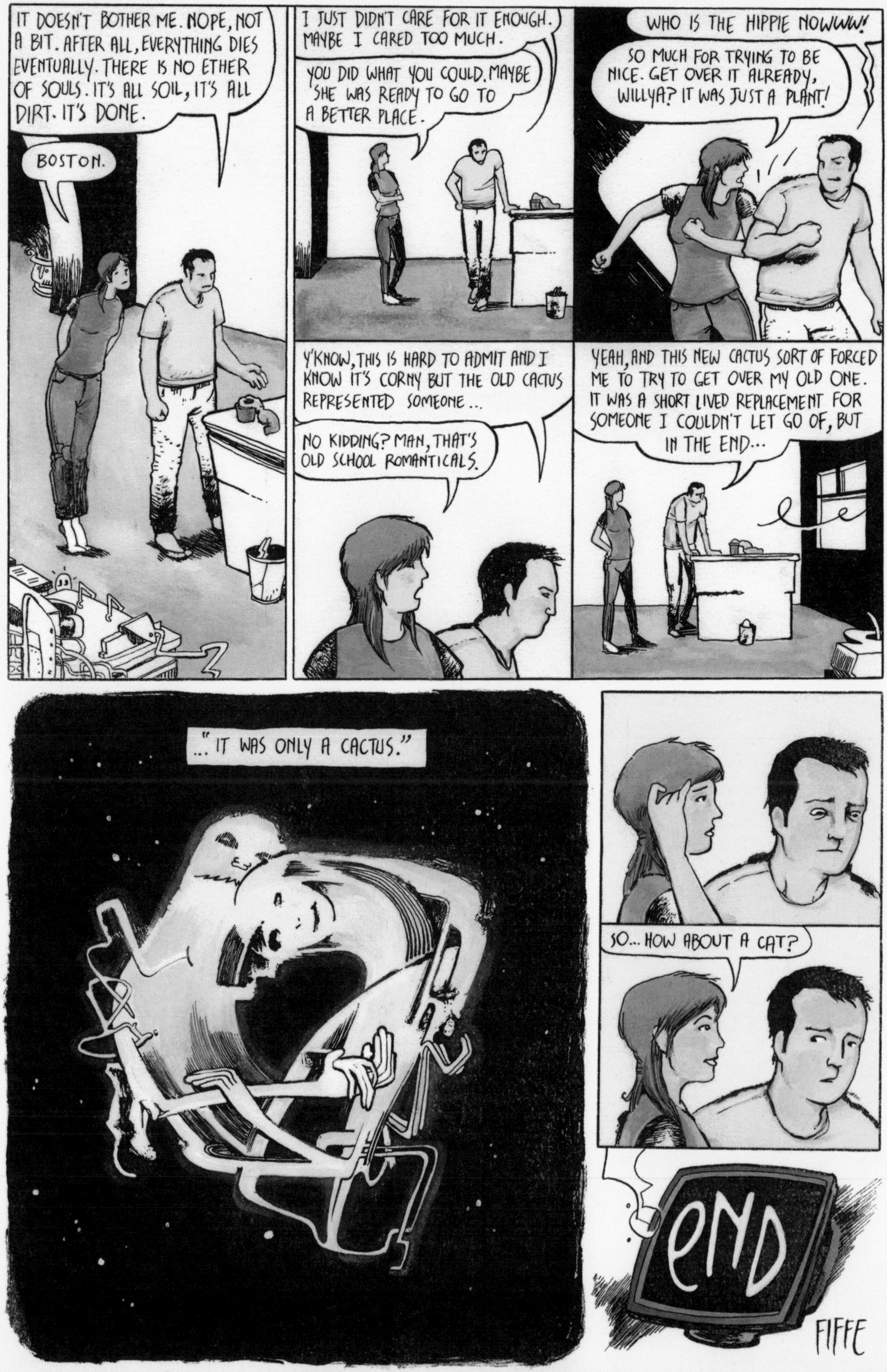
IT DOESN'T BOTHER ME. NOPE, NOT A BIT. AFTER ALL, EVERYTHING DIES EVENTUALLY. THERE IS NO ETHER OF SOULS. IT'S ALL SOIL, IT'S ALL DIRT. IT'S DONE.
BOSTON.
I JUST DIDN'T CARE FOR IT ENOUGH. MAYBE I CARED TOO MUCH.
YOU DID WHAT YOU COULD. MAYBE SHE WAS READY TO GO TO A BETTER PLACE.
WHO IS THE HIPPIE NOWWW!
SO MUCH FOR TRYING TO BE NICE. GET OVER IT ALREADY, WILLYA? IT WAS JUST A PLANT!
Y'KNOW, THIS IS HARD TO ADMIT AND I KNOW IT'S CORNY BUT THE OLD CACTUS REPRESENTED SOMEONE...
NO KIDDING? MAN, THAT'S OLD SCHOOL ROMANTICALS.
YEAH, AND THIS NEW CACTUS SORT OF FORCED ME TO TRY TO GET OVER MY OLD ONE. IT WAS A SHORT LIVED REPLACEMENT FOR SOMEONE I COULDN'T LET GO OF, BUT IN THE END...
..."IT WAS ONLY A CACTUS."
SO... HOW ABOUT A CAT?
END
FIFFE

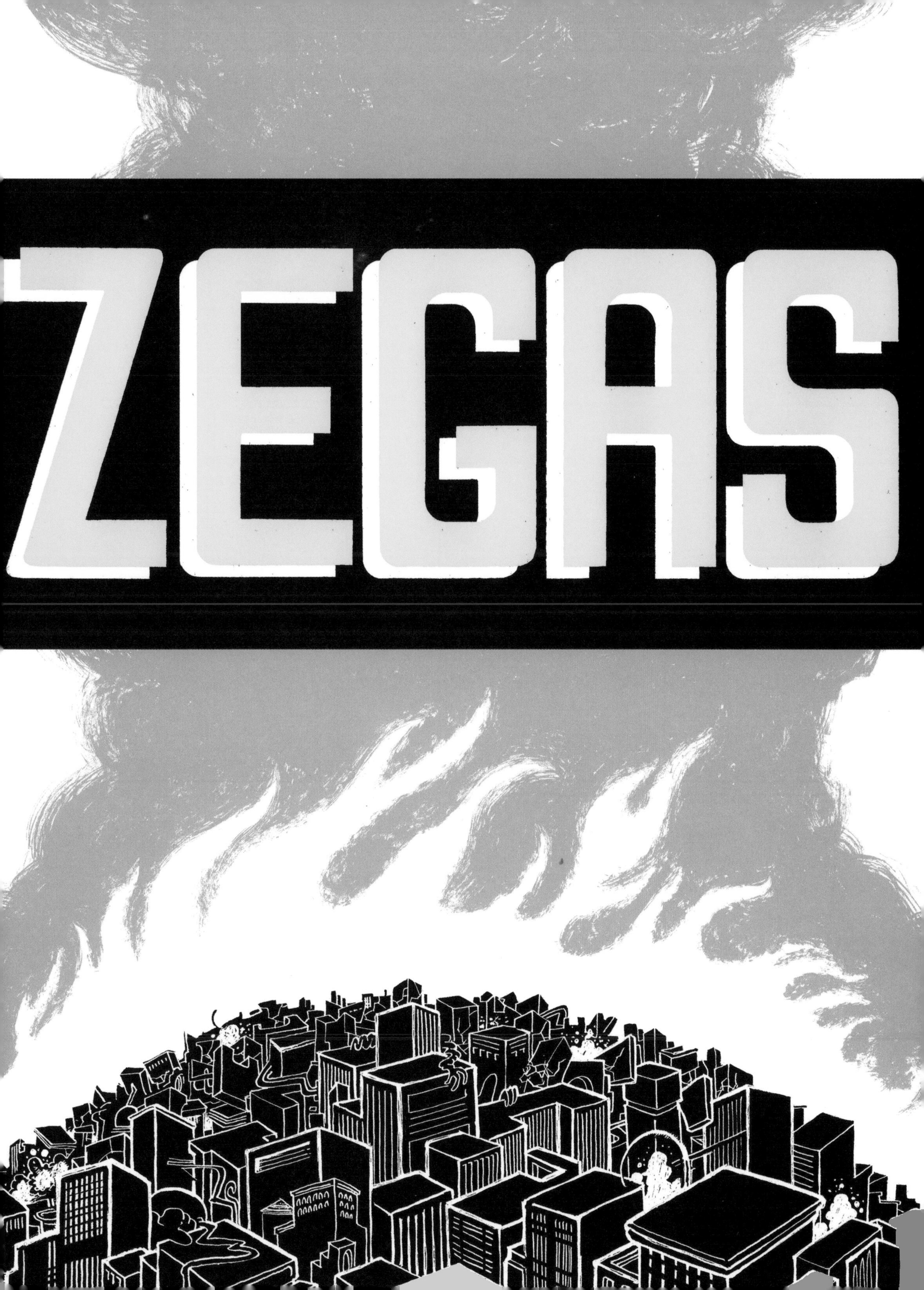
ZEGAS

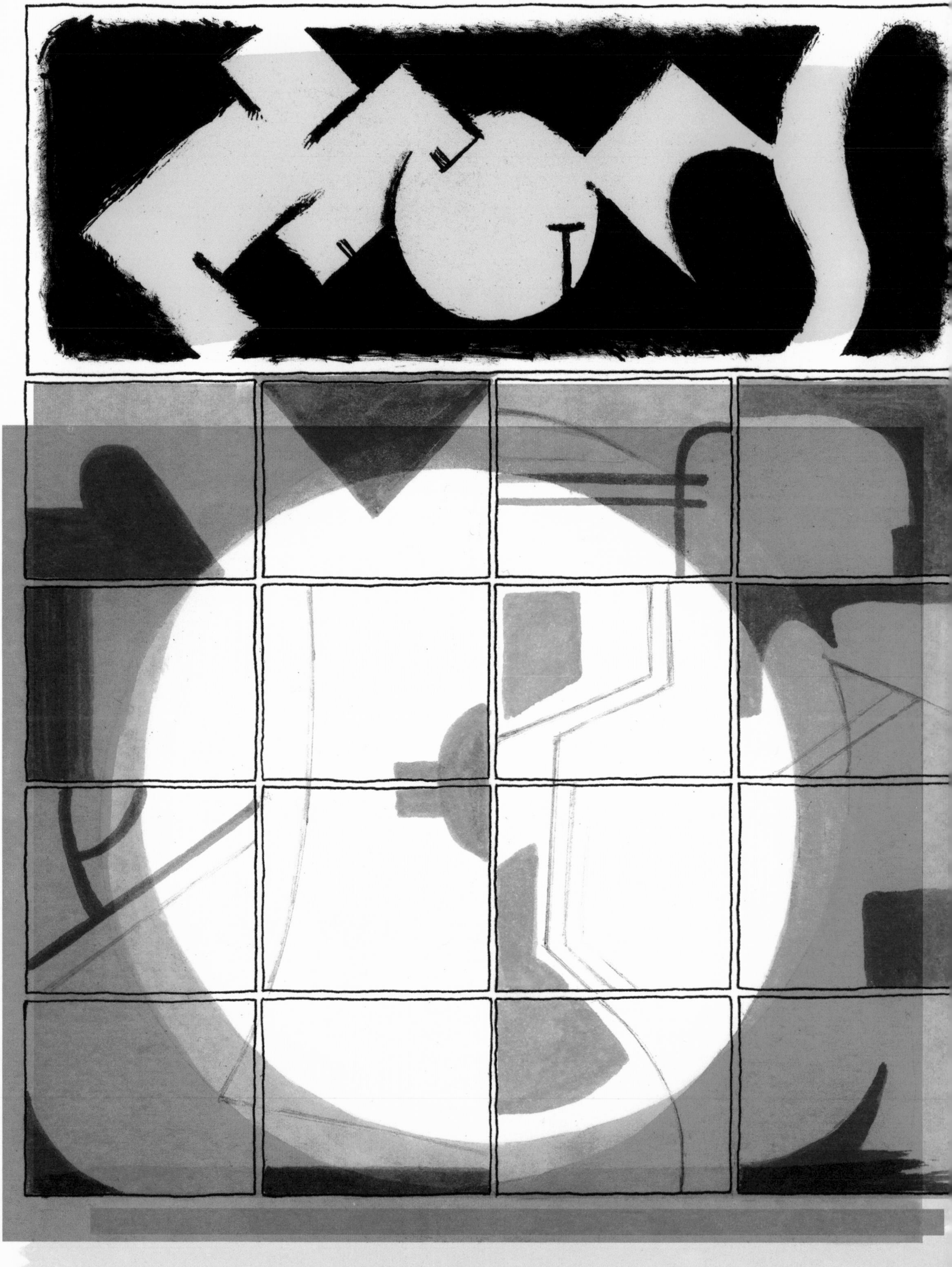

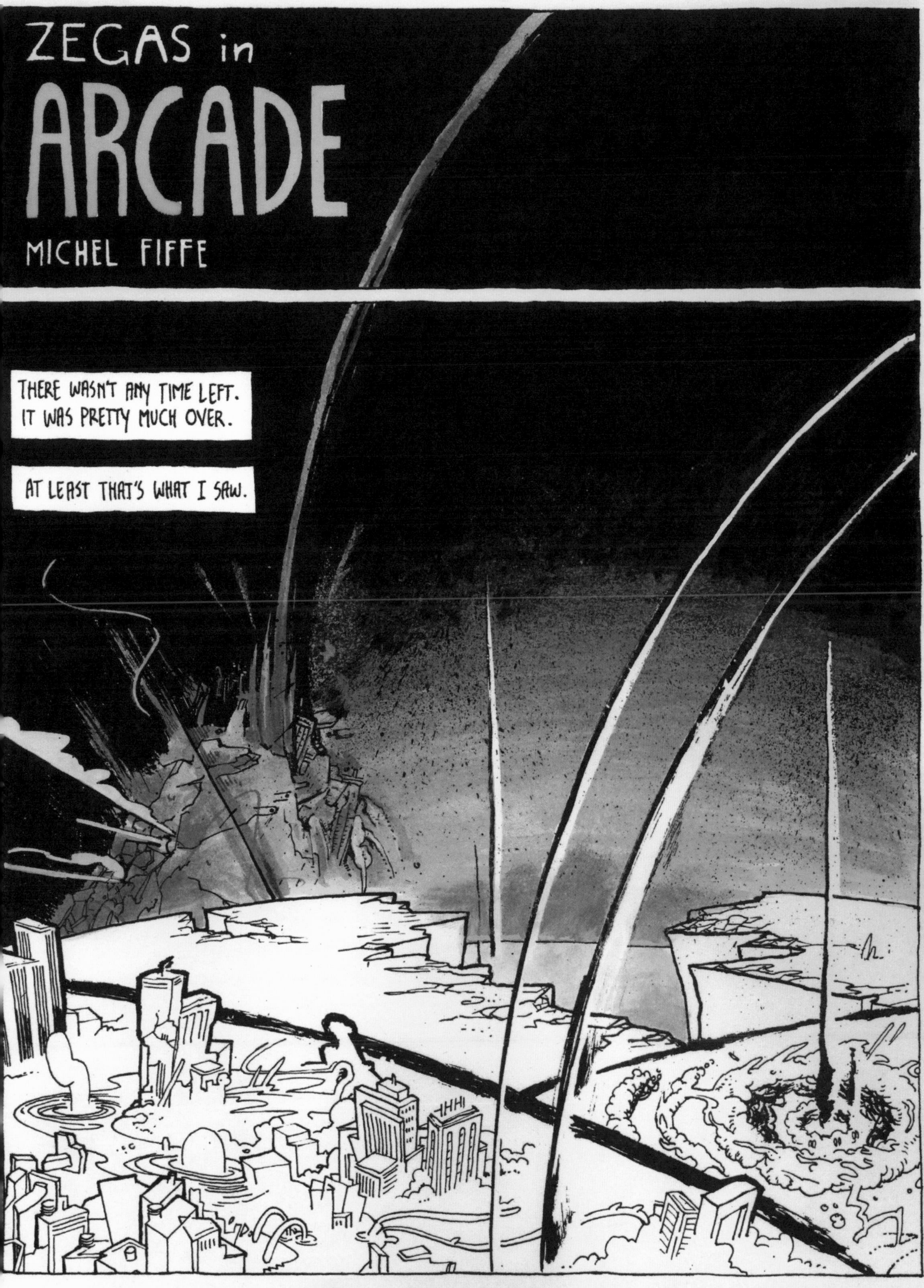
ZEGAS in
ARCADE
MICHEL FIFFE
THERE WASN'T ANY TIME LEFT. IT WAS PRETTY MUCH OVER.
AT LEAST THAT'S WHAT I SAW.

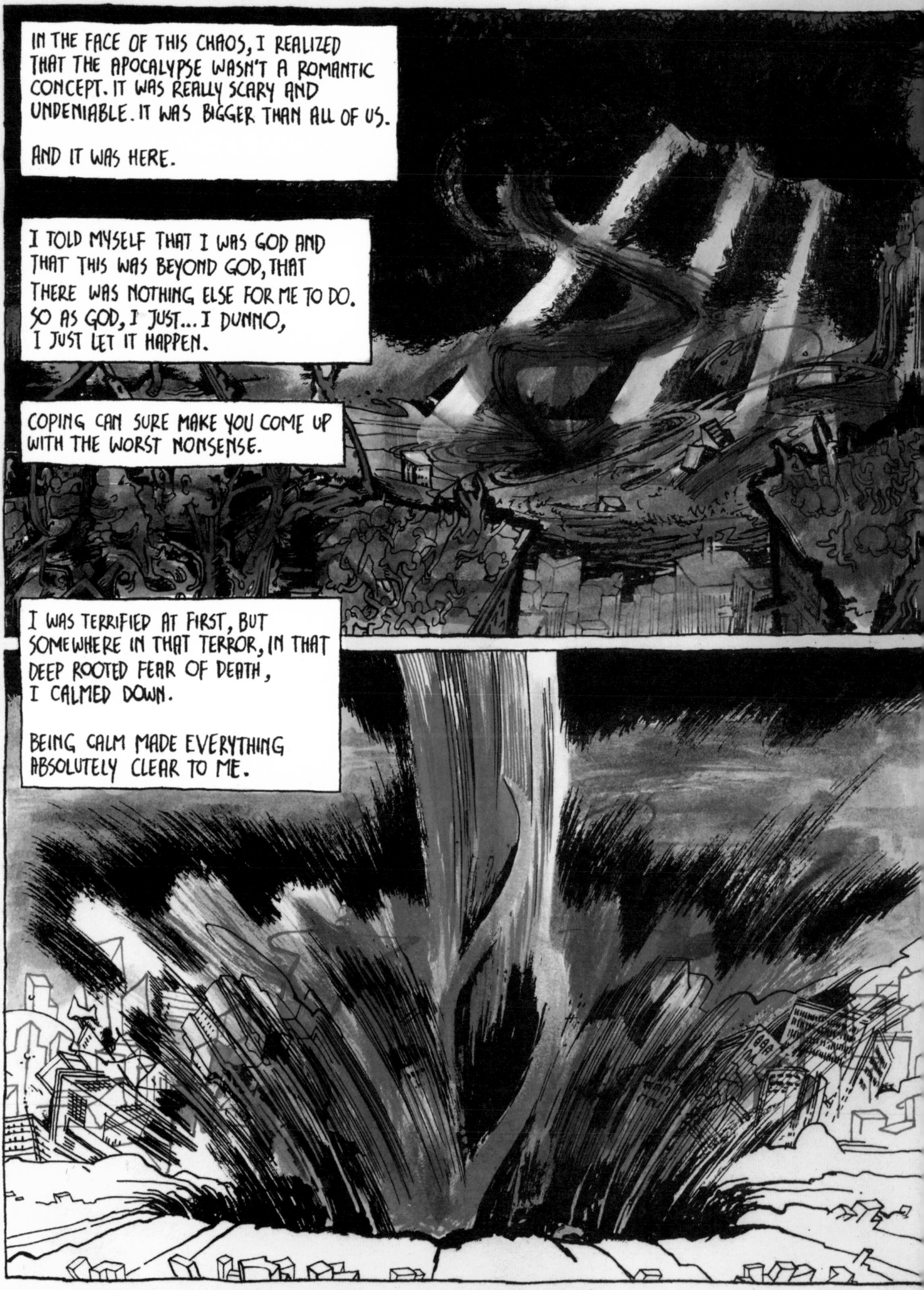
IN THE FACE OF THIS CHAOS, I REALIZED THAT THE APOCALYPSE WASN'T A ROMANTIC CONCEPT. IT WAS REALLY SCARY AND UNDENIABLE. IT WAS BIGGER THAN ALL OF US.
AND IT WAS HERE.
I TOLD MYSELF THAT I WAS GOD AND THAT THIS WAS BEYOND GOD, THAT THERE WAS NOTHING ELSE FOR ME TO DO. SO AS GOD, I JUST... I DUNNO, I JUST LET IT HAPPEN.
COPING CAN SURE MAKE YOU COME UP WITH THE WORST NONSENSE.
I WAS TERRIFIED AT FIRST, BUT SOMEWHERE IN THAT TERROR, IN THAT DEEP ROOTED FEAR OF DEATH, I CALMED DOWN.
BEING CALM MADE EVERYTHING ABSOLUTELY CLEAR TO ME.

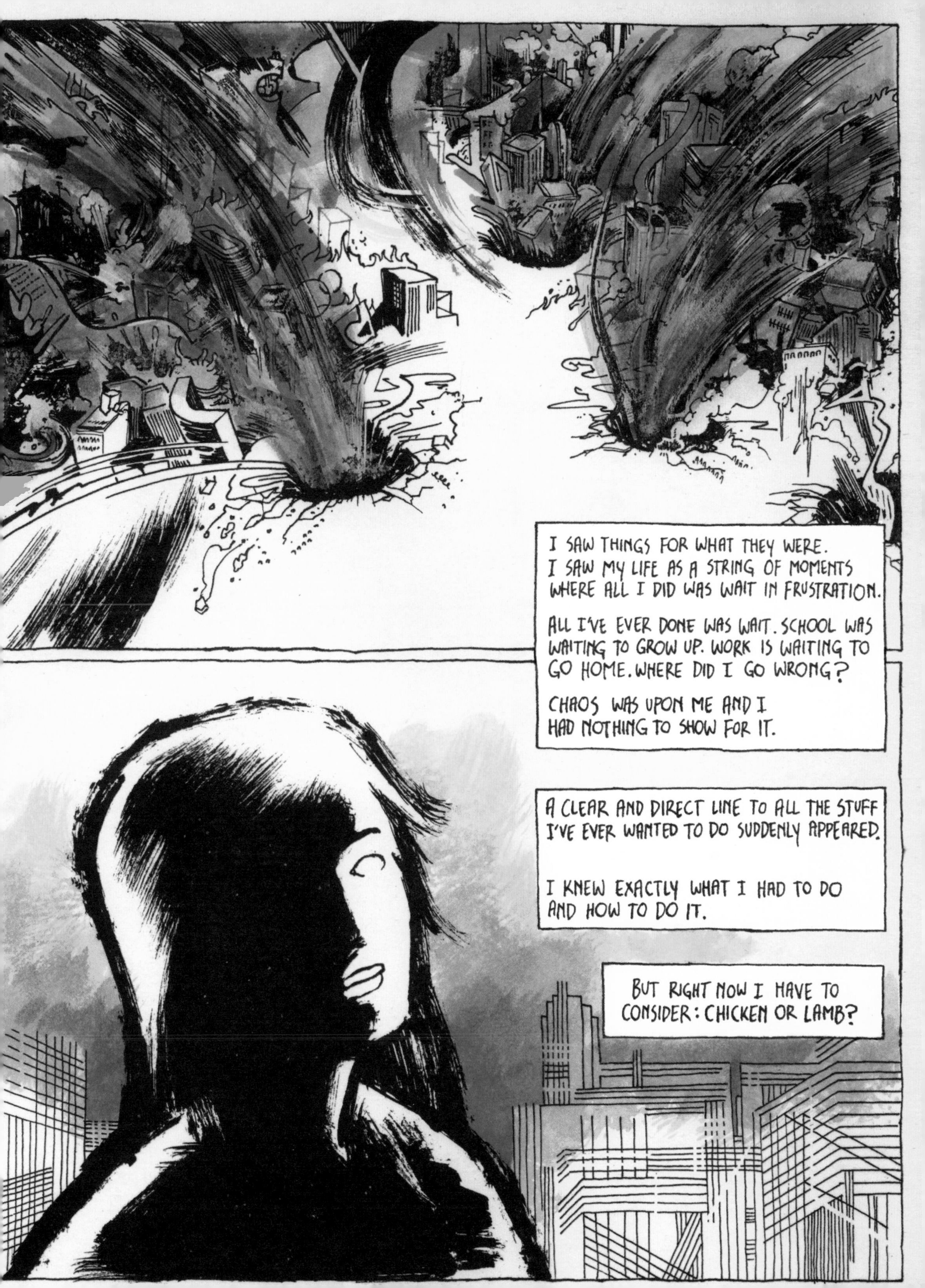
I SAW THINGS FOR WHAT THEY WERE. I SAW MY LIFE AS A STRING OF MOMENTS WHERE ALL I DID WAS WAIT IN FRUSTRATION.
ALL I'VE EVER DONE WAS WAIT. SCHOOL WAS WAITING TO GROW UP. WORK IS WAITING TO GO HOME. WHERE DID I GO WRONG?
CHAOS WAS UPON ME AND I HAD NOTHING TO SHOW FOR IT.
A CLEAR AND DIRECT LINE TO ALL THE STUFF I'VE EVER WANTED TO DO SUDDENLY APPEARED.
I KNEW EXACTLY WHAT I HAD TO DO AND HOW TO DO IT.
BUT RIGHT NOW I HAVE TO CONSIDER: CHICKEN OR LAMB?

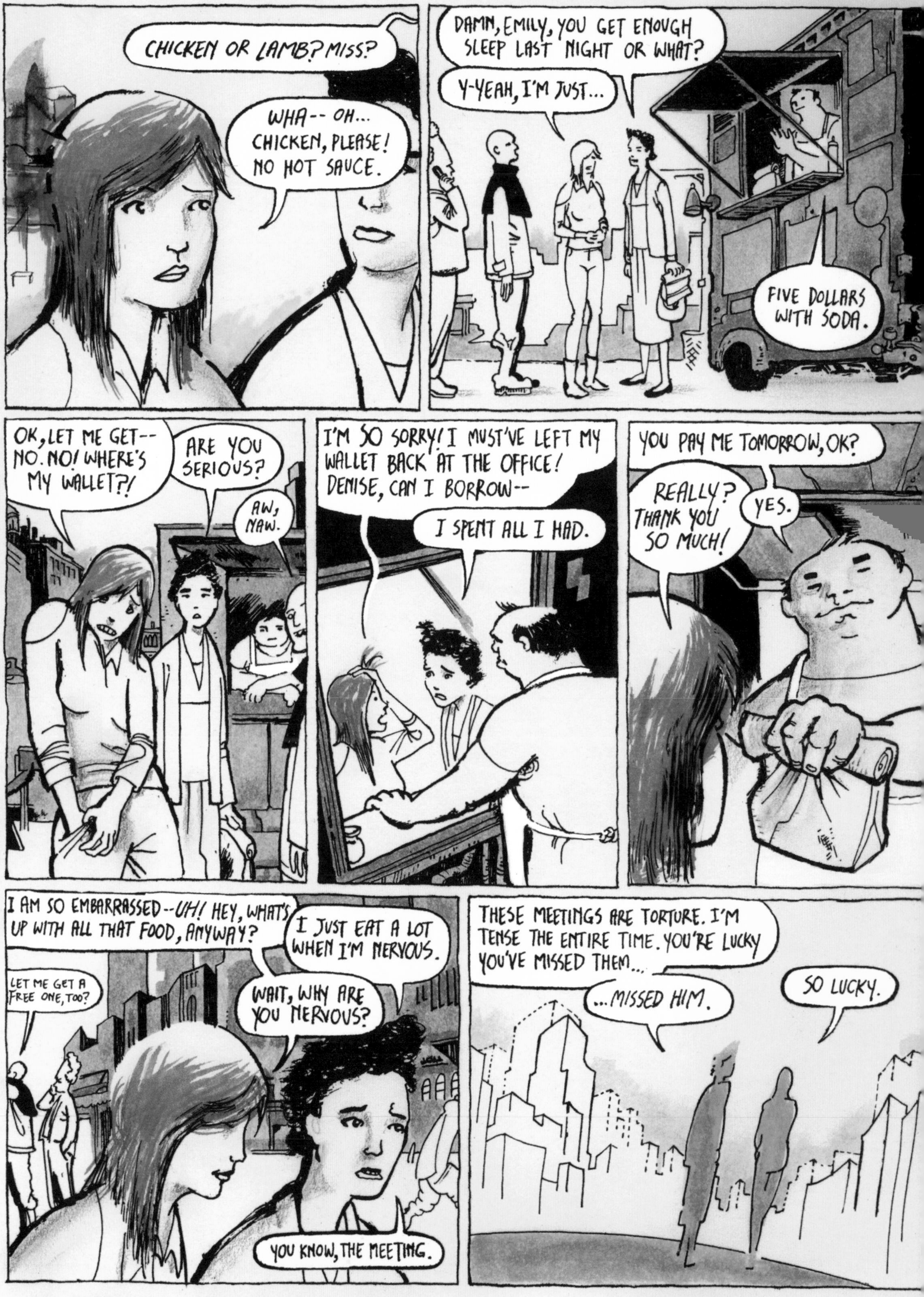
CHICKEN OR LAMB? MISS?
WHA-- OH... CHICKEN, PLEASE! NO HOT SAUCE.
DAMN, EMILY, YOU GET ENOUGH SLEEP LAST NIGHT OR WHAT?
Y-YEAH, I'M JUST...
FIVE DOLLARS WITH SODA.
OK, LET ME GET-- NO. NO! WHERE'S MY WALLET?!
ARE YOU SERIOUS?
AW, NAW.
I'M SO SORRY! I MUST'VE LEFT MY WALLET BACK AT THE OFFICE! DENISE, CAN I BORROW--
I SPENT ALL I HAD.
YOU PAY ME TOMORROW, OK?
REALLY? THANK YOU SO MUCH!
YES.
I AM SO EMBARRASSED--UH! HEY, WHAT'S UP WITH ALL THAT FOOD, ANYWAY?
I JUST EAT A LOT WHEN I'M NERVOUS.
LET ME GET A FREE ONE, TOO?
WAIT, WHY ARE YOU NERVOUS?
YOU KNOW, THE MEETING.
THESE MEETINGS ARE TORTURE. I'M TENSE THE ENTIRE TIME. YOU'RE LUCKY YOU'VE MISSED THEM...
...MISSED HIM.
SO LUCKY.

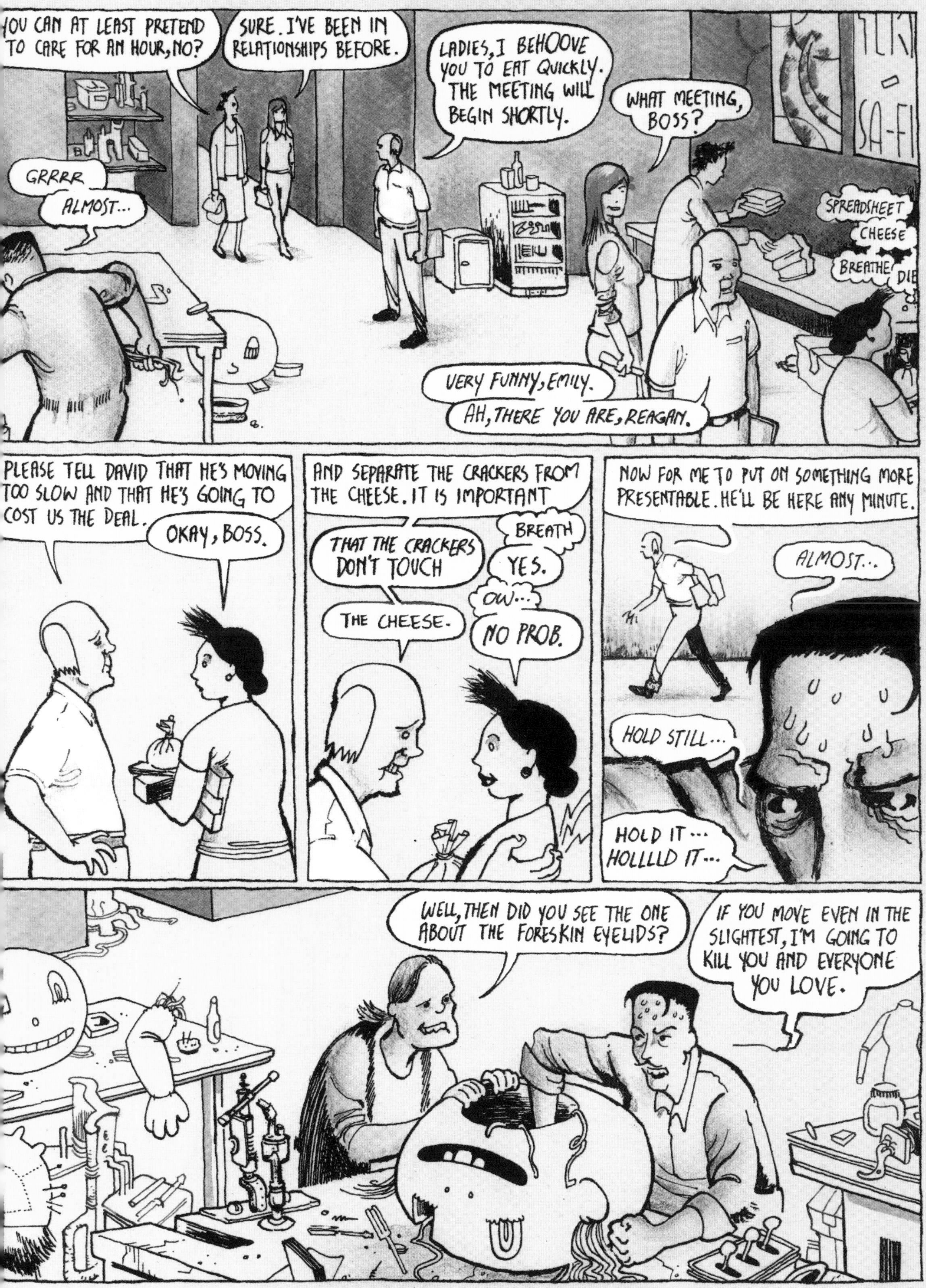
YOU CAN AT LEAST PRETEND TO CARE FOR AN HOUR, NO?
SURE. I'VE BEEN IN RELATIONSHIPS BEFORE.
LADIES, I BEHOOVE YOU TO EAT QUICKLY. THE MEETING WILL BEGIN SHORTLY.
WHAT MEETING, BOSS?
GRRRR
ALMOST...
SPREADSHEET
CHEESE
BREATHE
DIE
VERY FUNNY, EMILY.
AH, THERE YOU ARE, REAGAN.
PLEASE TELL DAVID THAT HE'S MOVING TOO SLOW AND THAT HE'S GOING TO COST US THE DEAL.
OKAY, BOSS.
AND SEPARATE THE CRACKERS FROM THE CHEESE. IT IS IMPORTANT
THAT THE CRACKERS DON'T TOUCH
BREATH
YES.
OW...
THE CHEESE.
NO PROB.
NOW FOR ME TO PUT ON SOMETHING MORE PRESENTABLE. HE'LL BE HERE ANY MINUTE.
ALMOST...
HOLD STILL...
HOLD IT... HOLLLLD IT...
WELL, THEN DID YOU SEE THE ONE ABOUT THE FORESKIN EYELIDS?
IF YOU MOVE EVEN IN THE SLIGHTEST, I'M GOING TO KILL YOU AND EVERYONE YOU LOVE.

YOU GOTTA LOOSEN UP ALREADY! WE SHOULD GO DANCING ONE OF THESE NIGHTS.

YEAH! I WANNA SEE YOU DANCE MERENGUE!

I'LL DANCE TO WHATEVER. LET'S AT LEAST GO OUT TO GET A DRINK.

HOW ABOUT LATER? WANNA GET ONE AFTER WORK? I'LL NEED IT...

NAH--I'M BROKE. MAYBE ON PAY DAY... NEXT WEEK.

SERIOUSLY.

DAVE! HOW'S IT GOIN'?

THIS IS UNBELIEVABLE. THIS INVESTOR GUY, HE REALLY WANTS ALL OF THE CHANGES?

OK, LET GO ALREADY.

YES, HE WANTS THE EYES SHIFTED AND THE CAMERA PLACEMENT CHANGED.

THAT ALONE WILL TAKE WEEKS!

YOU HAVE 15 MINUTES.

DAVE, IT'S NOT OUR FAULT.

DOES HE NOT KNOW THAT THIS TAKES TIME, OR DID YOU GET THE GUTS TO TELL HIM? STAND UP TO HIM, YOU WIMPS!

SO WE CAN BE OUT OF OUR JOBS? THAT'S NOT BRAVERY!

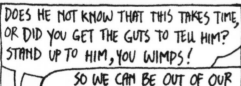

SCREW THIS KIDS MOVIE! I DESERVE BETTER! I'VE WORKED WITH HENSON! WORKED WITH BAIRD!!

THEN PLEASE LEAVE AFTER YOU'VE FIXED THOSE CAMERAS.

FWSHHT

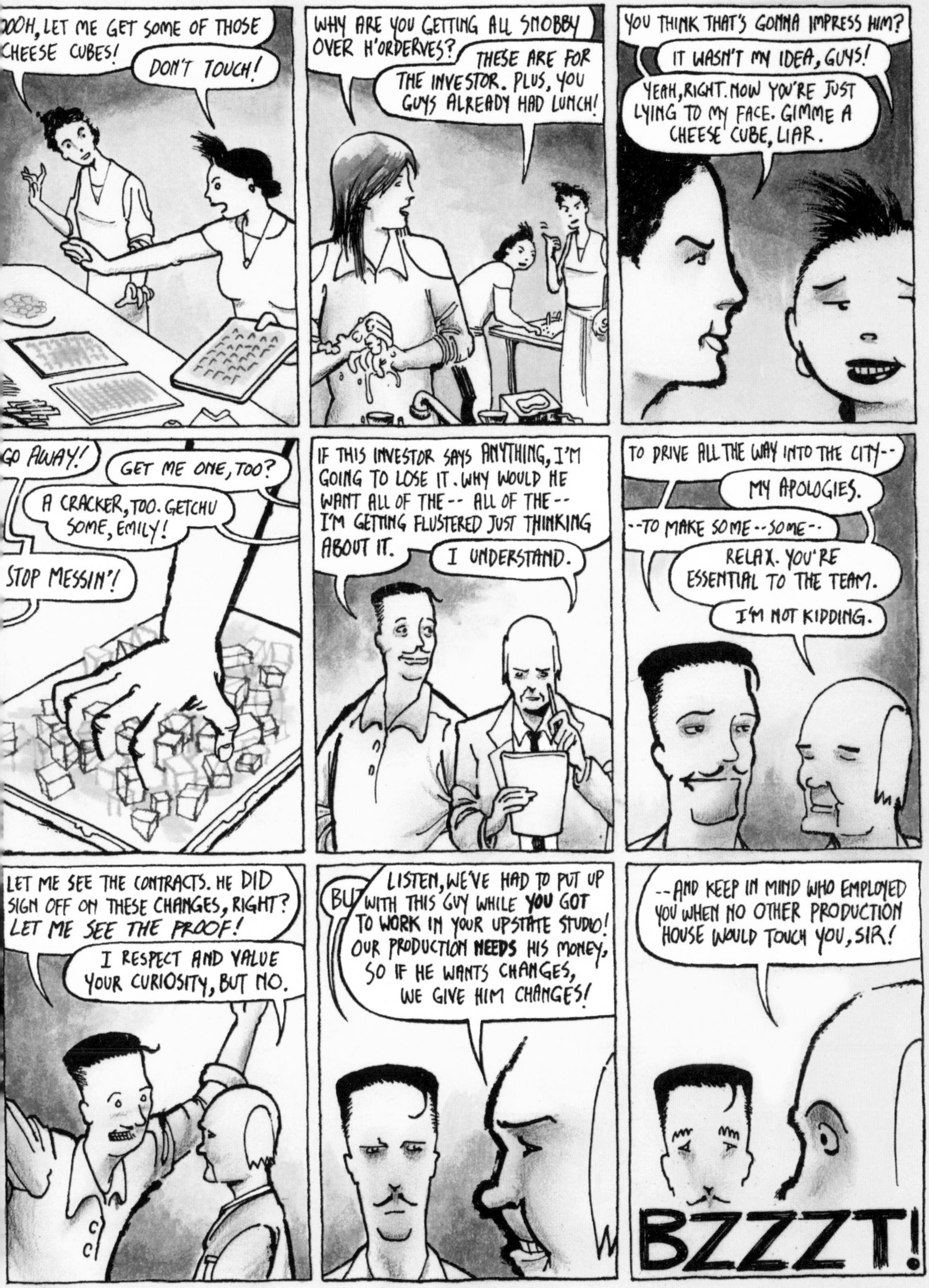
OOOH, LET ME GET SOME OF THOSE CHEESE CUBES!
DON'T TOUCH!
WHY ARE YOU GETTING ALL SNOBBY OVER H'ORDERVES?
THESE ARE FOR THE INVESTOR. PLUS, YOU GUYS ALREADY HAD LUNCH!
YOU THINK THAT'S GONNA IMPRESS HIM?
IT WASN'T MY IDEA, GUYS!
YEAH, RIGHT. NOW YOU'RE JUST LYING TO MY FACE. GIMME A CHEESE CUBE, LIAR.
GO AWAY!
GET ME ONE, TOO?
A CRACKER, TOO. GETCHU SOME, EMILY!
STOP MESSIN'!
IF THIS INVESTOR SAYS ANYTHING, I'M GOING TO LOSE IT. WHY WOULD HE WANT ALL OF THE-- ALL OF THE-- I'M GETTING FLUSTERED JUST THINKING ABOUT IT.
I UNDERSTAND.
TO DRIVE ALL THE WAY INTO THE CITY--
MY APOLOGIES.
--TO MAKE SOME--SOME--
RELAX. YOU'RE ESSENTIAL TO THE TEAM.
I'M NOT KIDDING.
LET ME SEE THE CONTRACTS. HE DID SIGN OFF ON THESE CHANGES, RIGHT? LET ME SEE THE PROOF!
I RESPECT AND VALUE YOUR CURIOSITY, BUT NO.
BUT
LISTEN, WE'VE HAD TO PUT UP WITH THIS GUY WHILE YOU GOT TO WORK IN YOUR UPSTATE STUDIO! OUR PRODUCTION NEEDS HIS MONEY, SO IF HE WANTS CHANGES, WE GIVE HIM CHANGES!
--AND KEEP IN MIND WHO EMPLOYED YOU WHEN NO OTHER PRODUCTION HOUSE WOULD TOUCH YOU, SIR!
BZZZT!

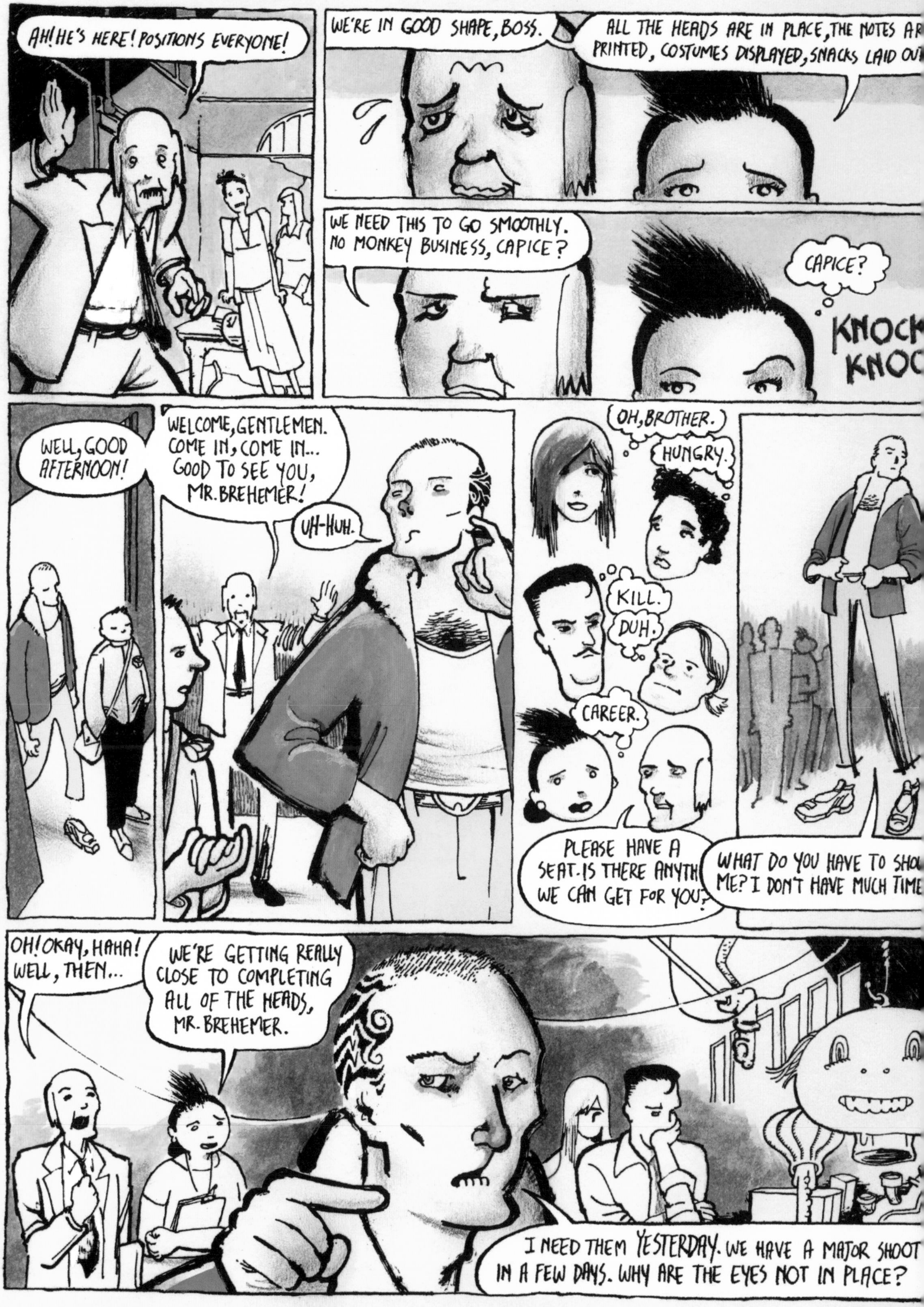
AH! HE'S HERE! POSITIONS EVERYONE!
WE'RE IN GOOD SHAPE, BOSS.
ALL THE HEADS ARE IN PLACE, THE NOTES AR
PRINTED, COSTUMES DISPLAYED, SNACKS LAID OU
WE NEED THIS TO GO SMOOTHLY. NO MONKEY BUSINESS, CAPICE?
CAPICE?
KNOCK
KNOC
WELL, GOOD AFTERNOON!
WELCOME, GENTLEMEN. COME IN, COME IN... GOOD TO SEE YOU, MR. BREHEMER!
UH-HUH.
OH, BROTHER.
HUNGRY.
KILL.
DUH.
CAREER.
PLEASE HAVE A SEAT. IS THERE ANYTH WE CAN GET FOR YOU?
WHAT DO YOU HAVE TO SHO ME? I DON'T HAVE MUCH TIME
OH! OKAY, HAHA! WELL, THEN...
WE'RE GETTING REALLY CLOSE TO COMPLETING ALL OF THE HEADS, MR. BREHEMER.
I NEED THEM YESTERDAY. WE HAVE A MAJOR SHOOT IN A FEW DAYS. WHY ARE THE EYES NOT IN PLACE?

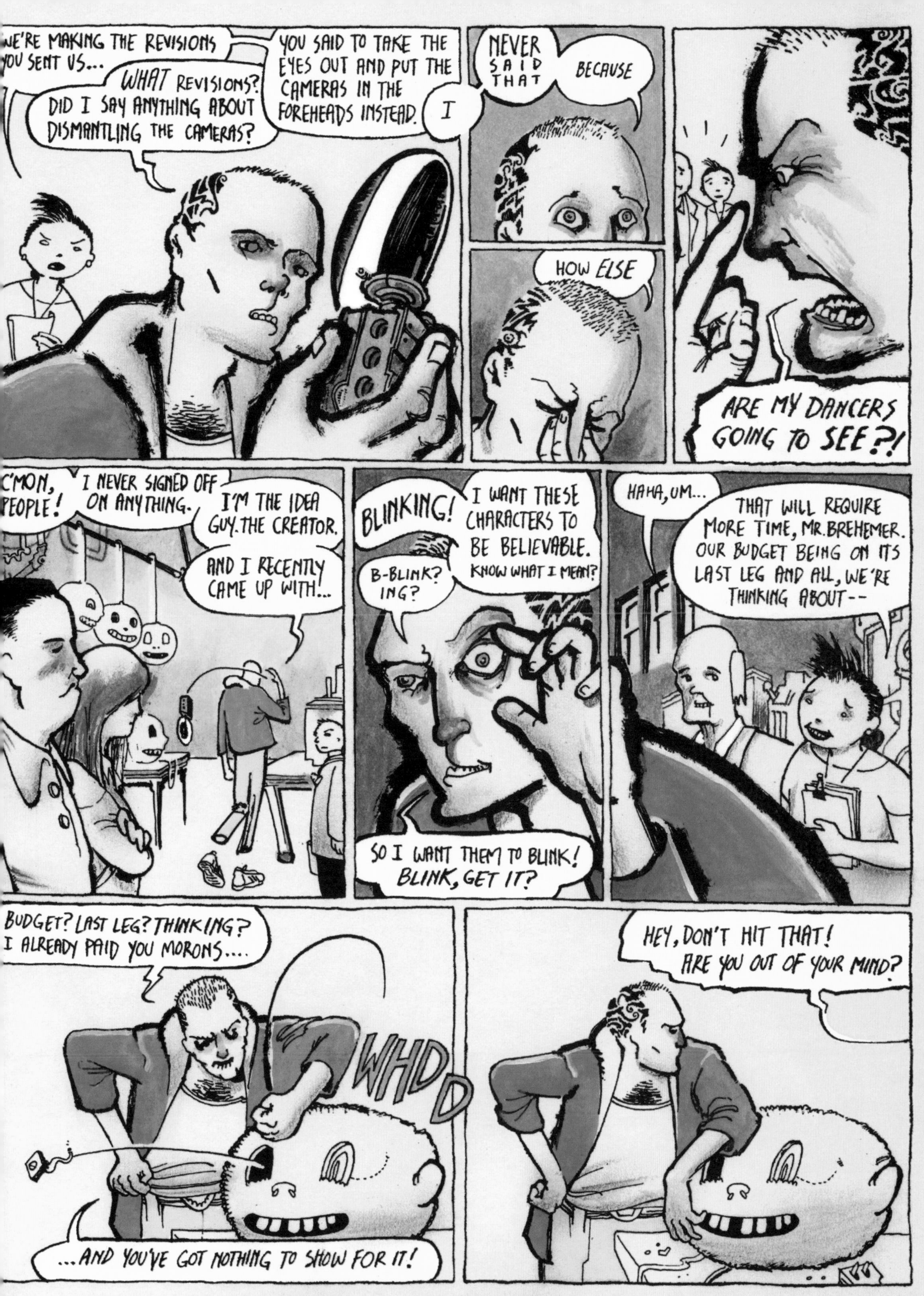
WE'RE MAKING THE REVISIONS YOU SENT US...
WHAT REVISIONS? DID I SAY ANYTHING ABOUT DISMANTLING THE CAMERAS?
YOU SAID TO TAKE THE EYES OUT AND PUT THE CAMERAS IN THE FOREHEADS INSTEAD.
I
NEVER SAID THAT
BECAUSE
HOW ELSE
ARE MY DANCERS GOING TO SEE?!
C'MON, PEOPLE!
I NEVER SIGNED OFF ON ANYTHING.
I'M THE IDEA GUY. THE CREATOR.
AND I RECENTLY CAME UP WITH...
BLINKING!
I WANT THESE CHARACTERS TO BE BELIEVABLE. KNOW WHAT I MEAN?
B-BLINK? ING?
SO I WANT THEM TO BLINK! BLINK, GET IT?
HAHA, UM...
THAT WILL REQUIRE MORE TIME, MR. BREHEMER. OUR BUDGET BEING ON ITS LAST LEG AND ALL, WE'RE THINKING ABOUT--
BUDGET? LAST LEG? THINKING? I ALREADY PAID YOU MORONS....
WHDD
...AND YOU'VE GOT NOTHING TO SHOW FOR IT!
HEY, DON'T HIT THAT! ARE YOU OUT OF YOUR MIND?

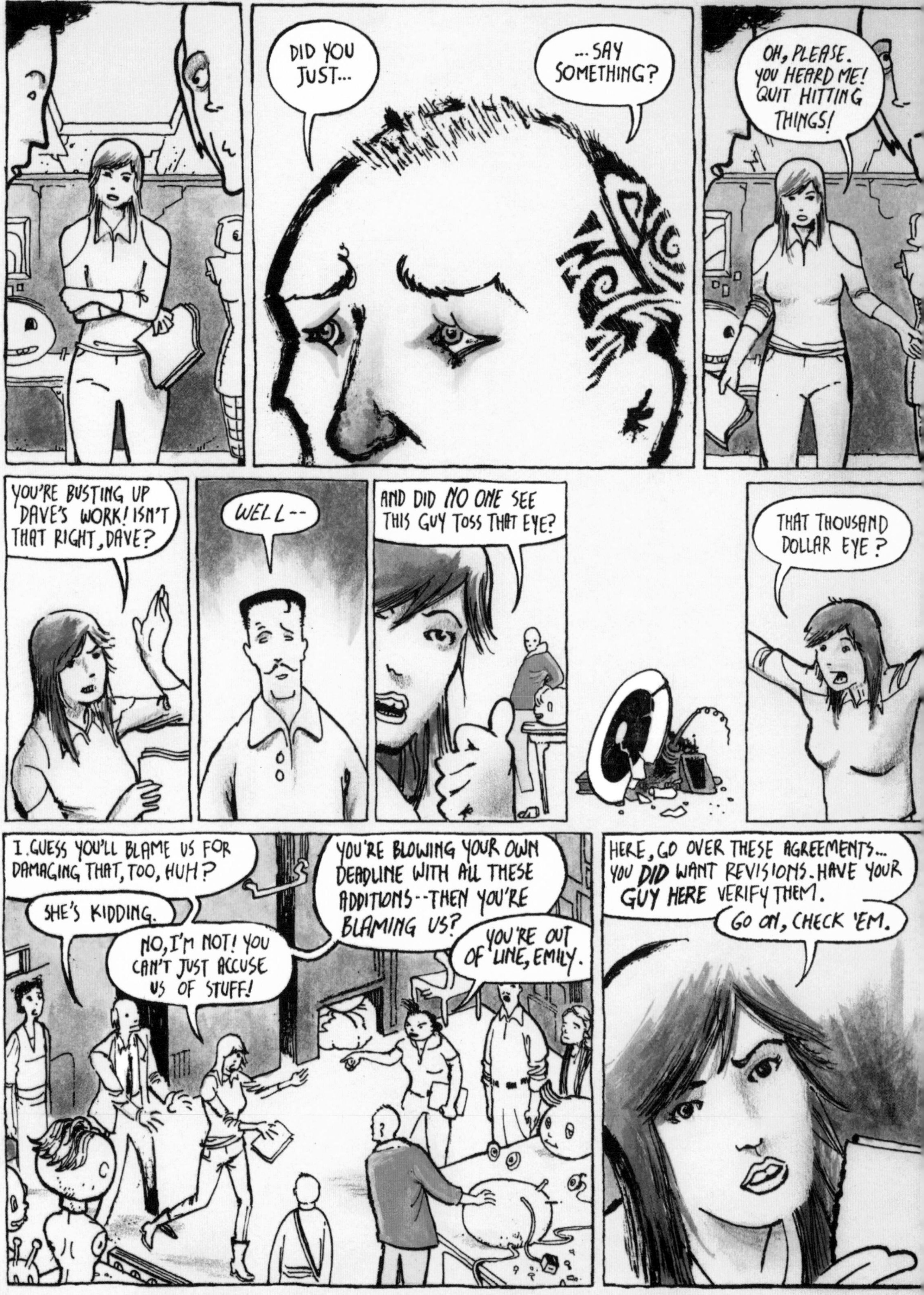
DID YOU JUST...
...SAY SOMETHING?
OH, PLEASE. YOU HEARD ME! QUIT HITTING THINGS!
YOU'RE BUSTING UP DAVE'S WORK! ISN'T THAT RIGHT, DAVE?
WELL--
AND DID NO ONE SEE THIS GUY TOSS THAT EYE?
THAT THOUSAND DOLLAR EYE?
I GUESS YOU'LL BLAME US FOR DAMAGING THAT, TOO, HUH?
SHE'S KIDDING.
NO, I'M NOT! YOU CAN'T JUST ACCUSE US OF STUFF!
YOU'RE BLOWING YOUR OWN DEADLINE WITH ALL THESE ADDITIONS--THEN YOU'RE BLAMING US?
YOU'RE OUT OF LINE, EMILY.
HERE, GO OVER THESE AGREEMENTS... YOU DID WANT REVISIONS. HAVE YOUR GUY HERE VERIFY THEM.
GO ON, CHECK 'EM.

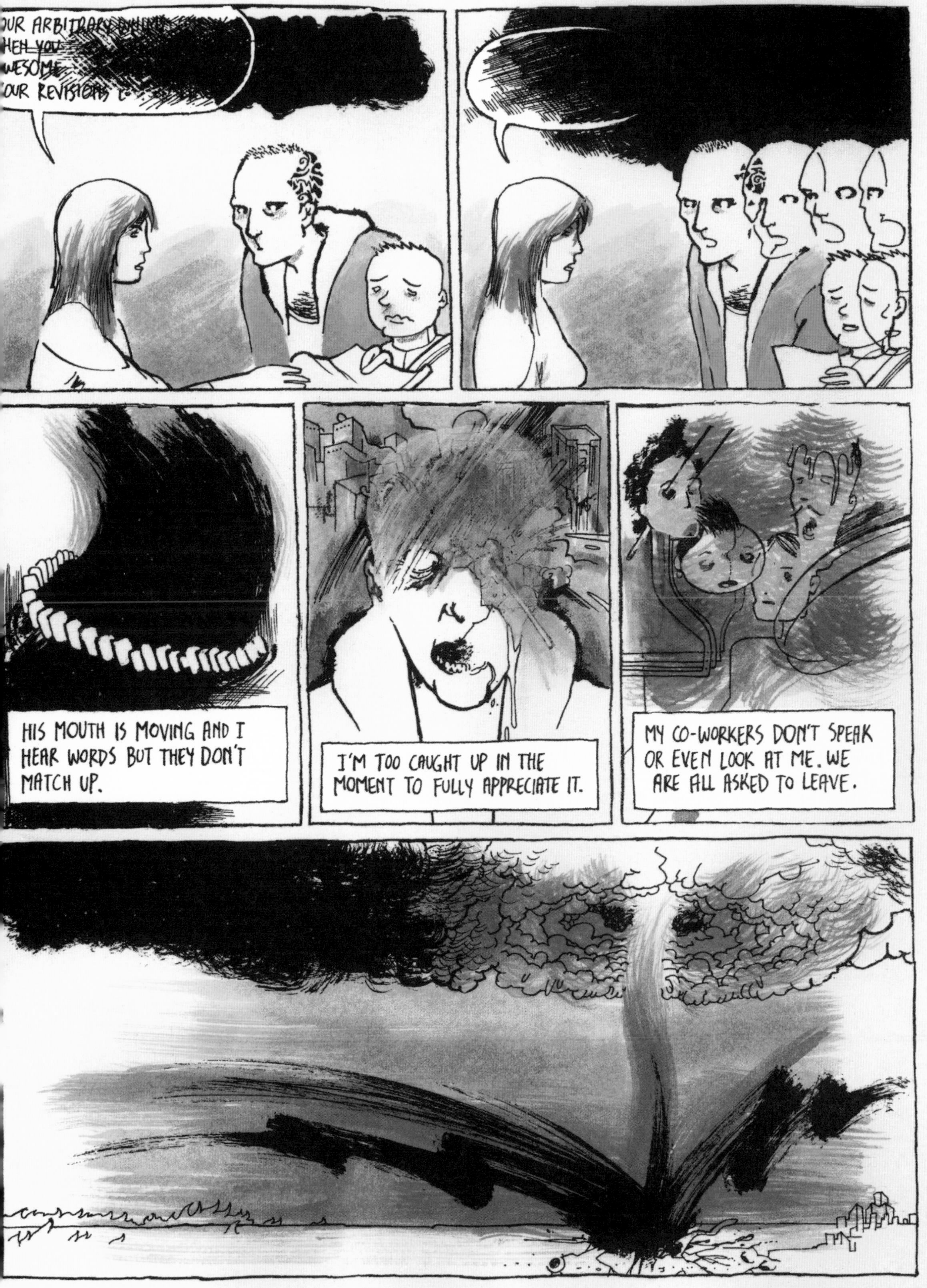
HIS MOUTH IS MOVING AND I HEAR WORDS BUT THEY DON'T MATCH UP.
I'M TOO CAUGHT UP IN THE MOMENT TO FULLY APPRECIATE IT.
MY CO-WORKERS DON'T SPEAK OR EVEN LOOK AT ME. WE ARE ALL ASKED TO LEAVE.

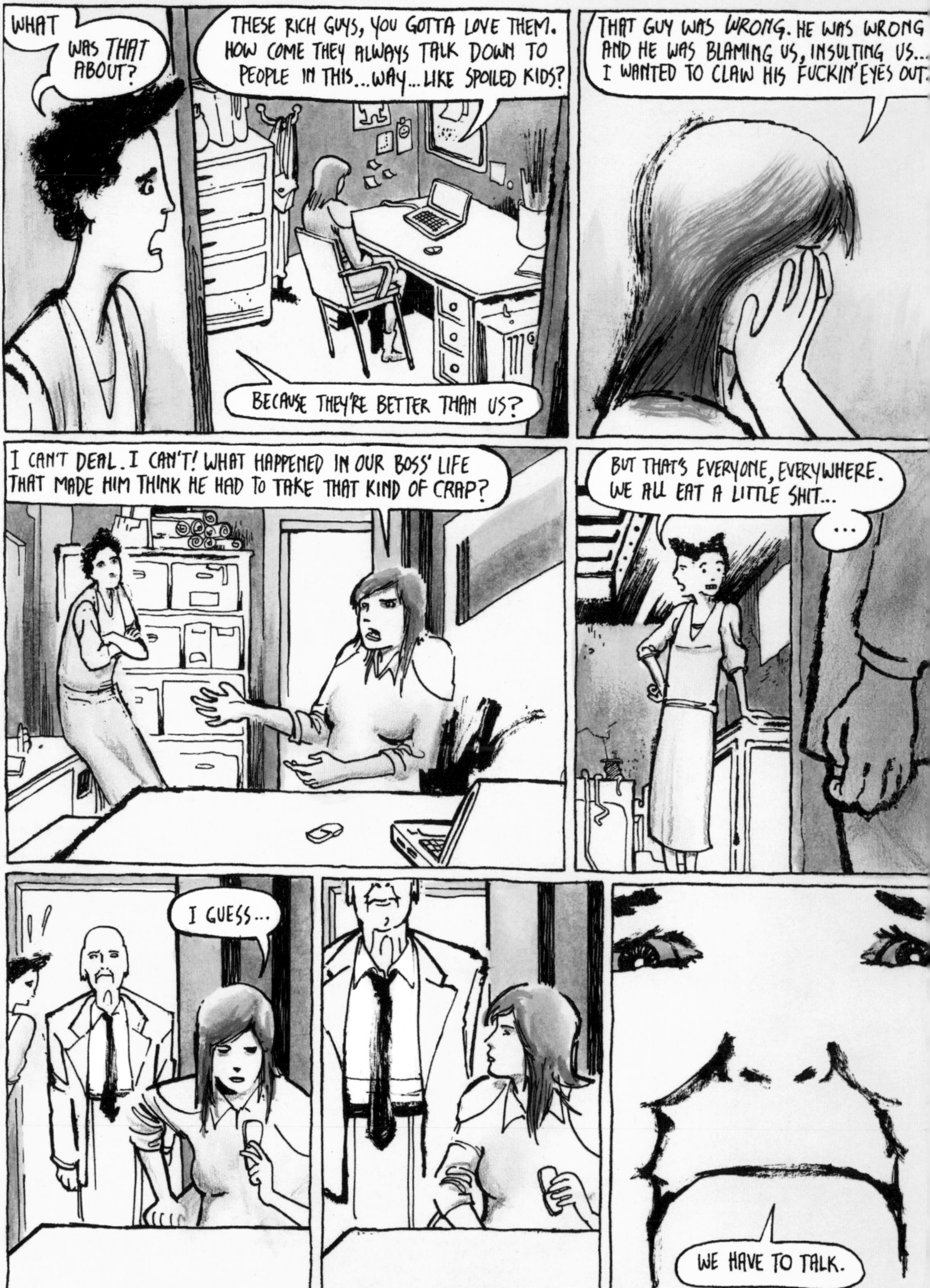
WHAT WAS THAT ABOUT?
THESE RICH GUYS, YOU GOTTA LOVE THEM. HOW COME THEY ALWAYS TALK DOWN TO PEOPLE IN THIS...WAY...LIKE SPOILED KIDS?
BECAUSE THEY'RE BETTER THAN US?
THAT GUY WAS WRONG. HE WAS WRONG AND HE WAS BLAMING US, INSULTING US... I WANTED TO CLAW HIS FUCKIN' EYES OUT.
I CAN'T DEAL. I CAN'T! WHAT HAPPENED IN OUR BOSS' LIFE THAT MADE HIM THINK HE HAD TO TAKE THAT KIND OF CRAP?
BUT THAT'S EVERYONE, EVERYWHERE. WE ALL EAT A LITTLE SHIT...
...
I GUESS...
WE HAVE TO TALK.

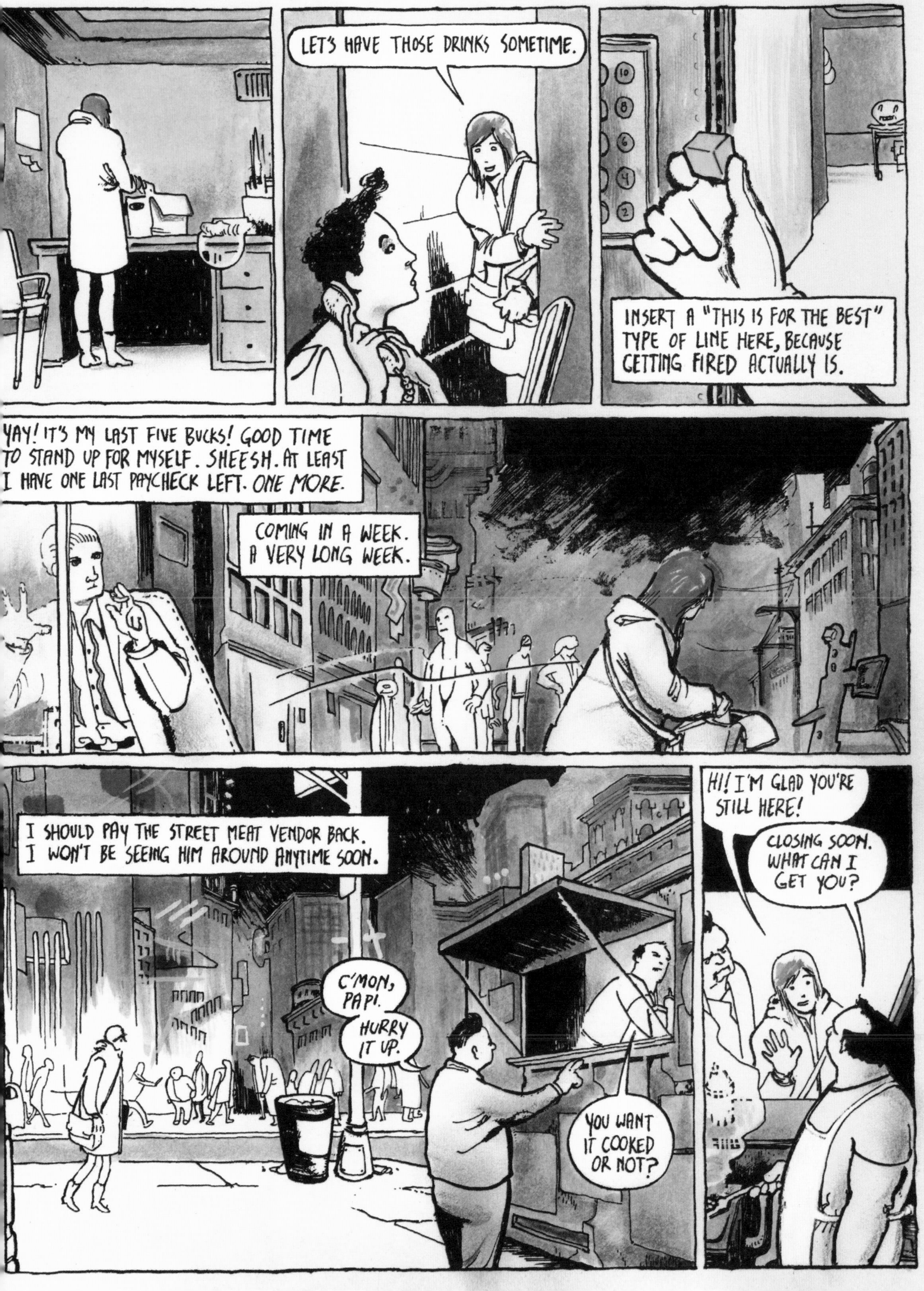
LET'S HAVE THOSE DRINKS SOMETIME.
INSERT A "THIS IS FOR THE BEST" TYPE OF LINE HERE, BECAUSE GETTING FIRED ACTUALLY IS.
YAY! IT'S MY LAST FIVE BUCKS! GOOD TIME TO STAND UP FOR MYSELF. SHEESH. AT LEAST I HAVE ONE LAST PAYCHECK LEFT. ONE MORE.
COMING IN A WEEK. A VERY LONG WEEK.
I SHOULD PAY THE STREET MEAT VENDOR BACK. I WON'T BE SEEING HIM AROUND ANYTIME SOON.
C'MON, PAPI.
HURRY IT UP.
YOU WANT IT COOKED OR NOT?
HI! I'M GLAD YOU'RE STILL HERE!
CLOSING SOON. WHAT CAN I GET YOU?

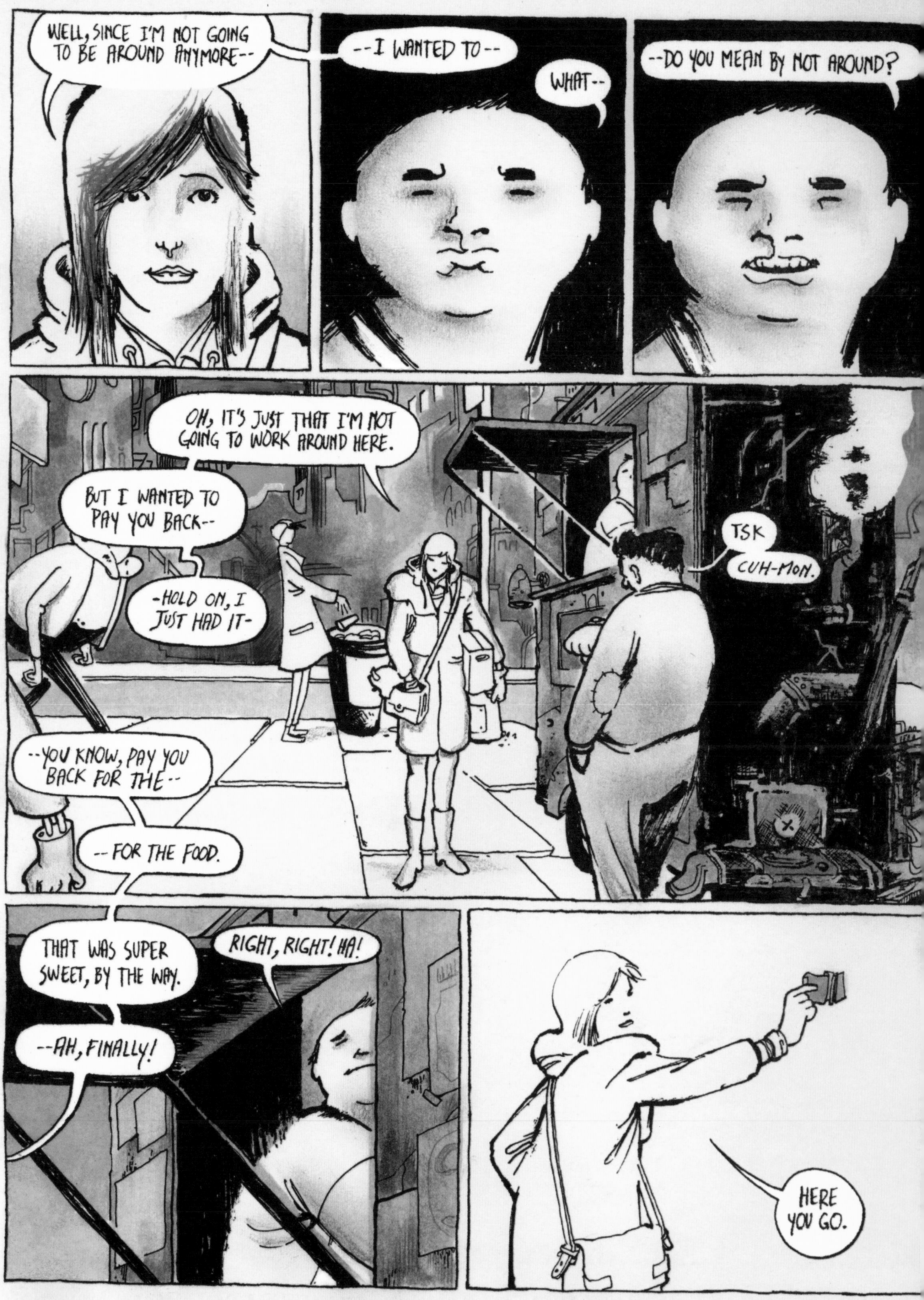
WELL, SINCE I'M NOT GOING TO BE AROUND ANYMORE--
--I WANTED TO--
WHAT--
--DO YOU MEAN BY NOT AROUND?
OH, IT'S JUST THAT I'M NOT GOING TO WORK AROUND HERE.
BUT I WANTED TO PAY YOU BACK--
-HOLD ON, I JUST HAD IT-
TSK
CUH-MON.
--YOU KNOW, PAY YOU BACK FOR THE--
--FOR THE FOOD.
THAT WAS SUPER SWEET, BY THE WAY.
RIGHT, RIGHT! HA!
--AH, FINALLY!
HERE YOU GO.

THIS BREAKS MY HEART. HE LOOKS LIKE HE ISN'T JUST TAKING HIS MONEY BACK...

THERE'S THIS--THIS DEEP GRATITUDE IN HIS FACE...AND NONE IS NEEDED. HE DID *ME* THE FAVOR AFTER ALL.

SHIT, IF THAT'S NOT CONDESCENDING OF ME.

HE PROBABLY GETS ALL OF THE WORST PEOPLE, ESPECIALLY AROUND HERE. THE MEATHEADS, THE CREEPS, THE INGRATES.

I DON'T SEE HIM AS JUST A VENDOR OR JUST ANOTHER CIVILIAN TRYING TO GET BY.

HE'S NOBLE. HE'S BEAUTIFUL.

AND HERE I AM WITH HIS FIVE BUCKS.

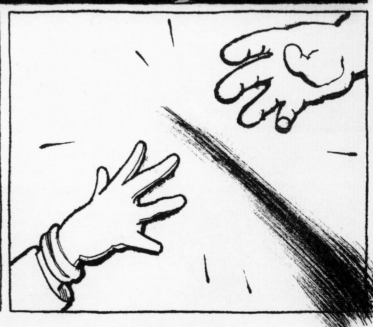

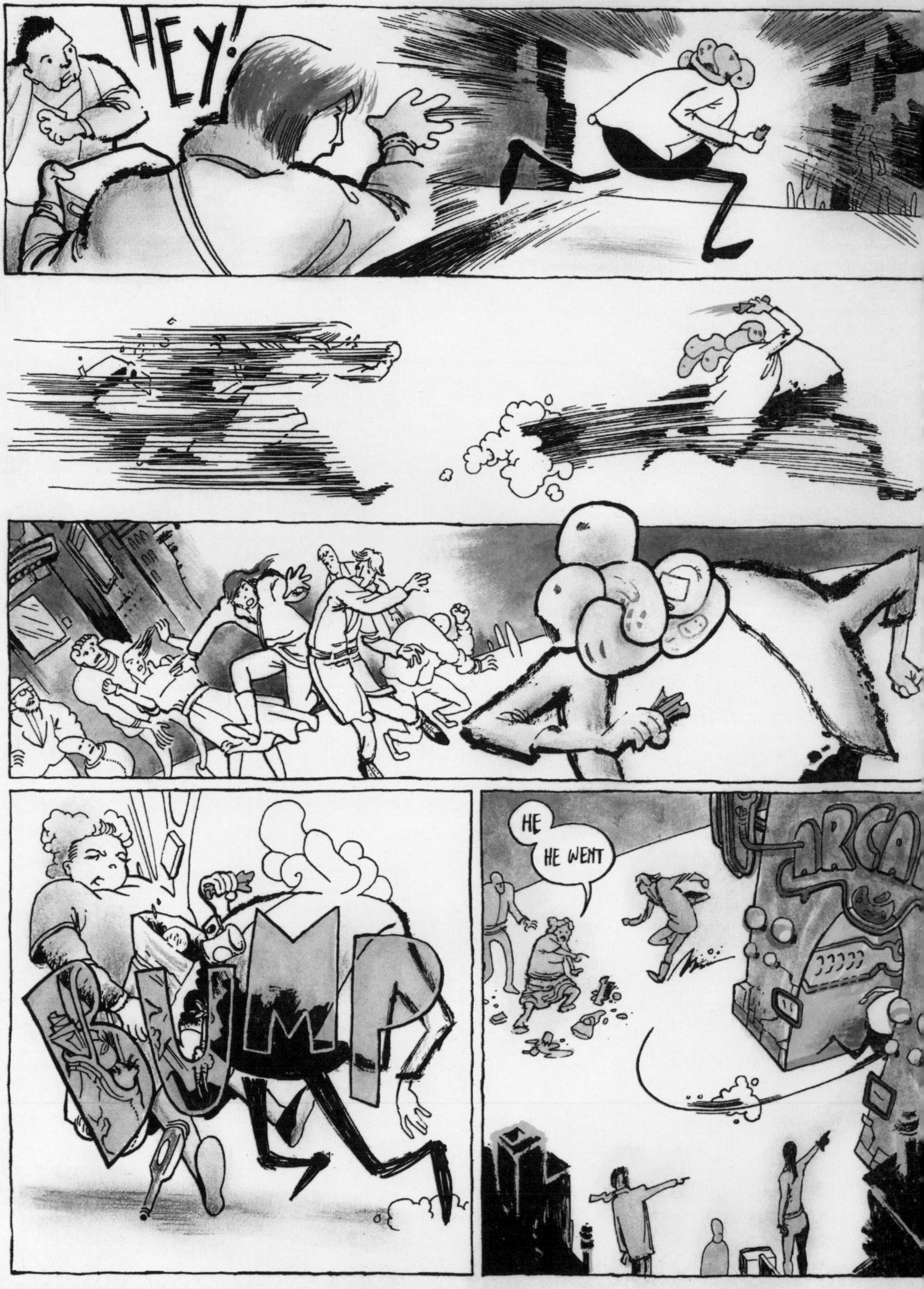
HEY!
BUMP
HE
HE WENT
ARCA

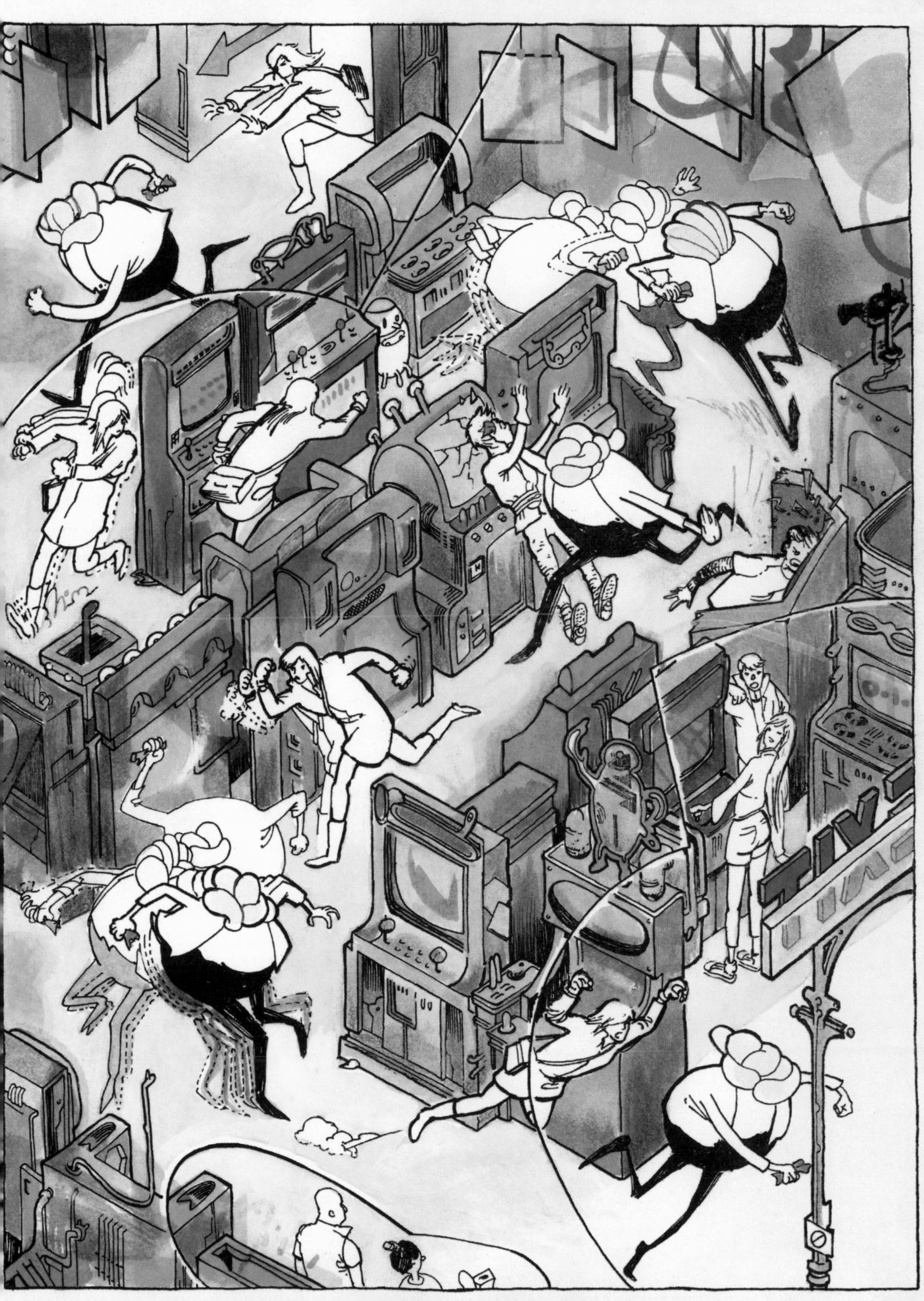

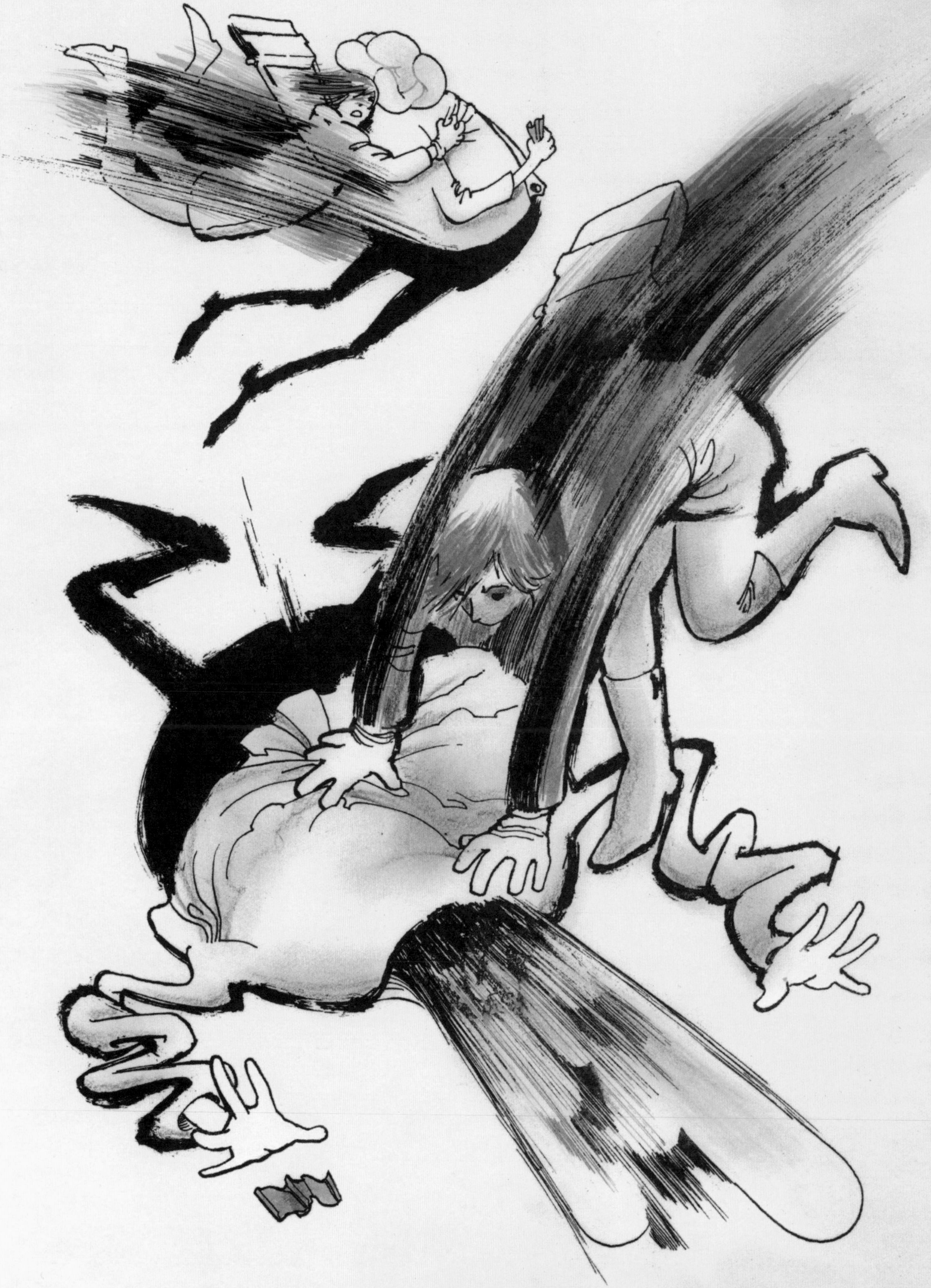

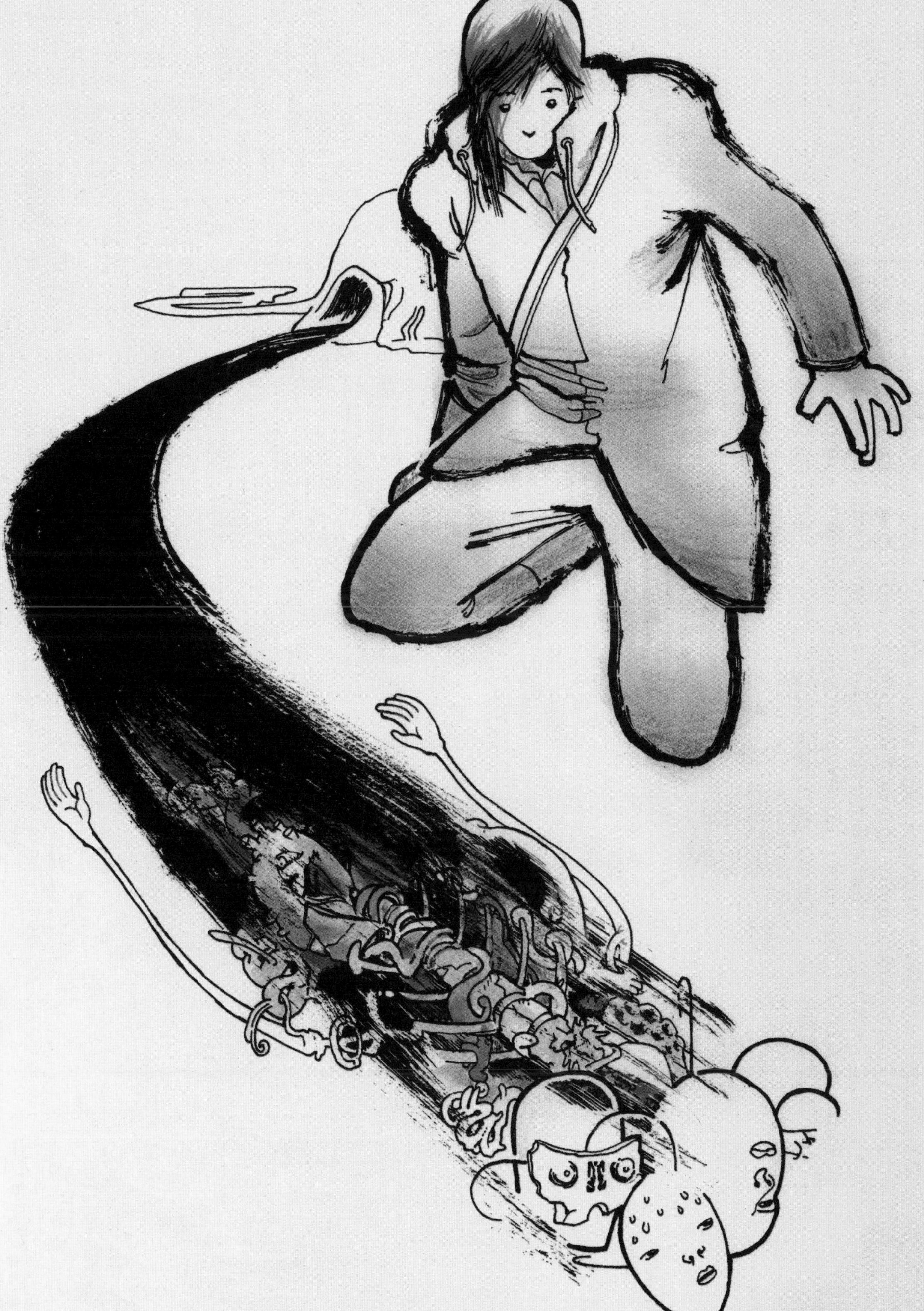

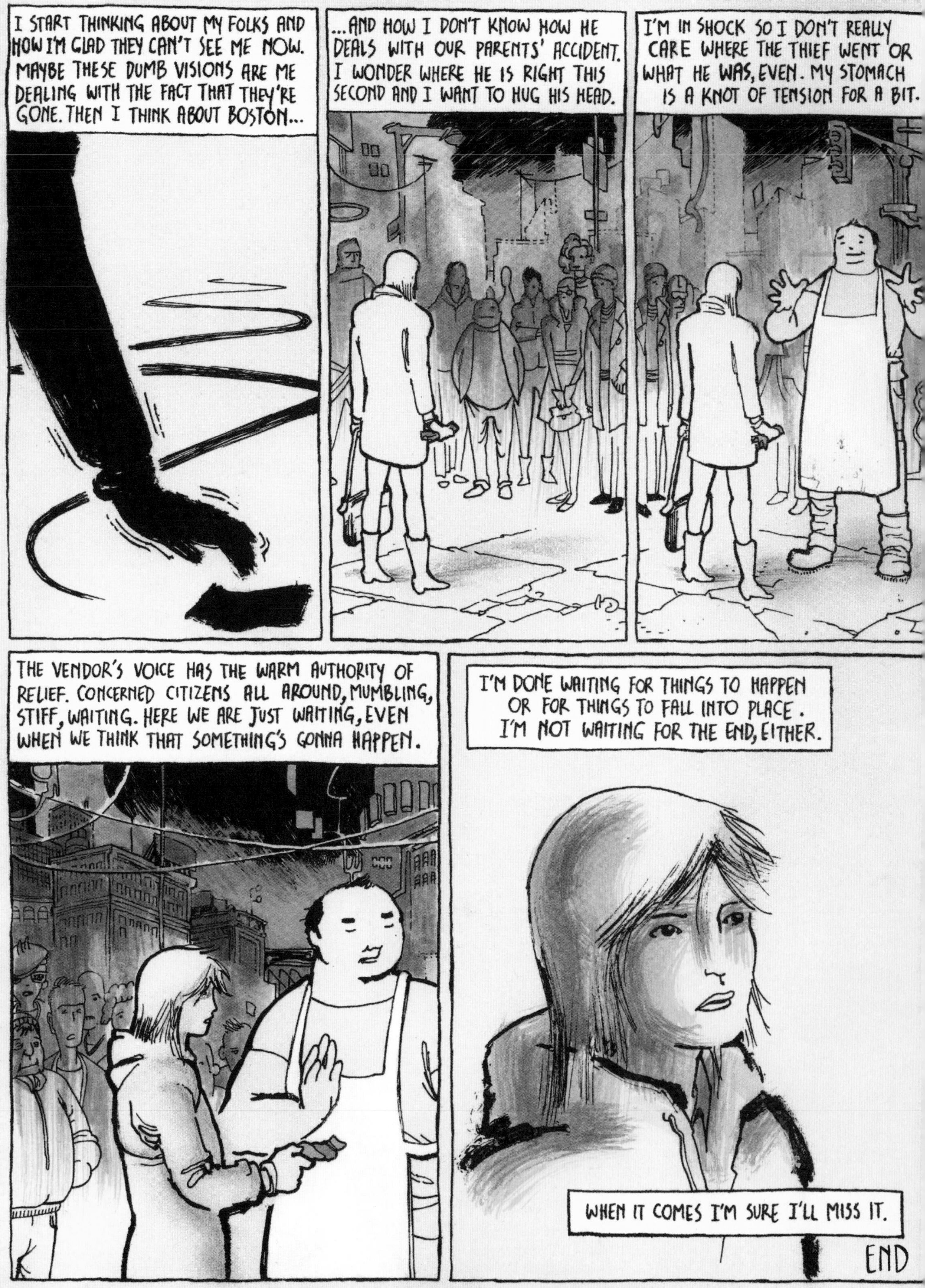
I START THINKING ABOUT MY FOLKS AND HOW I'M GLAD THEY CAN'T SEE ME NOW. MAYBE THESE DUMB VISIONS ARE ME DEALING WITH THE FACT THAT THEY'RE GONE. THEN I THINK ABOUT BOSTON...
...AND HOW I DON'T KNOW HOW HE DEALS WITH OUR PARENTS' ACCIDENT. I WONDER WHERE HE IS RIGHT THIS SECOND AND I WANT TO HUG HIS HEAD.
I'M IN SHOCK SO I DON'T REALLY CARE WHERE THE THIEF WENT OR WHAT HE WAS, EVEN. MY STOMACH IS A KNOT OF TENSION FOR A BIT.
THE VENDOR'S VOICE HAS THE WARM AUTHORITY OF RELIEF. CONCERNED CITIZENS ALL AROUND, MUMBLING, STIFF, WAITING. HERE WE ARE JUST WAITING, EVEN WHEN WE THINK THAT SOMETHING'S GONNA HAPPEN.
I'M DONE WAITING FOR THINGS TO HAPPEN OR FOR THINGS TO FALL INTO PLACE. I'M NOT WAITING FOR THE END, EITHER.
WHEN IT COMES I'M SURE I'LL MISS IT.
END

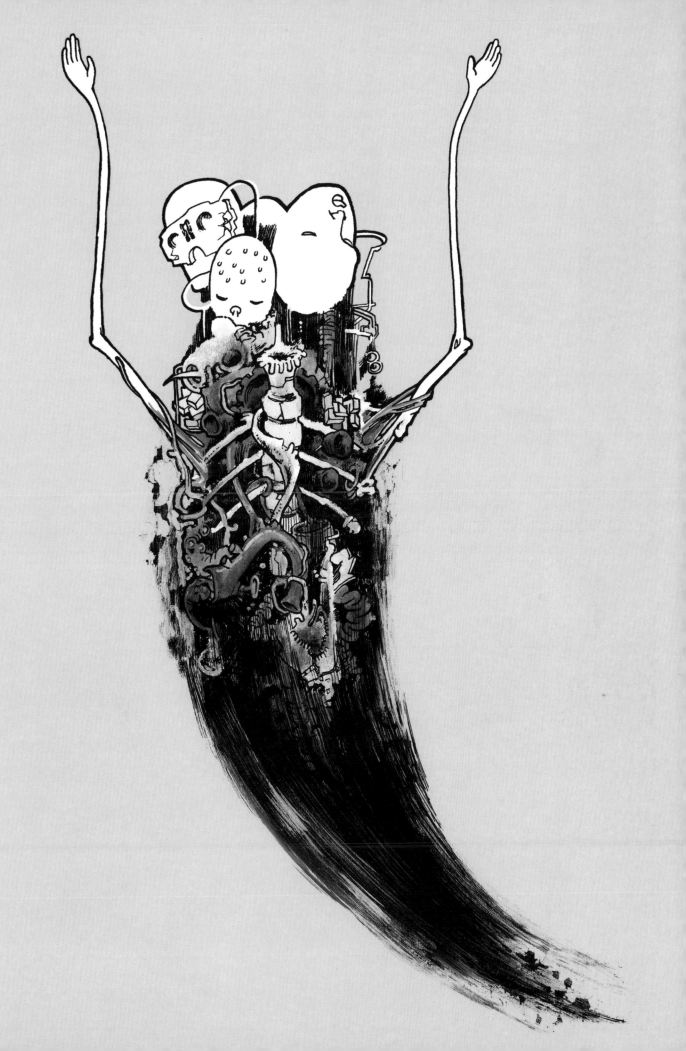

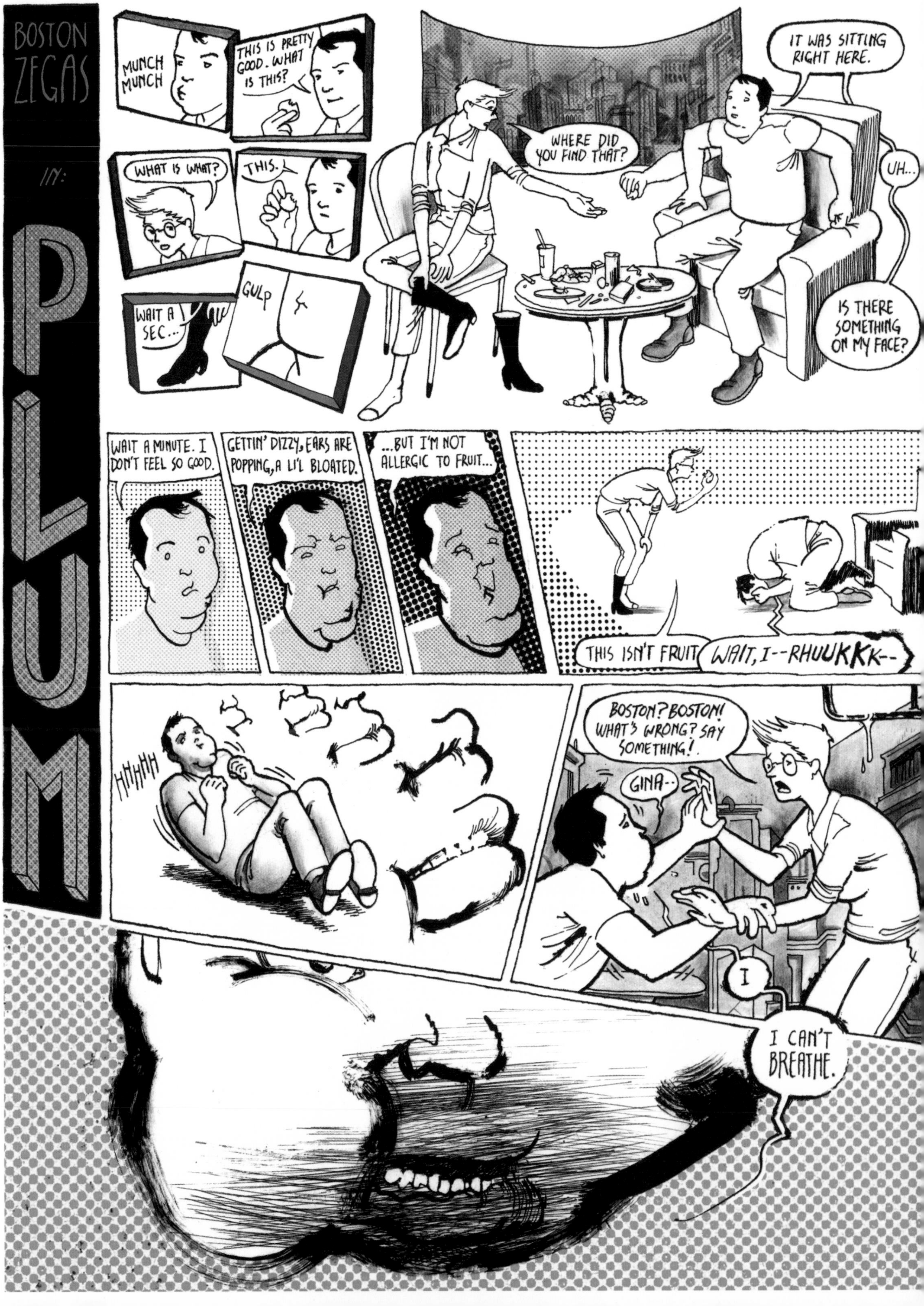
BOSTON ZEGAS
BY:
PLUM
MUNCH MUNCH
THIS IS PRETTY GOOD. WHAT IS THIS?
WHAT IS WHAT?
THIS.
WAIT A SEC...
GULP
WHERE DID YOU FIND THAT?
IT WAS SITTING RIGHT HERE.
UH...
IS THERE SOMETHING ON MY FACE?
WAIT A MINUTE. I DON'T FEEL SO GOOD.
GETTIN' DIZZY, EARS ARE POPPING, A LI'L BLOATED.
...BUT I'M NOT ALLERGIC TO FRUIT...
THIS ISN'T FRUIT
WAIT, I--RHUUKKK--
HHHHHH
BOSTON? BOSTON! WHAT'S WRONG? SAY SOMETHING!
GINA--
I
I CAN'T BREATHE.

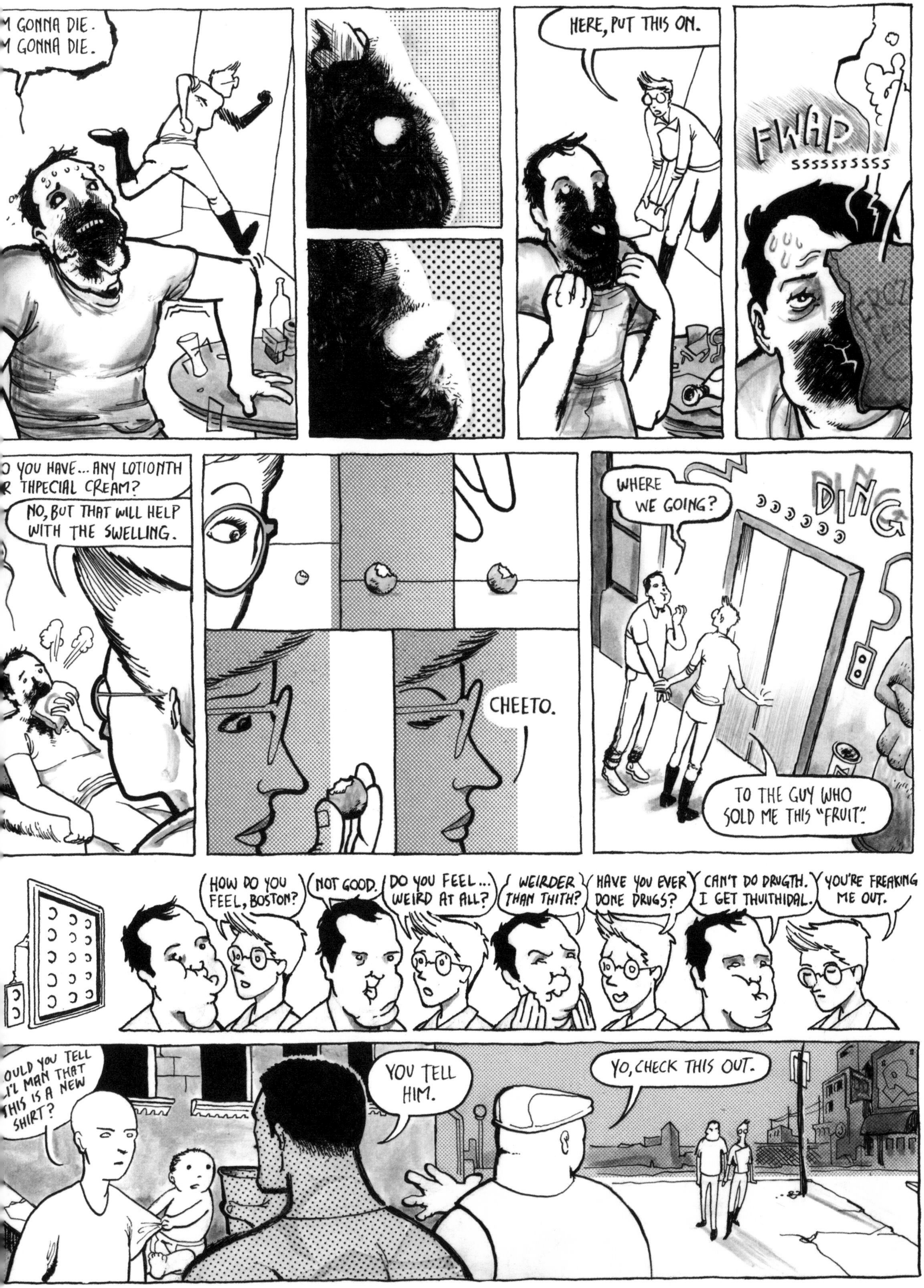
M GONNA DIE.
M GONNA DIE.
HERE, PUT THIS ON.
FWAP
SSSSSSSSSS
O YOU HAVE... ANY LOTIONTH
R THPECIAL CREAM?
NO, BUT THAT WILL HELP WITH THE SWELLING.
CHEETO.
WHERE WE GOING?
DING
TO THE GUY WHO SOLD ME THIS "FRUIT".
HOW DO YOU FEEL, BOSTON?
NOT GOOD.
DO YOU FEEL... WEIRD AT ALL?
WEIRDER THAN THITH?
HAVE YOU EVER DONE DRUGS?
CAN'T DO DRUGTH. I GET THUITHIDAL.
YOU'RE FREAKING ME OUT.
OULD YOU TELL
L'L MAN THAT
THIS IS A NEW
SHIRT?
YOU TELL HIM.
YO, CHECK THIS OUT.

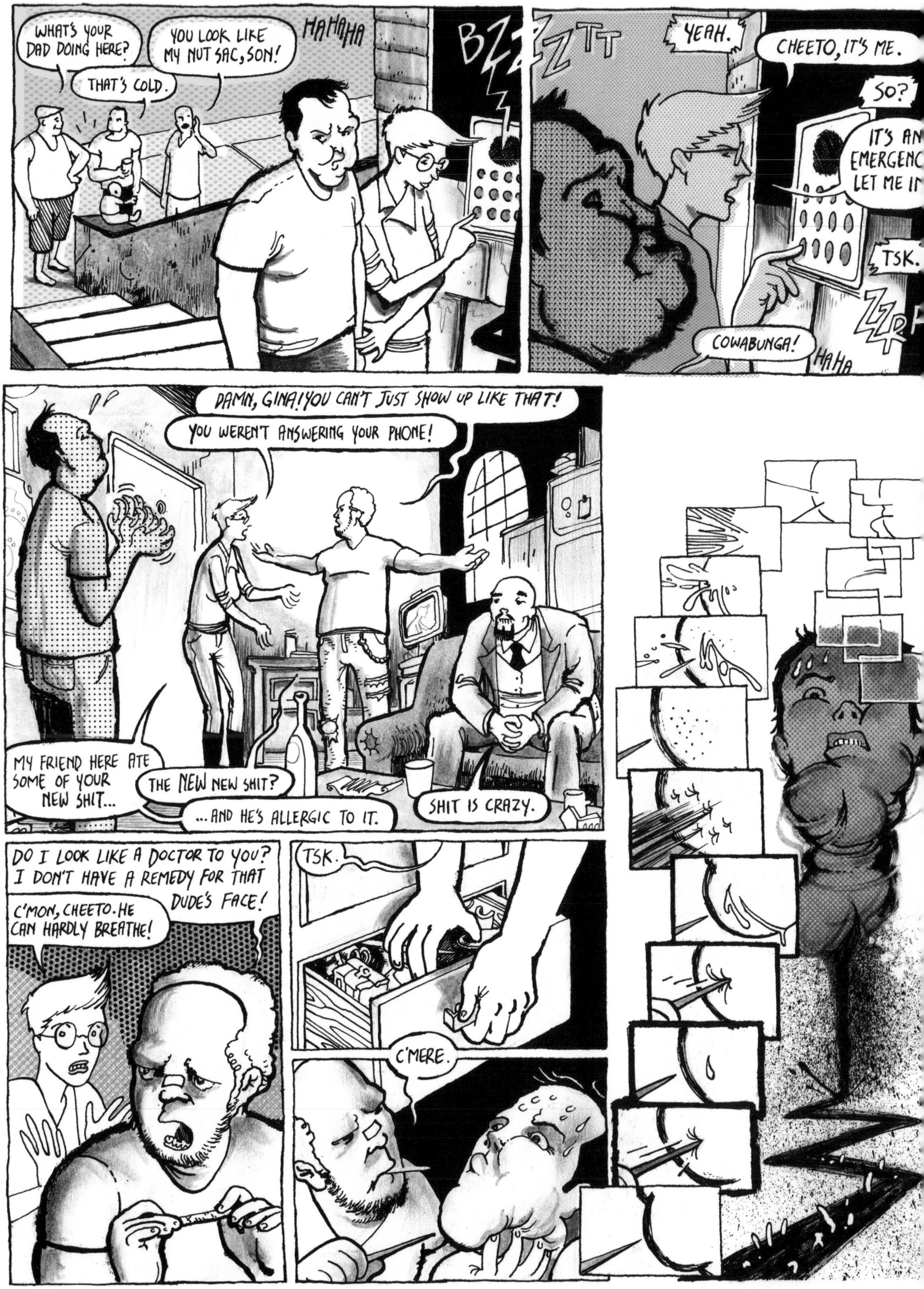
WHAT'S YOUR DAD DOING HERE?
YOU LOOK LIKE MY NUT SAC, SON!
HAHAHA
THAT'S COLD.
BZZZTT
YEAH.
CHEETO, IT'S ME.
SO?
IT'S AN EMERGENC LET ME IN
TSK.
ZZR
COWABUNGA!
HAHA
DAMN, GINA! YOU CAN'T JUST SHOW UP LIKE THAT!
YOU WEREN'T ANSWERING YOUR PHONE!
MY FRIEND HERE ATE SOME OF YOUR NEW SHIT...
THE NEW NEW SHIT?
...AND HE'S ALLERGIC TO IT.
SHIT IS CRAZY.
DO I LOOK LIKE A DOCTOR TO YOU? I DON'T HAVE A REMEDY FOR THAT DUDE'S FACE!
C'MON, CHEETO. HE CAN HARDLY BREATHE!
TSK.
C'MERE.

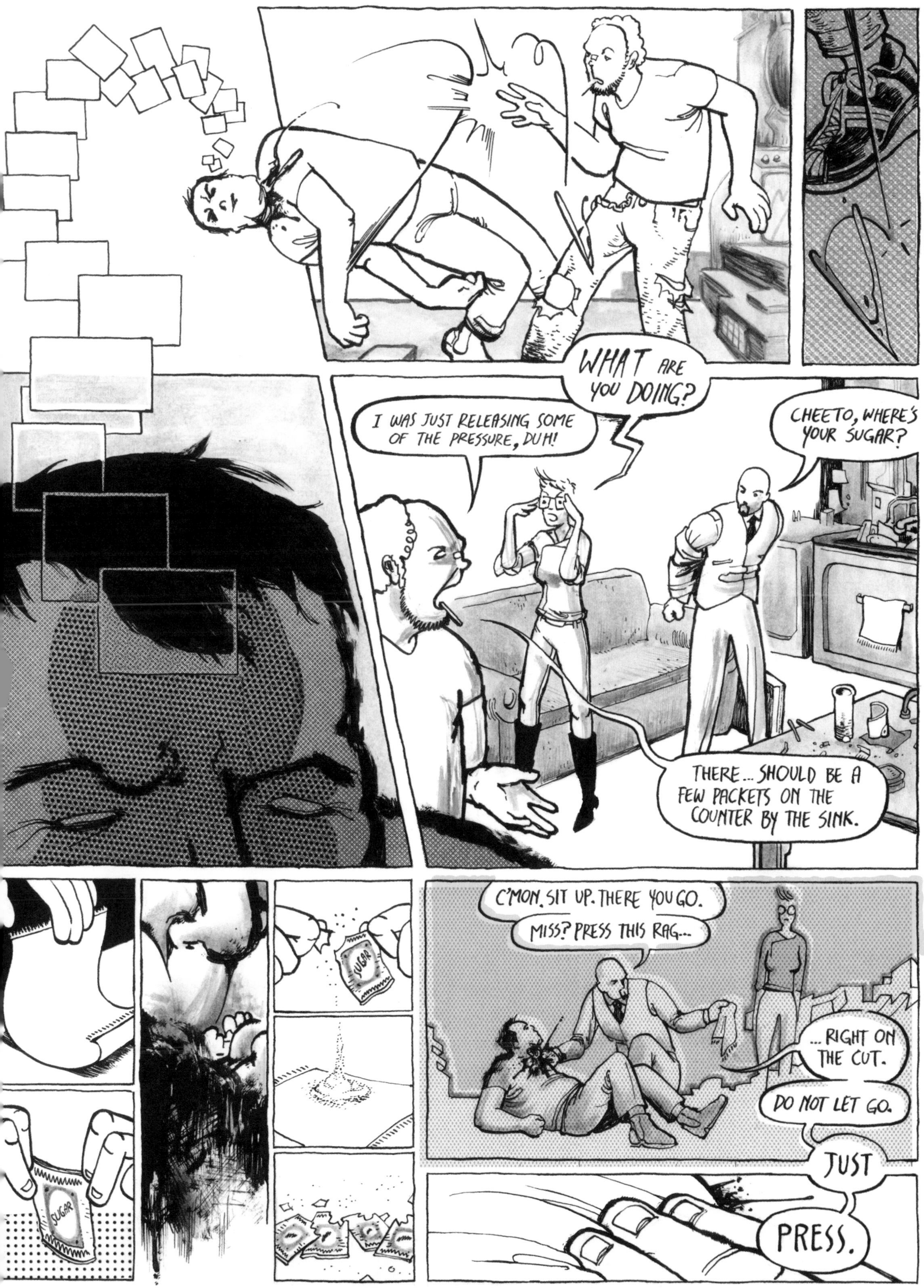
WHAT ARE YOU DOING?
I WAS JUST RELEASING SOME OF THE PRESSURE, DUH!
CHEETO, WHERE'S YOUR SUGAR?
THERE... SHOULD BE A FEW PACKETS ON THE COUNTER BY THE SINK.
SUGAR
SUGAR
C'MON. SIT UP. THERE YOU GO.
MISS? PRESS THIS RAG...
...RIGHT ON THE CUT.
DO NOT LET GO.
JUST
PRESS.

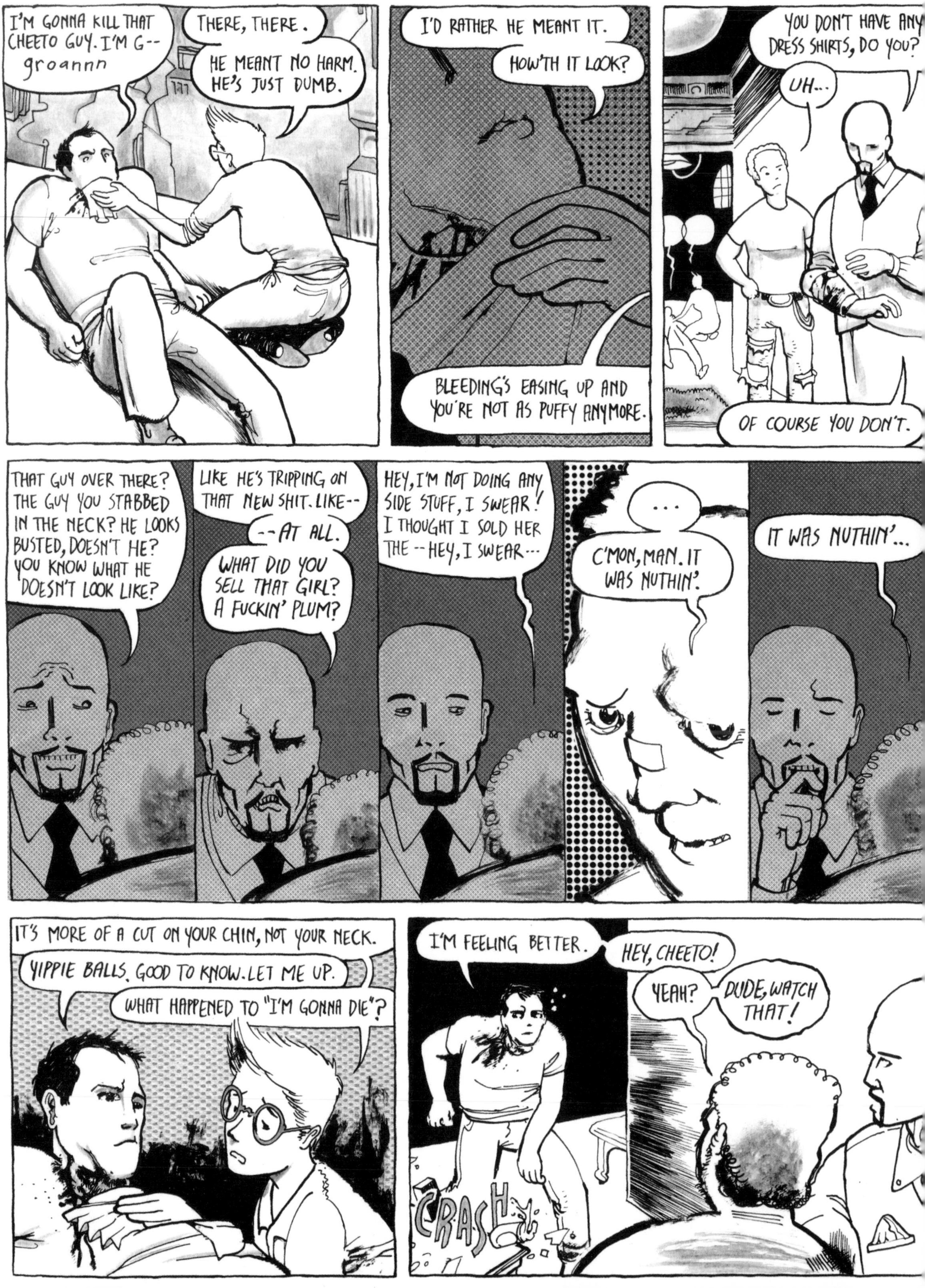
I'M GONNA KILL THAT CHEETO GUY. I'M G-- groannn
THERE, THERE.
HE MEANT NO HARM. HE'S JUST DUMB.
I'D RATHER HE MEANT IT.
HOW'TH IT LOOK?
BLEEDING'S EASING UP AND YOU'RE NOT AS PUFFY ANYMORE.
YOU DON'T HAVE ANY DRESS SHIRTS, DO YOU?
UH...
OF COURSE YOU DON'T.
THAT GUY OVER THERE? THE GUY YOU STABBED IN THE NECK? HE LOOKS BUSTED, DOESN'T HE? YOU KNOW WHAT HE DOESN'T LOOK LIKE?
LIKE HE'S TRIPPING ON THAT NEW SHIT. LIKE--
--AT ALL.
WHAT DID YOU SELL THAT GIRL? A FUCKIN' PLUM?
HEY, I'M NOT DOING ANY SIDE STUFF, I SWEAR! I THOUGHT I SOLD HER THE --HEY, I SWEAR...
...
C'MON, MAN. IT WAS NUTHIN'.
IT WAS NUTHIN'...
IT'S MORE OF A CUT ON YOUR CHIN, NOT YOUR NECK.
YIPPIE BALLS. GOOD TO KNOW. LET ME UP.
WHAT HAPPENED TO "I'M GONNA DIE"?
I'M FEELING BETTER.
HEY, CHEETO!
YEAH?
DUDE, WATCH THAT!
CRASH

YOU

YOU SHOULD GIVE THE LADY BACK HER MONEY.

GET THAT FINGER OUTTA MY FACE, MAN.

WARNING YOU...

OU SOLD HER DUDS. RIPPED HER OFF.

ALRIGHT, ALRIGHT.

WHAT IS THIS SHIT? IN MY OWN HOUSE?

GIVE IT BACK, CHEETO.

DID I ASK YOU TO SHOW UP AT MY HOUSE LOOKING LIKE A ASSHOLE? I EVEN TRIED TO HELP YOU OUT! BUT DO YOU CARE? NAW! NAW! YOU JUST START BREAKING SHIT!

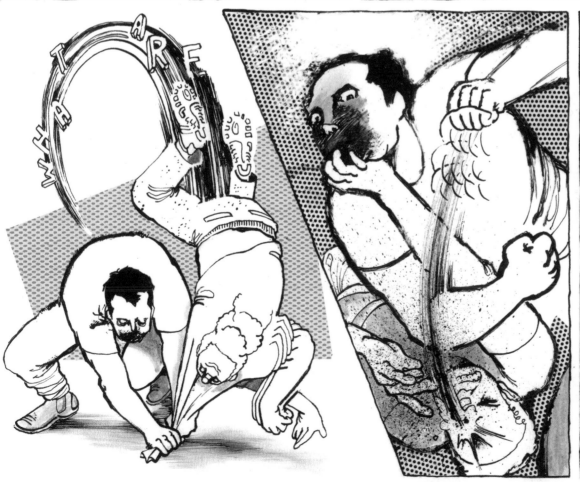

HEY, C'MON! BREAK IT UP!

HERE--

HERE...

JUST TAKE THIS. TAKE IT!

--AND GET OUTTA HERE ALREADY.

KOFF KOFF

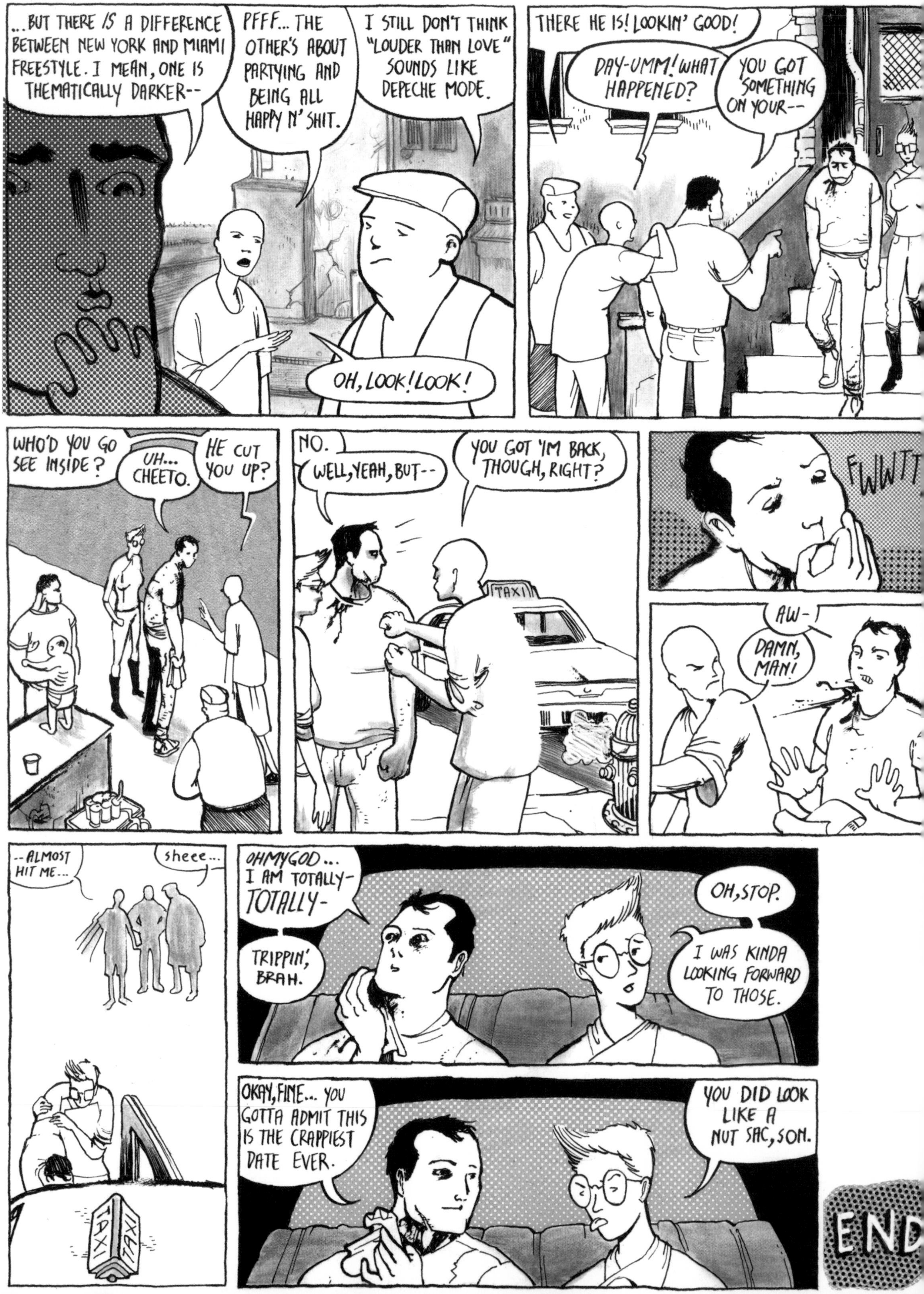
...BUT THERE IS A DIFFERENCE BETWEEN NEW YORK AND MIAMI FREESTYLE. I MEAN, ONE IS THEMATICALLY DARKER--
PFFF... THE OTHER'S ABOUT PARTYING AND BEING ALL HAPPY N' SHIT.
I STILL DON'T THINK "LOUDER THAN LOVE" SOUNDS LIKE DEPECHE MODE.
OH, LOOK! LOOK!
THERE HE IS! LOOKIN' GOOD!
DAY-UMM! WHAT HAPPENED?
YOU GOT SOMETHING ON YOUR--
WHO'D YOU GO SEE INSIDE?
UH... CHEETO.
HE CUT YOU UP?
NO.
WELL, YEAH, BUT--
YOU GOT 'IM BACK, THOUGH, RIGHT?
FWWTT
AW-
DAMN, MAN!
--ALMOST HIT ME...
sheee...
OHMYGOD... I AM TOTALLY- TOTALLY-
TRIPPIN', BRAH.
OH, STOP.
I WAS KINDA LOOKING FORWARD TO THOSE.
TAXI
OKAY, FINE... YOU GOTTA ADMIT THIS IS THE CRAPPIEST DATE EVER.
YOU DID LOOK LIKE A NUT SAC, SON.
END

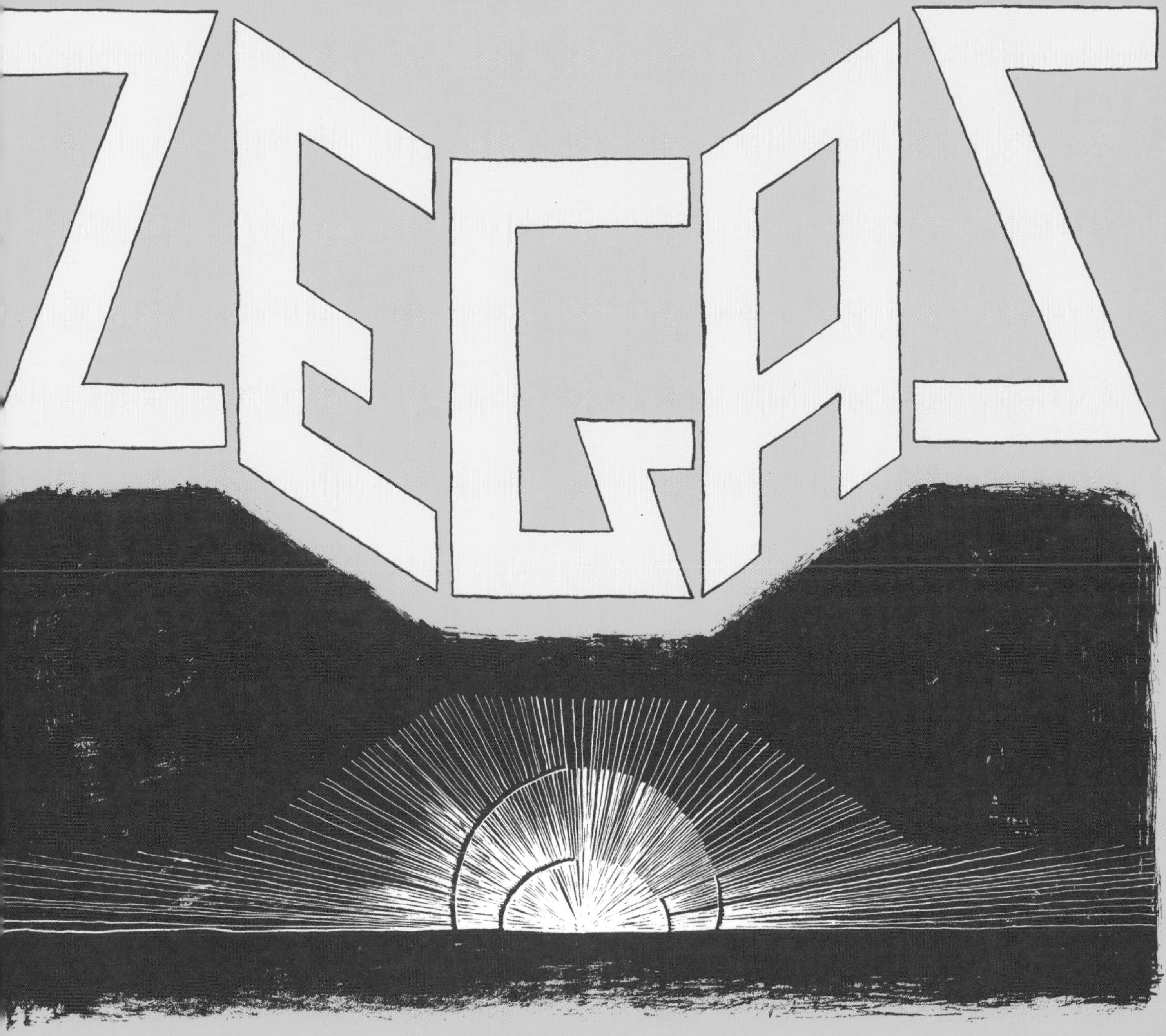

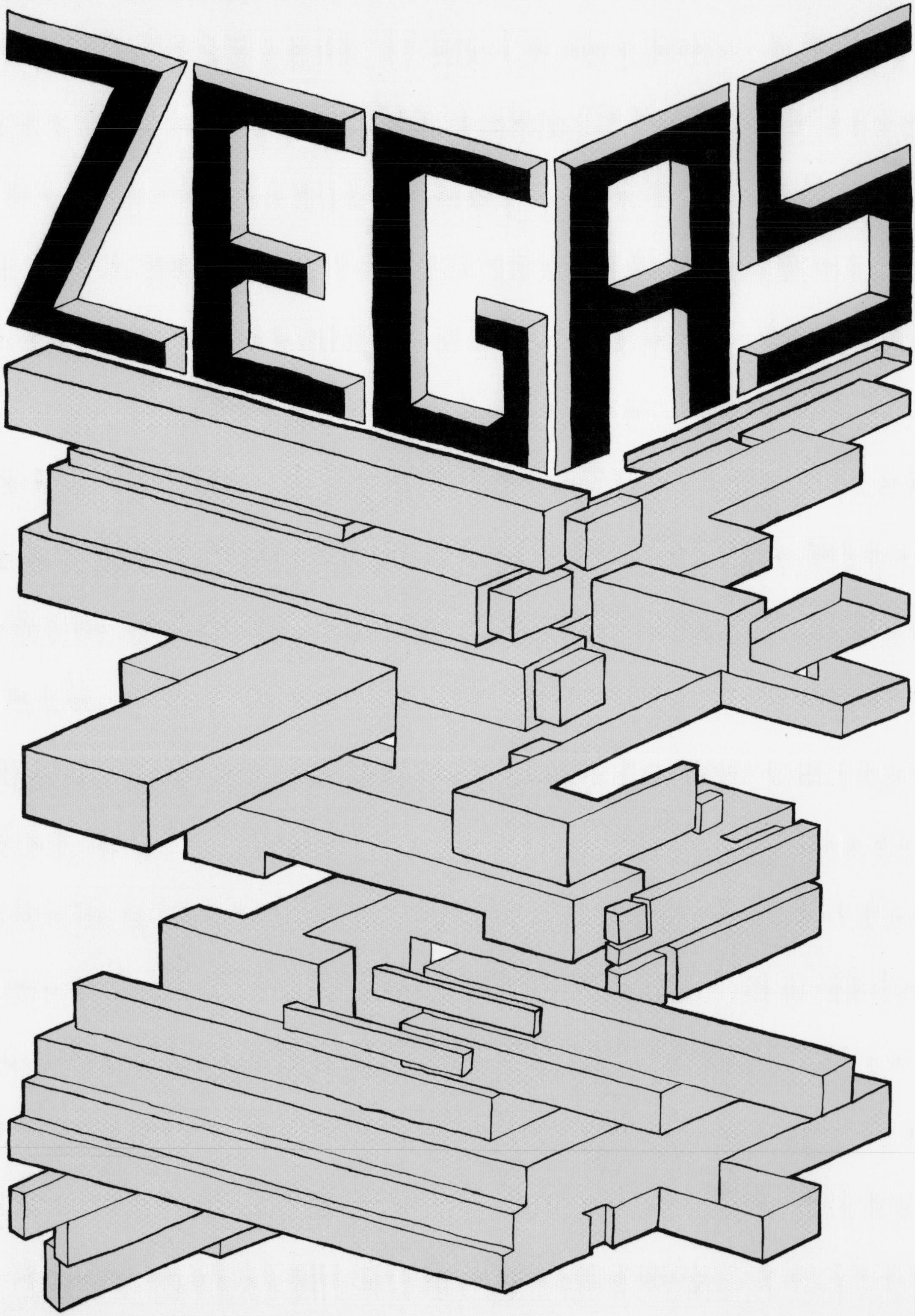
ZEGAS

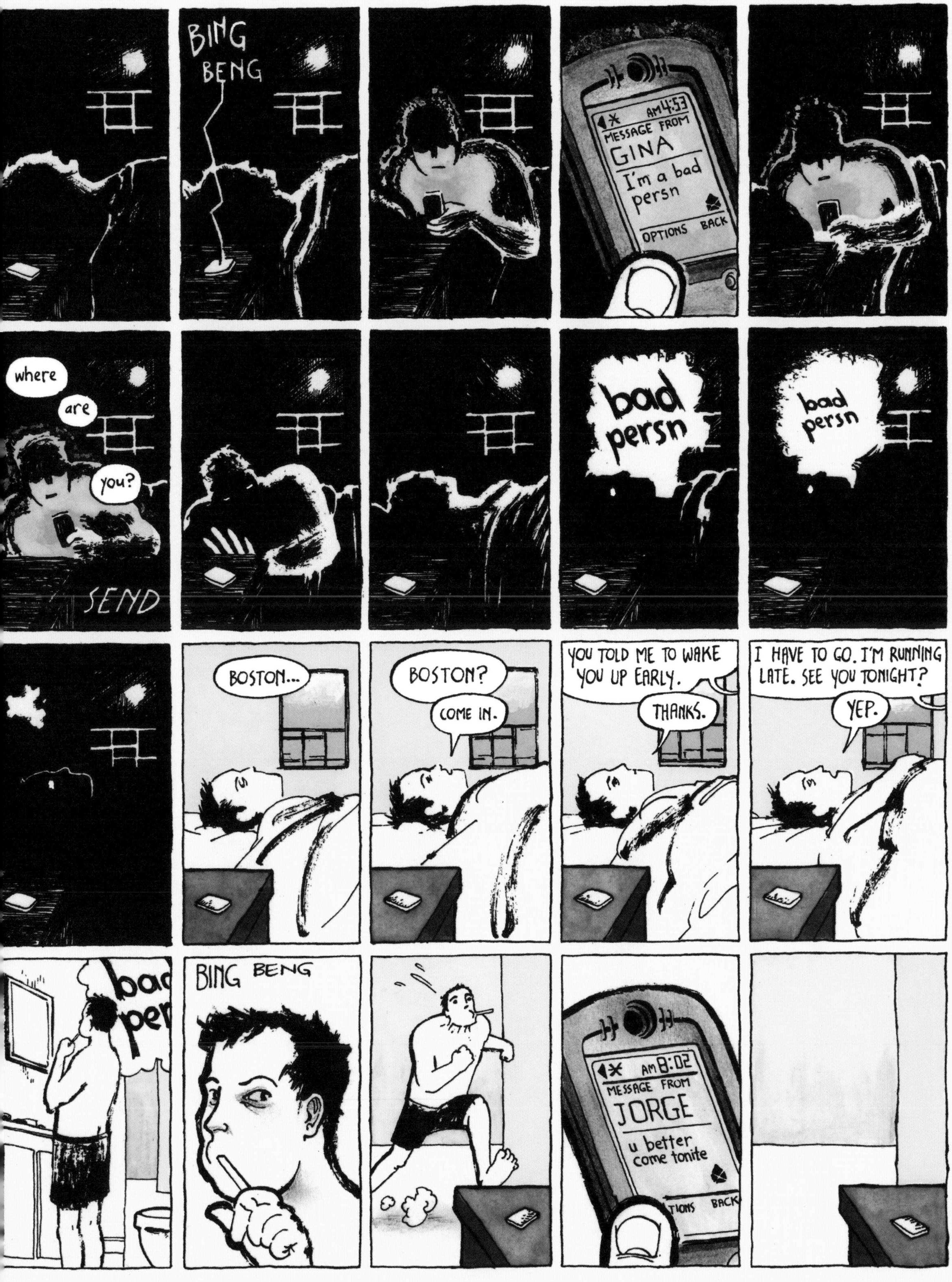
BING
BENG
AM4:53
MESSAGE FROM
GINA
I'm a bad persn
OPTIONS BACK
where
are
you?
SEND
bad persn
bad persn
BOSTON...
BOSTON?
COME IN.
YOU TOLD ME TO WAKE YOU UP EARLY.
THANKS.
I HAVE TO GO. I'M RUNNING LATE. SEE YOU TONIGHT?
YEP.
BING BENG
AM8:02
MESSAGE FROM
JORGE
u better come tonite
BACK

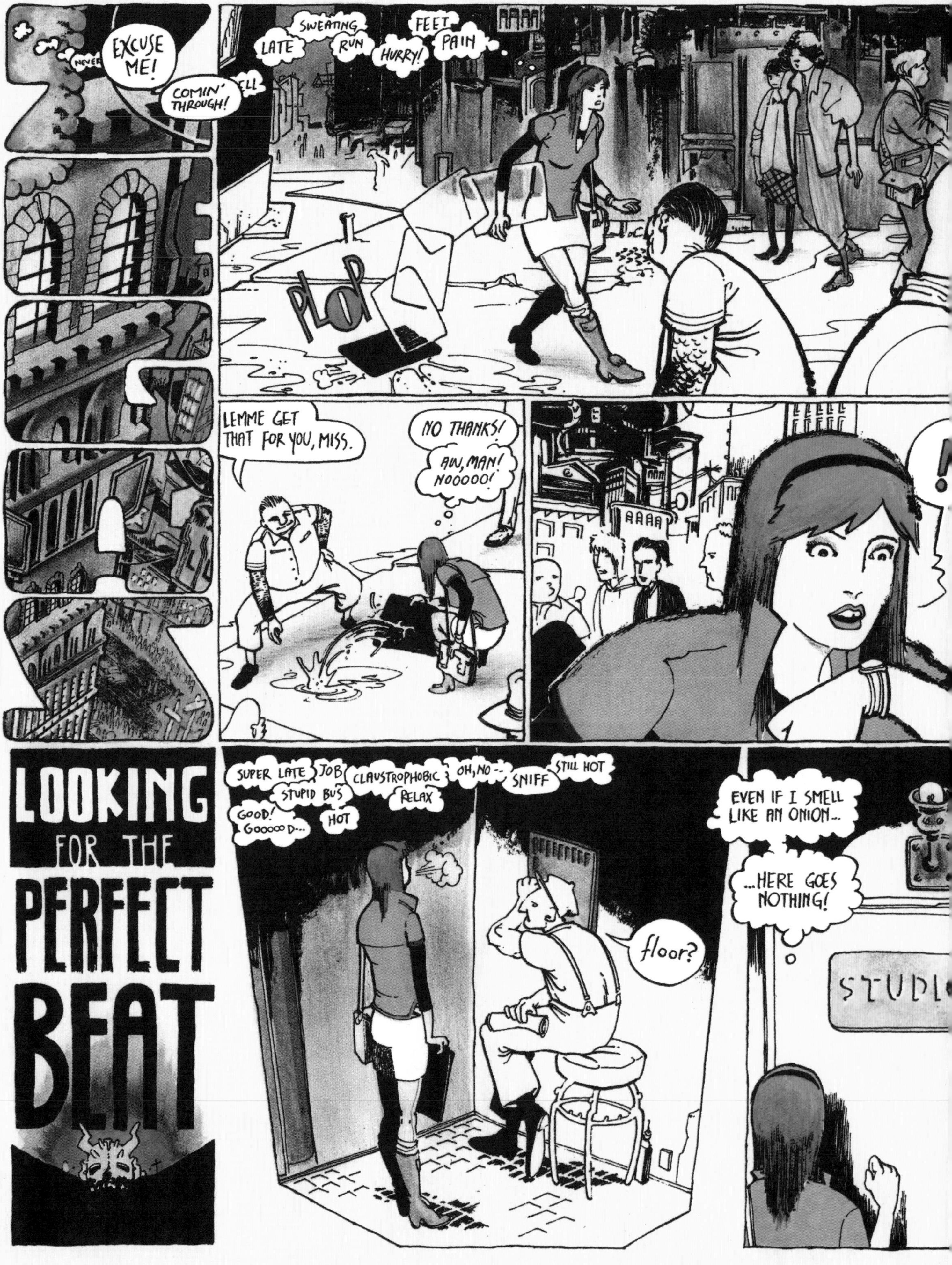

NEVER
EXCUSE ME!
COMIN' THROUGH!
LATE
SWEATING
RUN
HURRY!
FEET
PAIN
PLOP
LEMME GET THAT FOR YOU, MISS.
NO THANKS!
AW, MAN! NOOOOO!
!
LOOKING FOR THE PERFECT BEAT
SUPER LATE
JOB
STUPID BUS
CLAUSTROPHOBIC
RELAX
OH, NO --
SNIFF
STILL HOT
GOOD! GOOOOOD...
HOT
floor?
EVEN IF I SMELL LIKE AN ONION...
...HERE GOES NOTHING!
STUDI

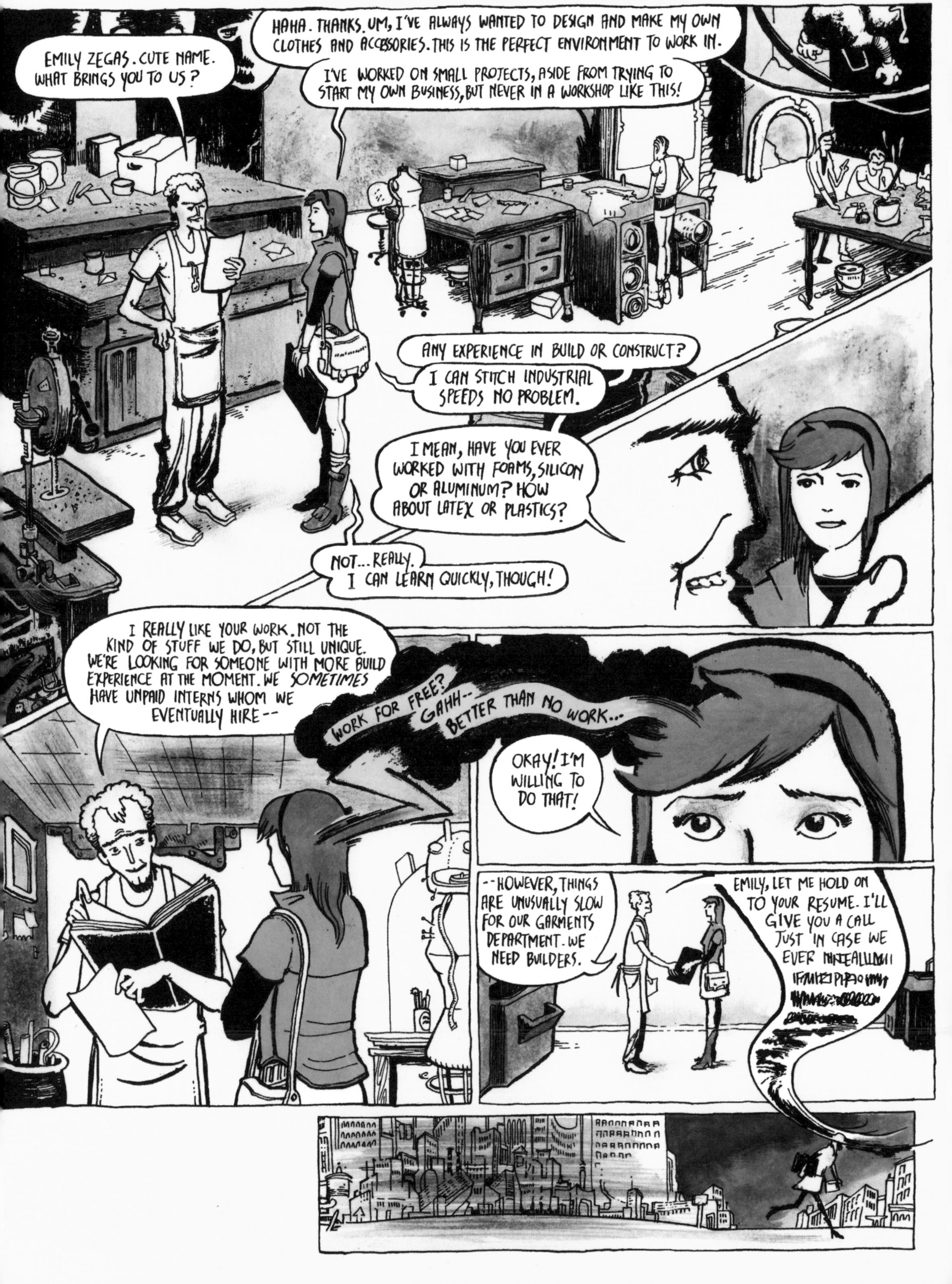
EMILY ZEGAS. CUTE NAME. WHAT BRINGS YOU TO US?
HAHA. THANKS. UM, I'VE ALWAYS WANTED TO DESIGN AND MAKE MY OWN CLOTHES AND ACCESSORIES. THIS IS THE PERFECT ENVIRONMENT TO WORK IN.
I'VE WORKED ON SMALL PROJECTS, ASIDE FROM TRYING TO START MY OWN BUSINESS, BUT NEVER IN A WORKSHOP LIKE THIS!
ANY EXPERIENCE IN BUILD OR CONSTRUCT?
I CAN STITCH INDUSTRIAL SPEEDS NO PROBLEM.
I MEAN, HAVE YOU EVER WORKED WITH FOAMS, SILICON OR ALUMINUM? HOW ABOUT LATEX OR PLASTICS?
NOT... REALLY. I CAN LEARN QUICKLY, THOUGH!
I REALLY LIKE YOUR WORK. NOT THE KIND OF STUFF WE DO, BUT STILL UNIQUE. WE'RE LOOKING FOR SOMEONE WITH MORE BUILD EXPERIENCE AT THE MOMENT. WE SOMETIMES HAVE UNPAID INTERNS WHOM WE EVENTUALLY HIRE--
WORK FOR FREE? GAHH-- BETTER THAN NO WORK...
OKAY! I'M WILLING TO DO THAT!
--HOWEVER, THINGS ARE UNUSUALLY SLOW FOR OUR GARMENTS DEPARTMENT. WE NEED BUILDERS.
EMILY, LET ME HOLD ON TO YOUR RESUME. I'LL GIVE YOU A CALL JUST IN CASE WE EVER

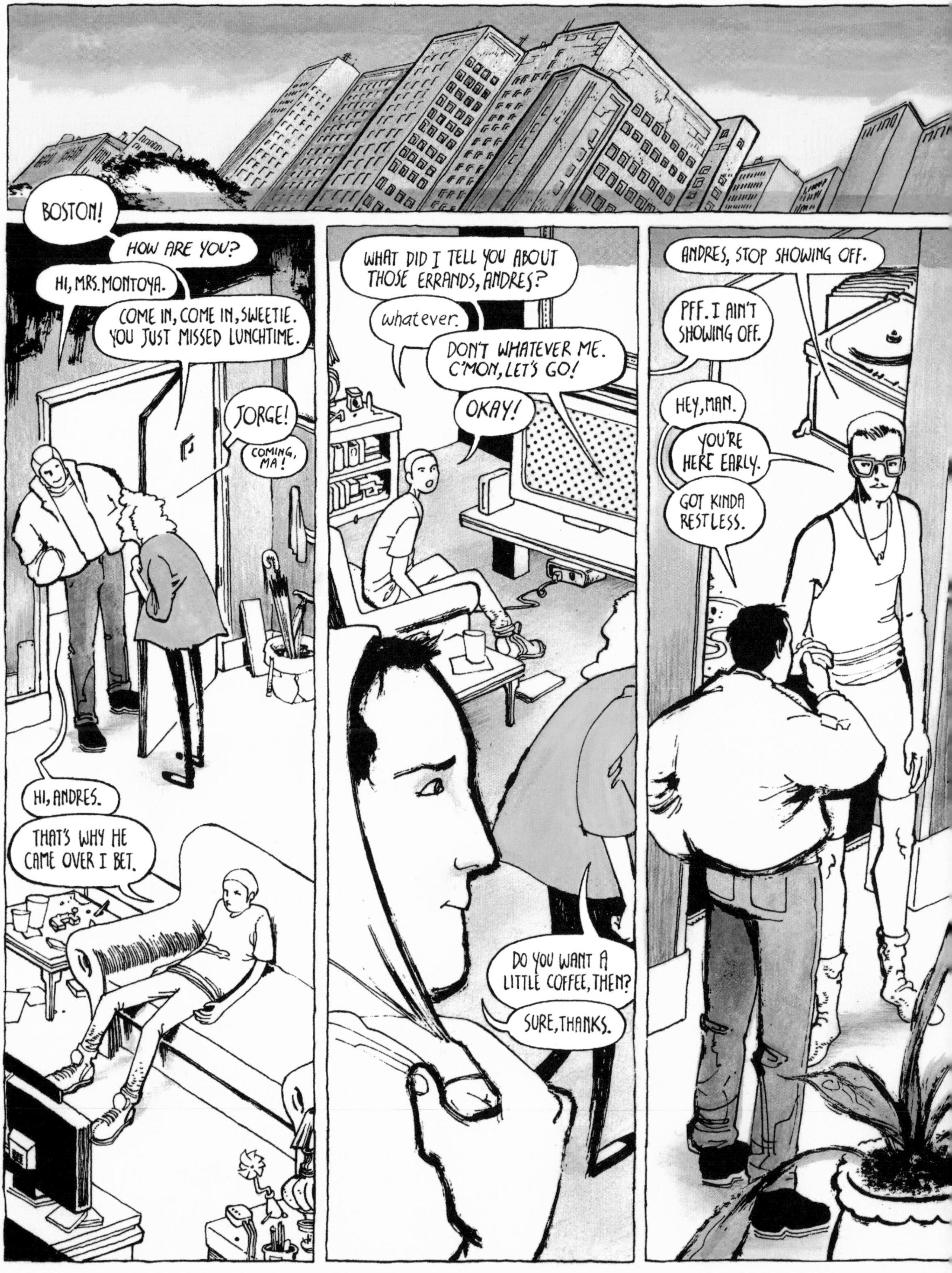
BOSTON!
HOW ARE YOU?
HI, MRS. MONTOYA.
COME IN, COME IN, SWEETIE. YOU JUST MISSED LUNCHTIME.
JORGE!
COMING, MA!
HI, ANDRES.
THAT'S WHY HE CAME OVER I BET.
WHAT DID I TELL YOU ABOUT THOSE ERRANDS, ANDRES?
whatever.
DON'T WHATEVER ME. C'MON, LET'S GO!
OKAY!
DO YOU WANT A LITTLE COFFEE, THEN?
SURE, THANKS.
ANDRES, STOP SHOWING OFF.
PFF. I AIN'T SHOWING OFF.
HEY, MAN.
YOU'RE HERE EARLY.
GOT KINDA RESTLESS.

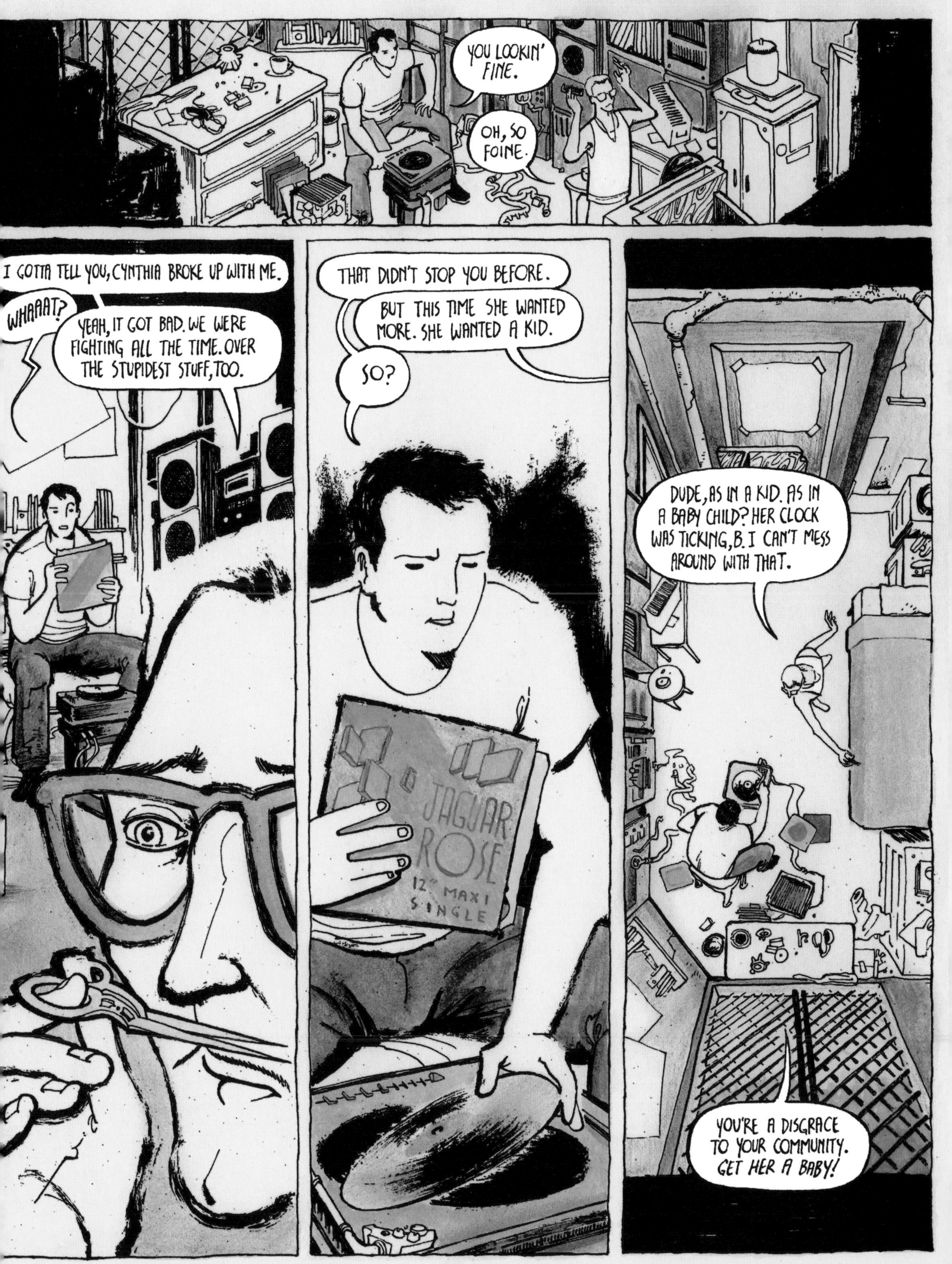
YOU LOOKIN' FINE.
OH, SO FOINE.
I GOTTA TELL YOU, CYNTHIA BROKE UP WITH ME.
WHAAAT?
YEAH, IT GOT BAD. WE WERE FIGHTING ALL THE TIME. OVER THE STUPIDEST STUFF, TOO.
THAT DIDN'T STOP YOU BEFORE.
BUT THIS TIME SHE WANTED MORE. SHE WANTED A KID.
SO?
JAGUAR ROSE
12" MAXI SINGLE
DUDE, AS IN A KID. AS IN A BABY CHILD? HER CLOCK WAS TICKING, B. I CAN'T MESS AROUND WITH THAT.
YOU'RE A DISGRACE TO YOUR COMMUNITY. GET HER A BABY!

HOW ABOUT YOU? FINALLY MADE IT HAPPEN WITH GINA?

SORTA, I THINK. EVERY TIME I BRING UP GETTING SERIOUS SHE CHANGES THE SUBJECT.

PROBABLY BECAUSE YOU SAY THINGS LIKE "GETTING SERIOUS".

SHE ALSO GETS WEIRD AND QUIET.

bad persn

I CAN SEE THAT. SHE'S GOT THE MEAT GAZE.

THE WHAT?

YOU KNOW, THE MEAT GAZE. LIKE YOU THINK SOMEONE'S BEING INTENSE AND DEEP BUT REALLY THEY JUST HAVE NOTHING TO SAY.

I MUST HAVE THE MEAT GAZE ALL THE TIME.

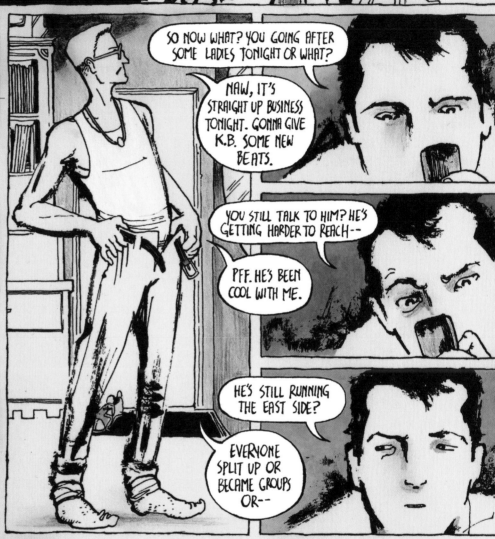

SO NOW WHAT? YOU GOING AFTER SOME LADIES TONIGHT OR WHAT?

NAW, IT'S STRAIGHT UP BUSINESS TONIGHT. GONNA GIVE K.B. SOME NEW BEATS.

YOU STILL TALK TO HIM? HE'S GETTING HARDER TO REACH--

PFF. HE'S BEEN COOL WITH ME.

HE'S STILL RUNNING THE EAST SIDE?

EVERYONE SPLIT UP OR BECAME GROUPS OR--

WHATEVER, MAN. K.B. IS DOWN TO EARTH. HE'S PUTTING OUT ALL THESE NEIGHBORHOOD BEEFS. HIS RECORDS ARE ABOUT PEOPLE... ABOUT DOWN TO EARTH TYPE SHIT.

HE'S GOT YOU BELIEVING IT, AT LEAST.

WHY YOU SO NEGATIVE?

I'M JUST SAYIN'.

I'M JUST SAYIN', I'M JUST SAYIN'.

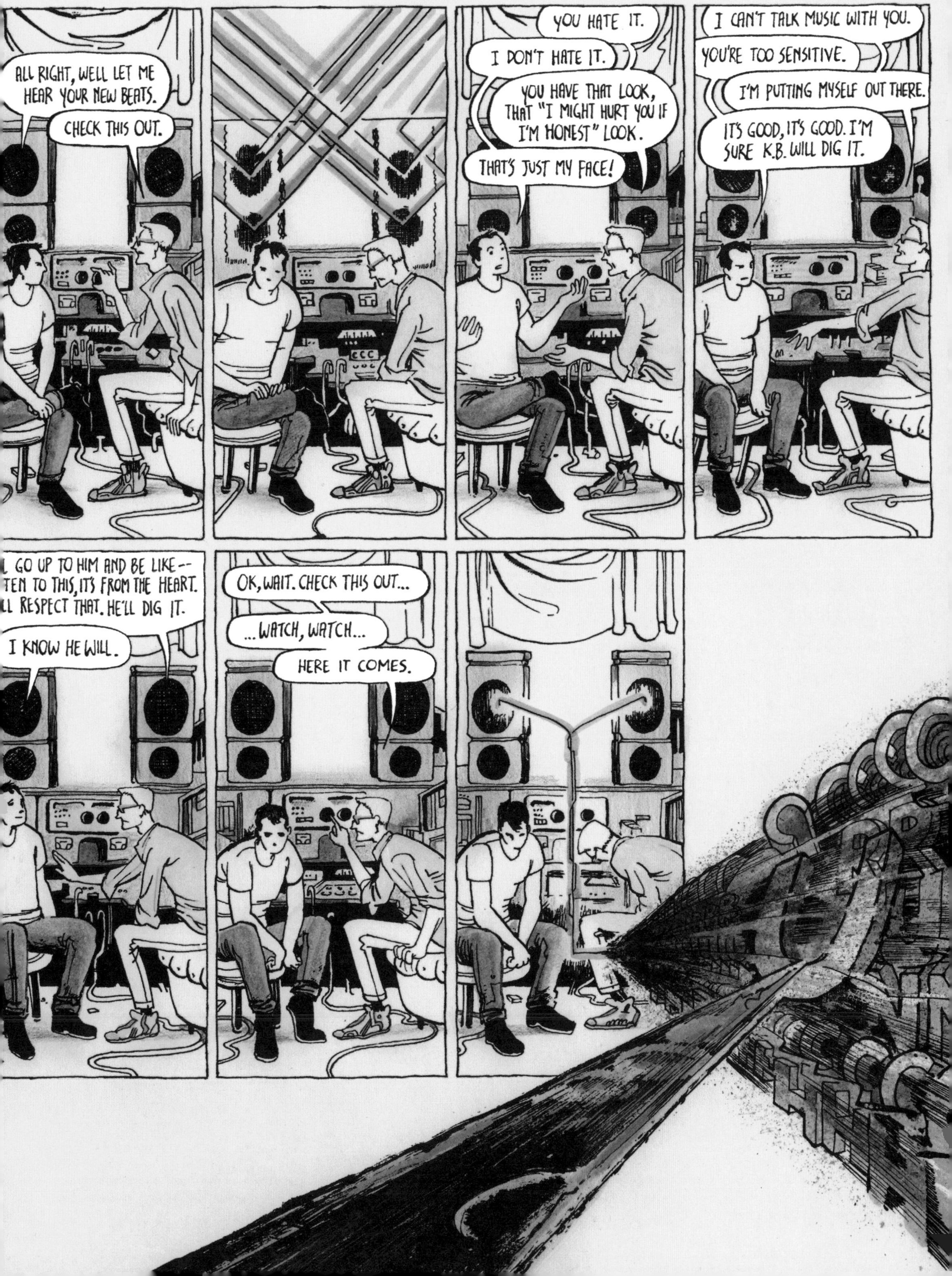
ALL RIGHT, WELL LET ME HEAR YOUR NEW BEATS.
CHECK THIS OUT.
YOU HATE IT.
I DON'T HATE IT.
YOU HAVE THAT LOOK, THAT "I MIGHT HURT YOU IF I'M HONEST" LOOK.
THAT'S JUST MY FACE!
I CAN'T TALK MUSIC WITH YOU.
YOU'RE TOO SENSITIVE.
I'M PUTTING MYSELF OUT THERE.
IT'S GOOD, IT'S GOOD. I'M SURE K.B. WILL DIG IT.
GO UP TO HIM AND BE LIKE--
TEN TO THIS, IT'S FROM THE HEART.
LL RESPECT THAT. HE'LL DIG IT.
I KNOW HE WILL.
OK, WAIT. CHECK THIS OUT...
...WATCH, WATCH...
HERE IT COMES.

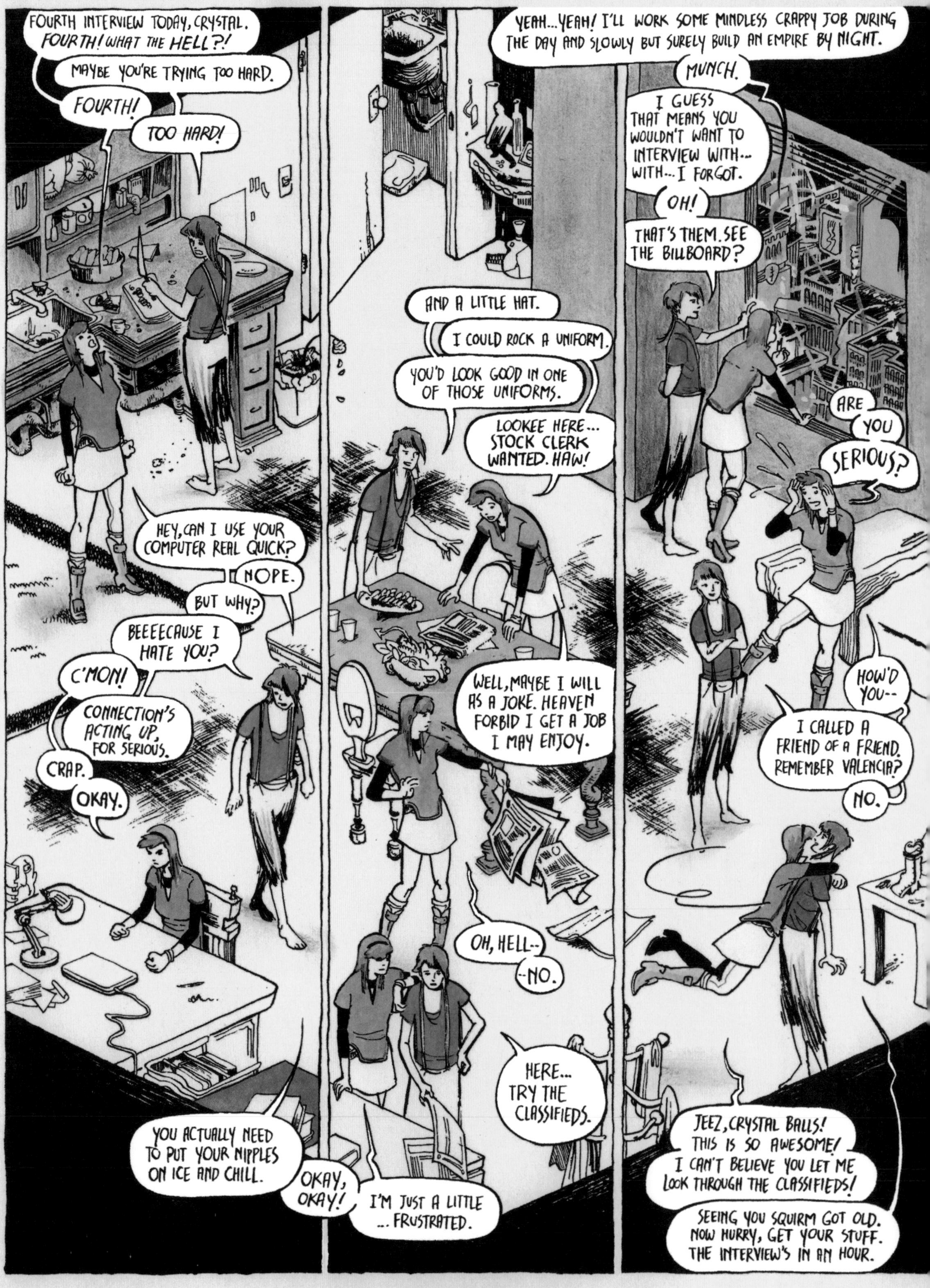
FOURTH INTERVIEW TODAY, CRYSTAL. FOURTH! WHAT THE HELL?!
MAYBE YOU'RE TRYING TOO HARD.
FOURTH!
TOO HARD!
HEY, CAN I USE YOUR COMPUTER REAL QUICK?
NOPE.
BUT WHY?
BEEEECAUSE I HATE YOU?
C'MON!
CONNECTION'S ACTING UP, FOR SERIOUS.
CRAP.
OKAY.
YOU ACTUALLY NEED TO PUT YOUR NIPPLES ON ICE AND CHILL.
OKAY, OKAY!
I'M JUST A LITTLE ...FRUSTRATED.
HERE... TRY THE CLASSIFIEDS.
OH, HELL--
--NO.
WELL, MAYBE I WILL AS A JOKE. HEAVEN FORBID I GET A JOB I MAY ENJOY.
LOOKEE HERE... STOCK CLERK WANTED. HAW!
YOU'D LOOK GOOD IN ONE OF THOSE UNIFORMS.
I COULD ROCK A UNIFORM.
AND A LITTLE HAT.
YEAH...YEAH! I'LL WORK SOME MINDLESS CRAPPY JOB DURING THE DAY AND SLOWLY BUT SURELY BUILD AN EMPIRE BY NIGHT.
MUNCH.
I GUESS THAT MEANS YOU WOULDN'T WANT TO INTERVIEW WITH... WITH... I FORGOT.
OH!
THAT'S THEM. SEE THE BILLBOARD?
ARE YOU SERIOUS?
HOW'D YOU--
I CALLED A FRIEND OF A FRIEND. REMEMBER VALENCIA?
NO.
JEEZ, CRYSTAL BALLS! THIS IS SO AWESOME! I CAN'T BELIEVE YOU LET ME LOOK THROUGH THE CLASSIFIEDS!
SEEING YOU SQUIRM GOT OLD. NOW HURRY, GET YOUR STUFF. THE INTERVIEW'S IN AN HOUR.

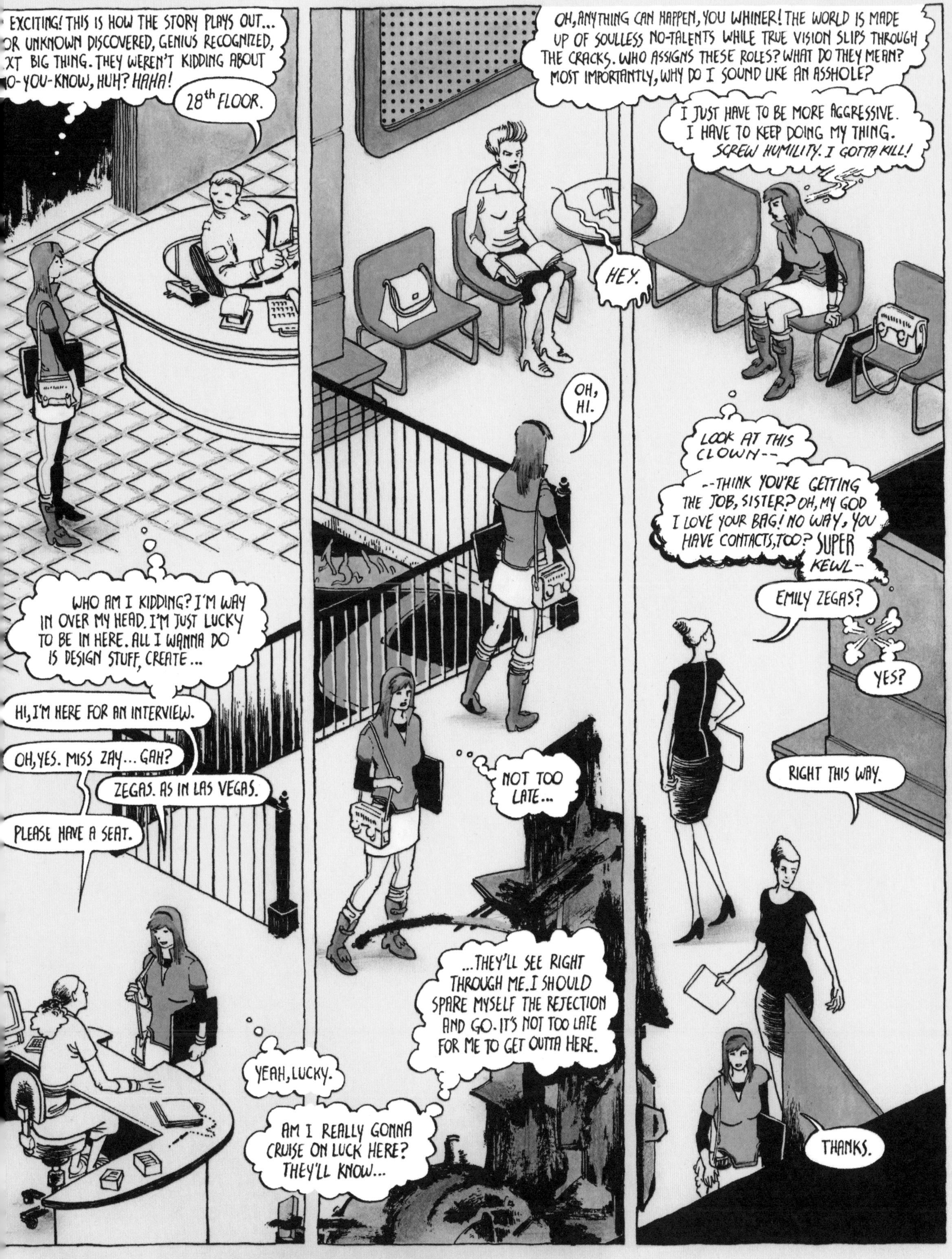
EXCITING! THIS IS HOW THE STORY PLAYS OUT... OR UNKNOWN DISCOVERED, GENIUS RECOGNIZED, XT BIG THING. THEY WEREN'T KIDDING ABOUT O-YOU-KNOW, HUH? HAHA!
28th FLOOR.
WHO AM I KIDDING? I'M WAY IN OVER MY HEAD. I'M JUST LUCKY TO BE IN HERE. ALL I WANNA DO IS DESIGN STUFF, CREATE...
HI, I'M HERE FOR AN INTERVIEW.
OH, YES. MISS ZAY... GAH?
ZEGAS. AS IN LAS VEGAS.
PLEASE HAVE A SEAT.
YEAH, LUCKY.
AM I REALLY GONNA CRUISE ON LUCK HERE? THEY'LL KNOW...
OH, HI.
NOT TOO LATE...
...THEY'LL SEE RIGHT THROUGH ME. I SHOULD SPARE MYSELF THE REJECTION AND GO. IT'S NOT TOO LATE FOR ME TO GET OUTTA HERE.
OH, ANYTHING CAN HAPPEN, YOU WHINER! THE WORLD IS MADE UP OF SOULLESS NO-TALENTS WHILE TRUE VISION SLIPS THROUGH THE CRACKS. WHO ASSIGNS THESE ROLES? WHAT DO THEY MEAN? MOST IMPORTANTLY, WHY DO I SOUND LIKE AN ASSHOLE?
I JUST HAVE TO BE MORE AGGRESSIVE. I HAVE TO KEEP DOING MY THING. SCREW HUMILITY. I GOTTA KILL!
HEY.
LOOK AT THIS CLOWN--
--THINK YOU'RE GETTING THE JOB, SISTER? OH, MY GOD I LOVE YOUR BAG! NO WAY, YOU HAVE CONTACTS, TOO? SUPER KEWL--
EMILY ZEGAS?
YES?
RIGHT THIS WAY.
THANKS.

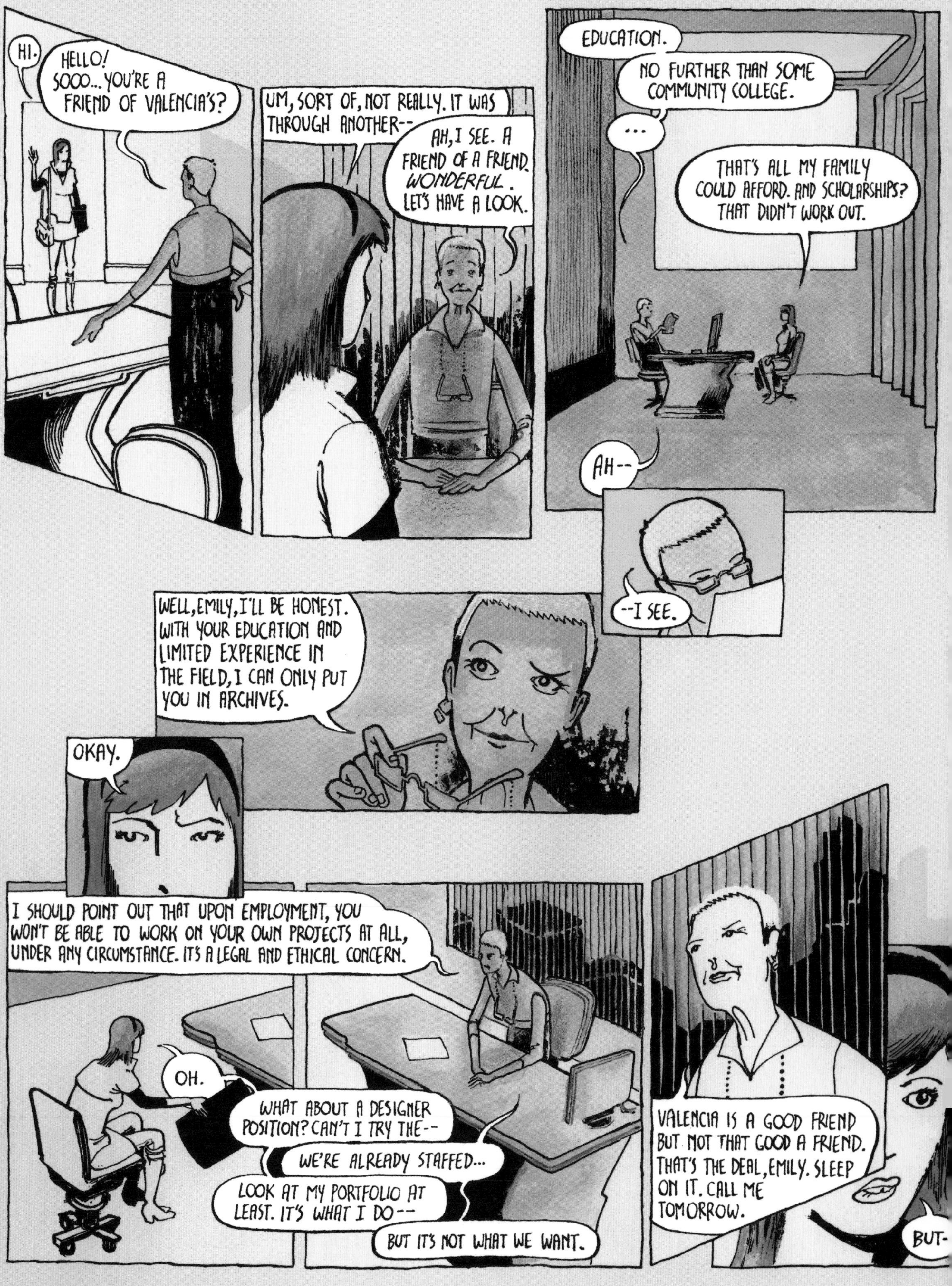
HI.
HELLO! SOOO... YOU'RE A FRIEND OF VALENCIA'S?
UM, SORT OF, NOT REALLY. IT WAS THROUGH ANOTHER--
AH, I SEE. A FRIEND OF A FRIEND. WONDERFUL. LET'S HAVE A LOOK.
EDUCATION.
NO FURTHER THAN SOME COMMUNITY COLLEGE.
...
THAT'S ALL MY FAMILY COULD AFFORD. AND SCHOLARSHIPS? THAT DIDN'T WORK OUT.
AH--
--I SEE.
WELL, EMILY, I'LL BE HONEST. WITH YOUR EDUCATION AND LIMITED EXPERIENCE IN THE FIELD, I CAN ONLY PUT YOU IN ARCHIVES.
OKAY.
I SHOULD POINT OUT THAT UPON EMPLOYMENT, YOU WON'T BE ABLE TO WORK ON YOUR OWN PROJECTS AT ALL, UNDER ANY CIRCUMSTANCE. IT'S A LEGAL AND ETHICAL CONCERN.
OH.
WHAT ABOUT A DESIGNER POSITION? CAN'T I TRY THE--
WE'RE ALREADY STAFFED...
LOOK AT MY PORTFOLIO AT LEAST. IT'S WHAT I DO--
BUT IT'S NOT WHAT WE WANT.
VALENCIA IS A GOOD FRIEND BUT NOT THAT GOOD A FRIEND. THAT'S THE DEAL, EMILY. SLEEP ON IT. CALL ME TOMORROW.
BUT-

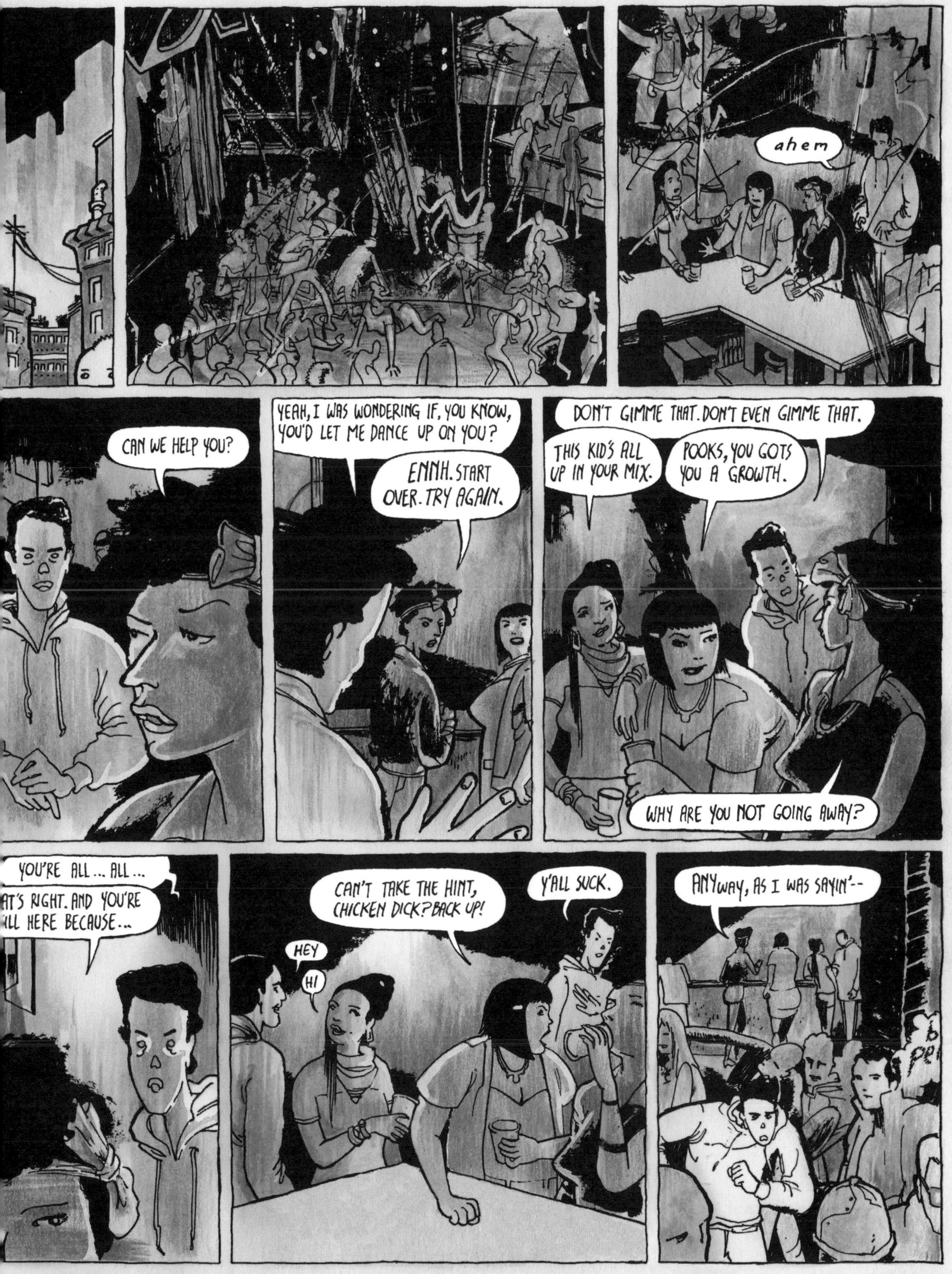
ahem
CAN WE HELP YOU?
YEAH, I WAS WONDERING IF, YOU KNOW, YOU'D LET ME DANCE UP ON YOU?
ENNH. START OVER. TRY AGAIN.
DON'T GIMME THAT. DON'T EVEN GIMME THAT.
THIS KID'S ALL UP IN YOUR MIX.
POOKS, YOU GOTS YOU A GROWTH.
WHY ARE YOU NOT GOING AWAY?
YOU'RE ALL... ALL...
AT'S RIGHT. AND YOU'RE
LL HERE BECAUSE...
CAN'T TAKE THE HINT, CHICKEN DICK? BACK UP!
HEY
HI
Y'ALL SUCK.
ANYway, AS I WAS SAYIN'--

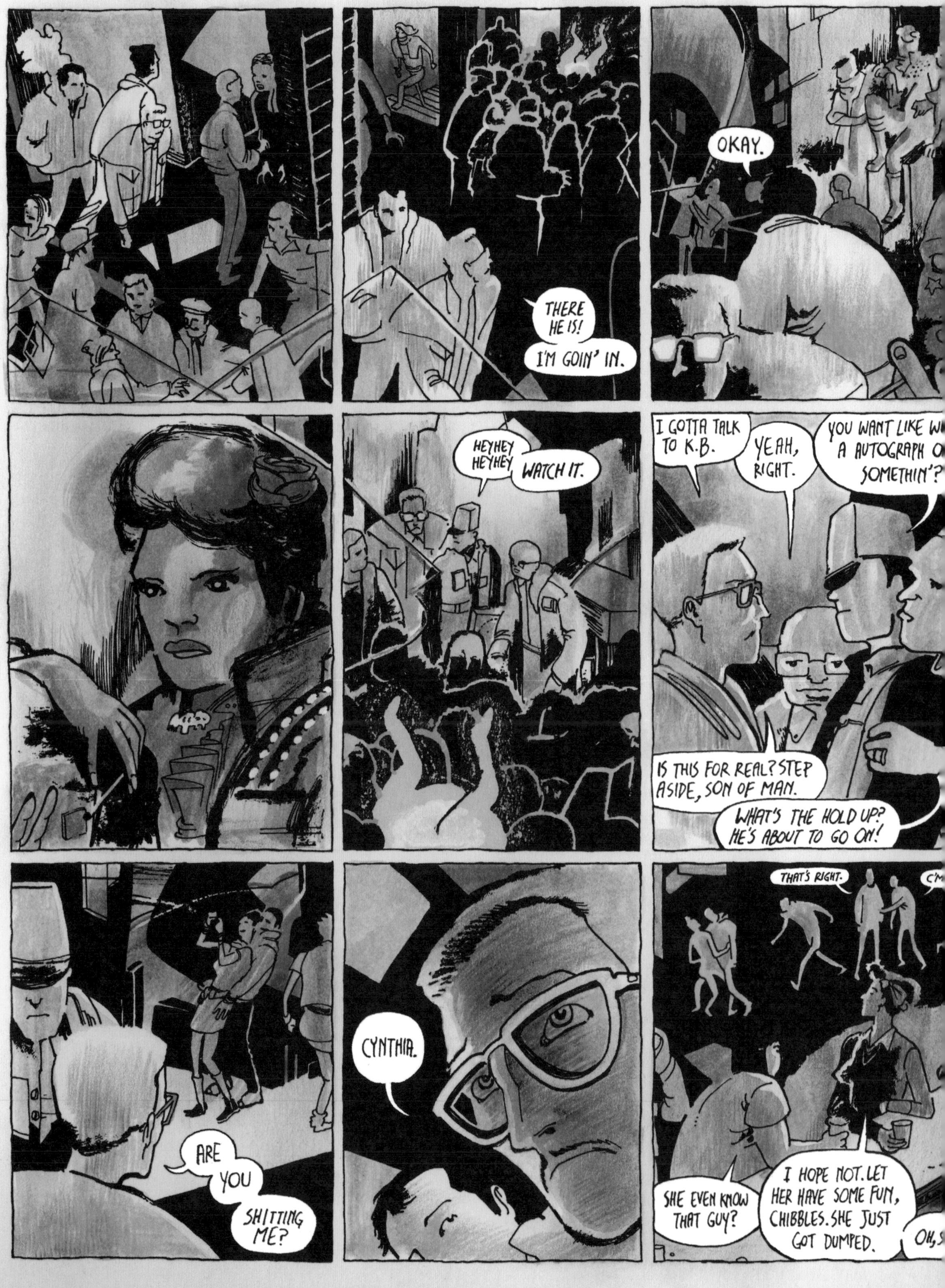

THERE HE IS!
I'M GOIN' IN.
OKAY.
HEYHEY HEYHEY
WATCH IT.
I GOTTA TALK TO K.B.
YEAH, RIGHT.
YOU WANT LIKE A AUTOGRAPH SOMETHIN'?
IS THIS FOR REAL? STEP ASIDE, SON OF MAN.
WHAT'S THE HOLD UP? HE'S ABOUT TO GO ON!
ARE YOU SHITTING ME?
CYNTHIA.
THAT'S RIGHT.
SHE EVEN KNOW THAT GUY?
I HOPE NOT. LET HER HAVE SOME FUN, CHIBBLES. SHE JUST GOT DUMPED.
OH,

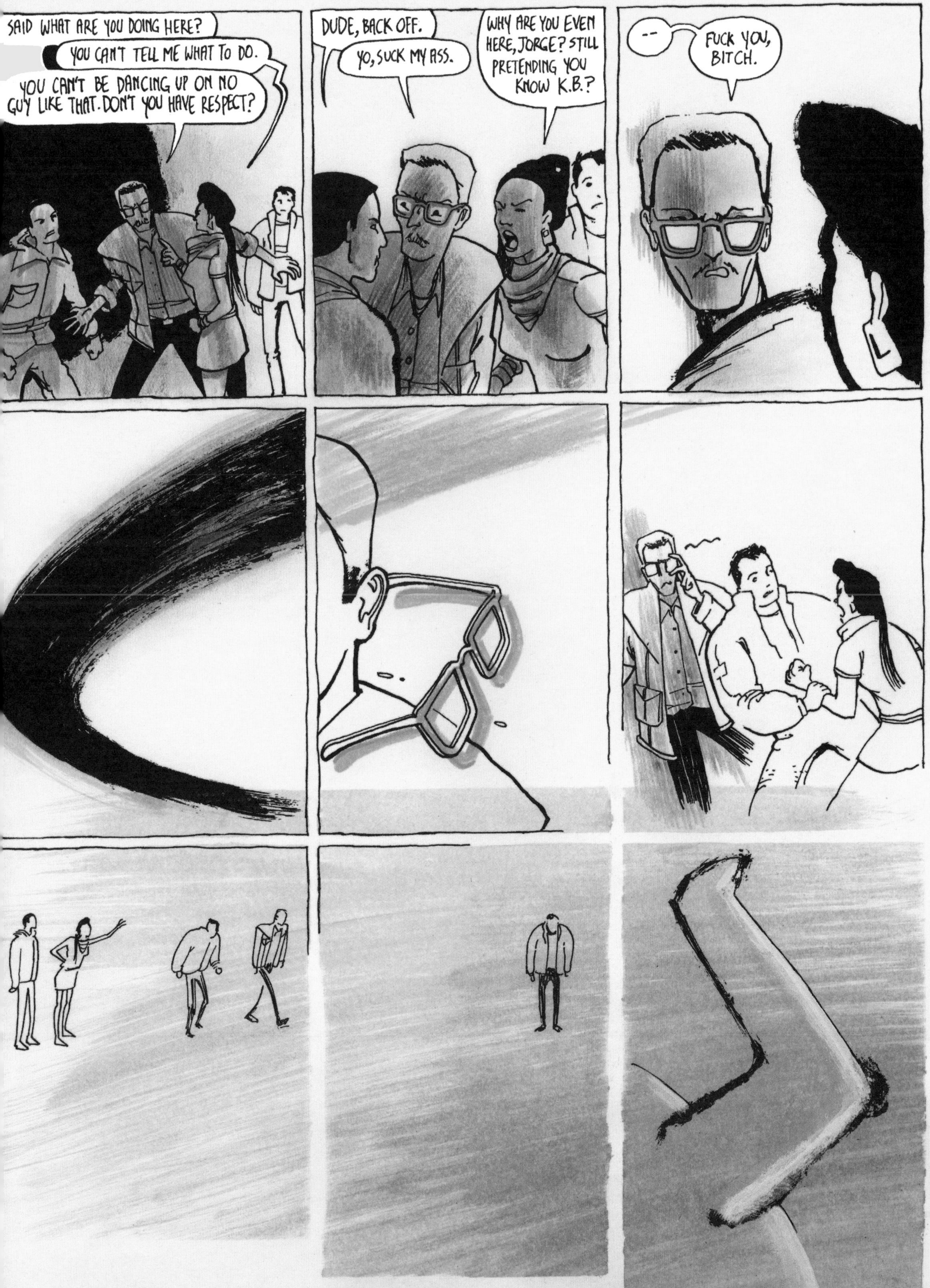
SAID WHAT ARE YOU DOING HERE?
YOU CAN'T TELL ME WHAT TO DO.
YOU CAN'T BE DANCING UP ON NO GUY LIKE THAT. DON'T YOU HAVE RESPECT?
DUDE, BACK OFF.
YO, SUCK MY ASS.
WHY ARE YOU EVEN HERE, JORGE? STILL PRETENDING YOU KNOW K.B.?
--
FUCK YOU, BITCH.

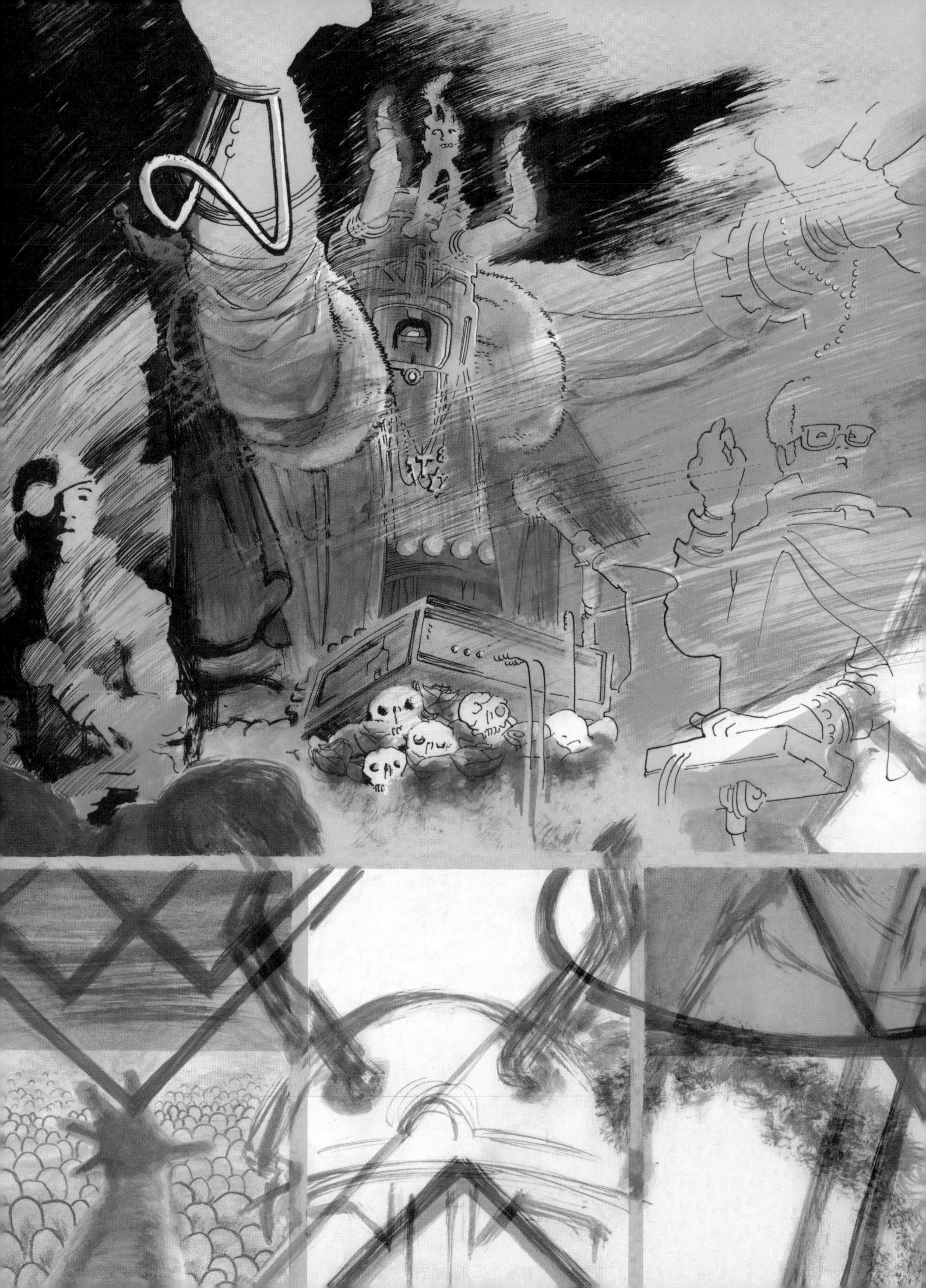

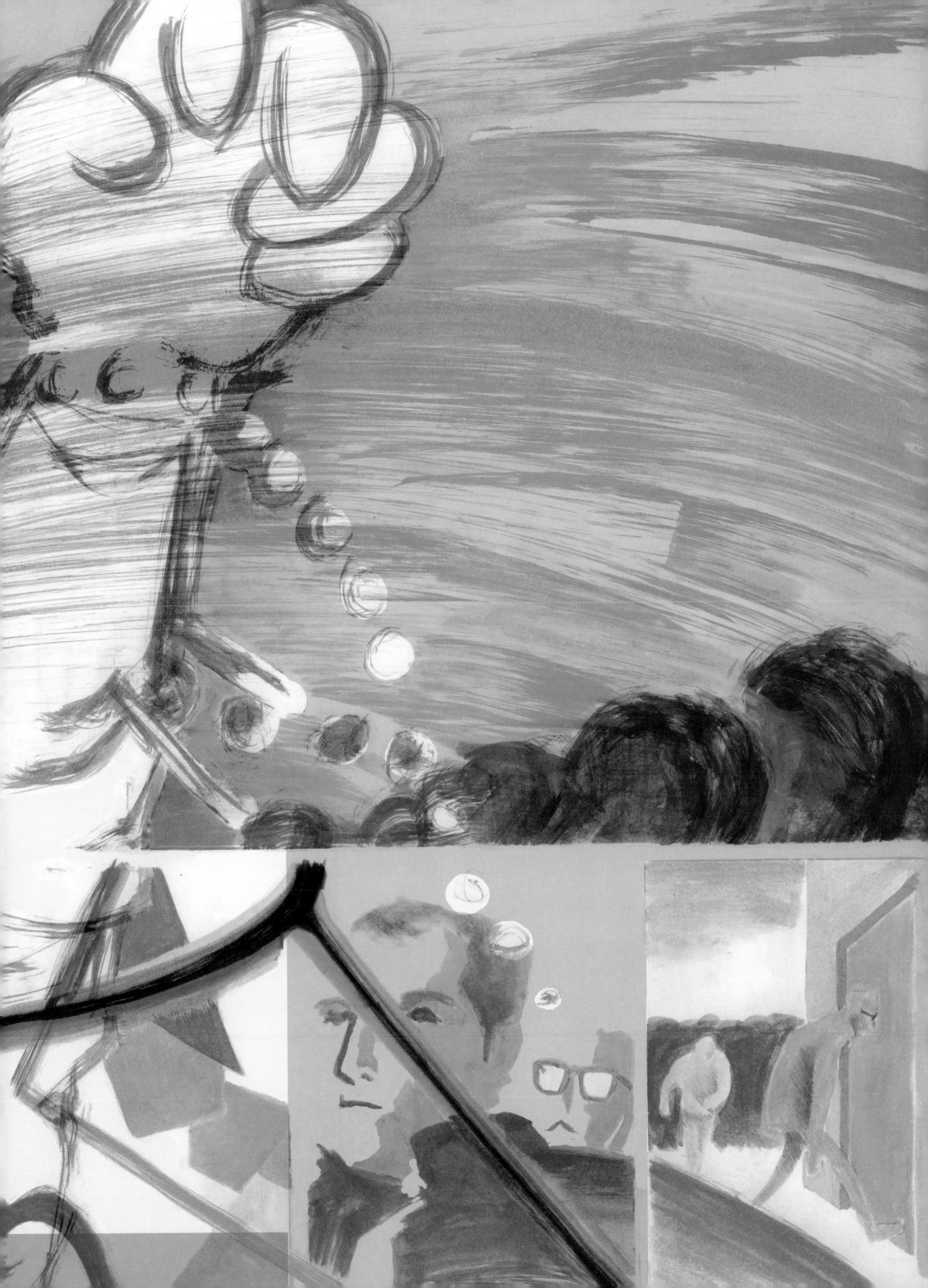

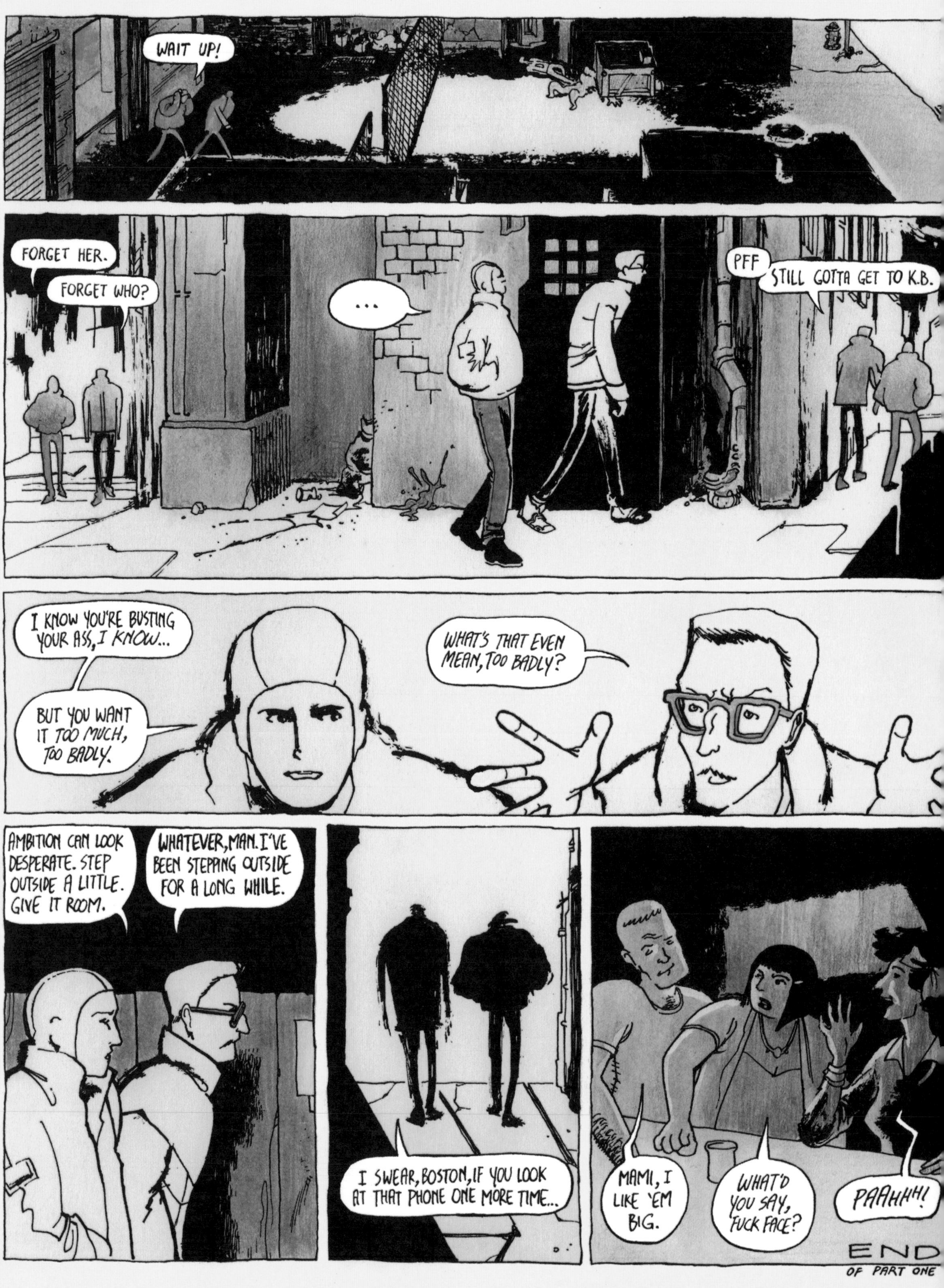
WAIT UP!
FORGET HER.
FORGET WHO?
...
PFF
STILL GOTTA GET TO K.B.
I KNOW YOU'RE BUSTING YOUR ASS, I KNOW...
BUT YOU WANT IT TOO MUCH, TOO BADLY.
WHAT'S THAT EVEN MEAN, TOO BADLY?
AMBITION CAN LOOK DESPERATE. STEP OUTSIDE A LITTLE. GIVE IT ROOM.
WHATEVER, MAN. I'VE BEEN STEPPING OUTSIDE FOR A LONG WHILE.
I SWEAR, BOSTON, IF YOU LOOK AT THAT PHONE ONE MORE TIME...
MAMI, I LIKE 'EM BIG.
WHAT'D YOU SAY, FUCK FACE?
PAAHHH!
END
OF PART ONE

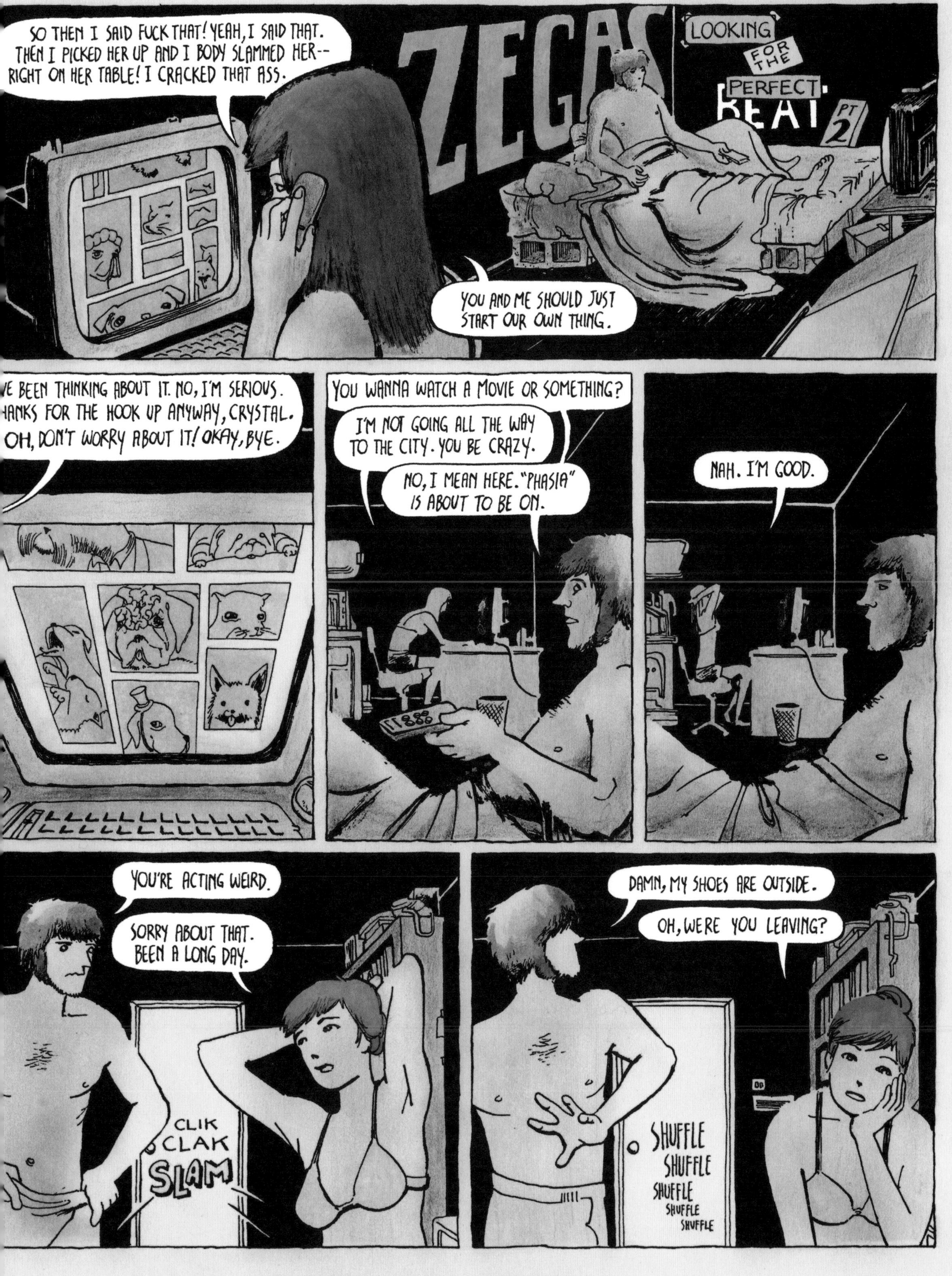
SO THEN I SAID FUCK THAT! YEAH, I SAID THAT. THEN I PICKED HER UP AND I BODY SLAMMED HER-- RIGHT ON HER TABLE! I CRACKED THAT ASS.
ZEGAS
LOOKING FOR THE PERFECT BEAT PT 2
YOU AND ME SHOULD JUST START OUR OWN THING.
VE BEEN THINKING ABOUT IT. NO, I'M SERIOUS. HANKS FOR THE HOOK UP ANYWAY, CRYSTAL. OH, DON'T WORRY ABOUT IT! OKAY, BYE.
YOU WANNA WATCH A MOVIE OR SOMETHING?
I'M NOT GOING ALL THE WAY TO THE CITY. YOU BE CRAZY.
NO, I MEAN HERE. "PHASIA" IS ABOUT TO BE ON.
NAH. I'M GOOD.
YOU'RE ACTING WEIRD.
SORRY ABOUT THAT. BEEN A LONG DAY.
CLIK
CLAK
SLAM
DAMN, MY SHOES ARE OUTSIDE.
OH, WERE YOU LEAVING?
SHUFFLE
SHUFFLE
SHUFFLE
SHUFFLE
SHUFFLE

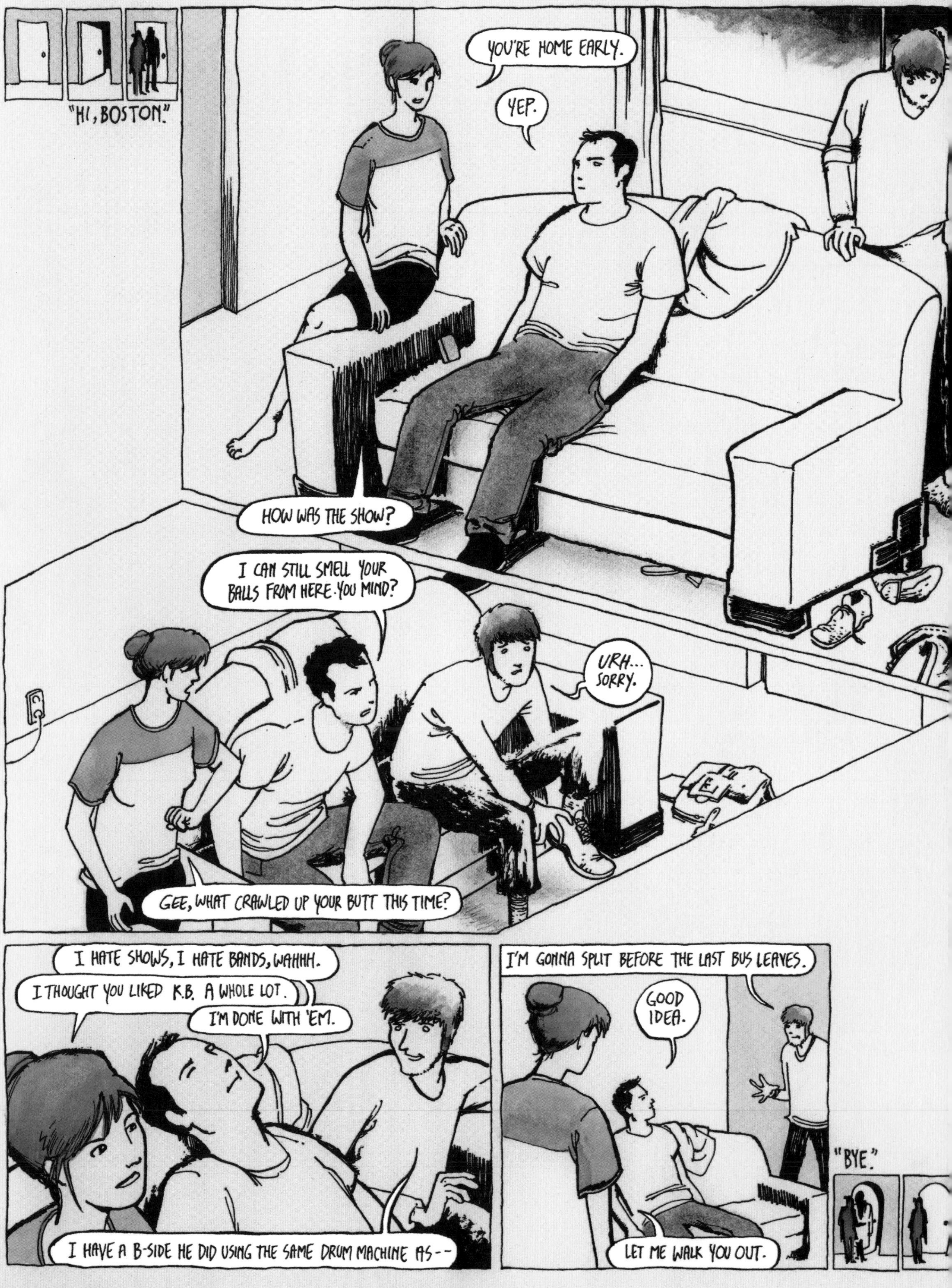
"HI, BOSTON."
YOU'RE HOME EARLY.
YEP.
HOW WAS THE SHOW?
I CAN STILL SMELL YOUR BALLS FROM HERE. YOU MIND?
URH... SORRY.
GEE, WHAT CRAWLED UP YOUR BUTT THIS TIME?
I HATE SHOWS, I HATE BANDS, WAHHH.
I THOUGHT YOU LIKED K.B. A WHOLE LOT.
I'M DONE WITH 'EM.
I HAVE A B-SIDE HE DID USING THE SAME DRUM MACHINE AS--
I'M GONNA SPLIT BEFORE THE LAST BUS LEAVES.
GOOD IDEA.
LET ME WALK YOU OUT.
"BYE."

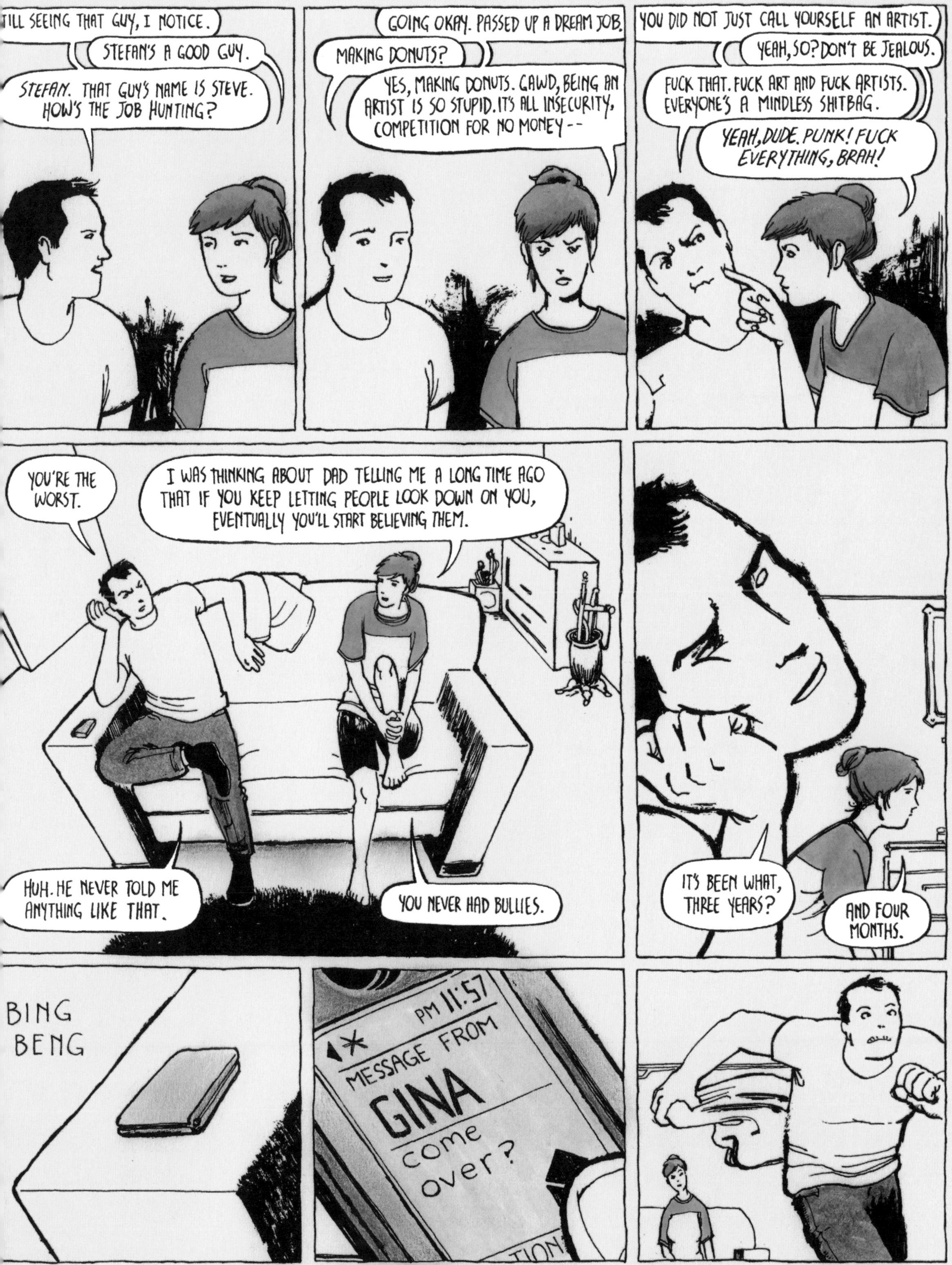
TILL SEEING THAT GUY, I NOTICE.
STEFAN'S A GOOD GUY.
STEFAN. THAT GUY'S NAME IS STEVE. HOW'S THE JOB HUNTING?
GOING OKAY. PASSED UP A DREAM JOB.
MAKING DONUTS?
YES, MAKING DONUTS. GAWD, BEING AN ARTIST IS SO STUPID. IT'S ALL INSECURITY, COMPETITION FOR NO MONEY --
YOU DID NOT JUST CALL YOURSELF AN ARTIST.
YEAH, SO? DON'T BE JEALOUS.
FUCK THAT. FUCK ART AND FUCK ARTISTS. EVERYONE'S A MINDLESS SHITBAG.
YEAH, DUDE. PUNK! FUCK EVERYTHING, BRAH!
YOU'RE THE WORST.
I WAS THINKING ABOUT DAD TELLING ME A LONG TIME AGO THAT IF YOU KEEP LETTING PEOPLE LOOK DOWN ON YOU, EVENTUALLY YOU'LL START BELIEVING THEM.
HUH. HE NEVER TOLD ME ANYTHING LIKE THAT.
YOU NEVER HAD BULLIES.
IT'S BEEN WHAT, THREE YEARS?
AND FOUR MONTHS.
BING BENG
PM 11:57
MESSAGE FROM
GINA
come over?

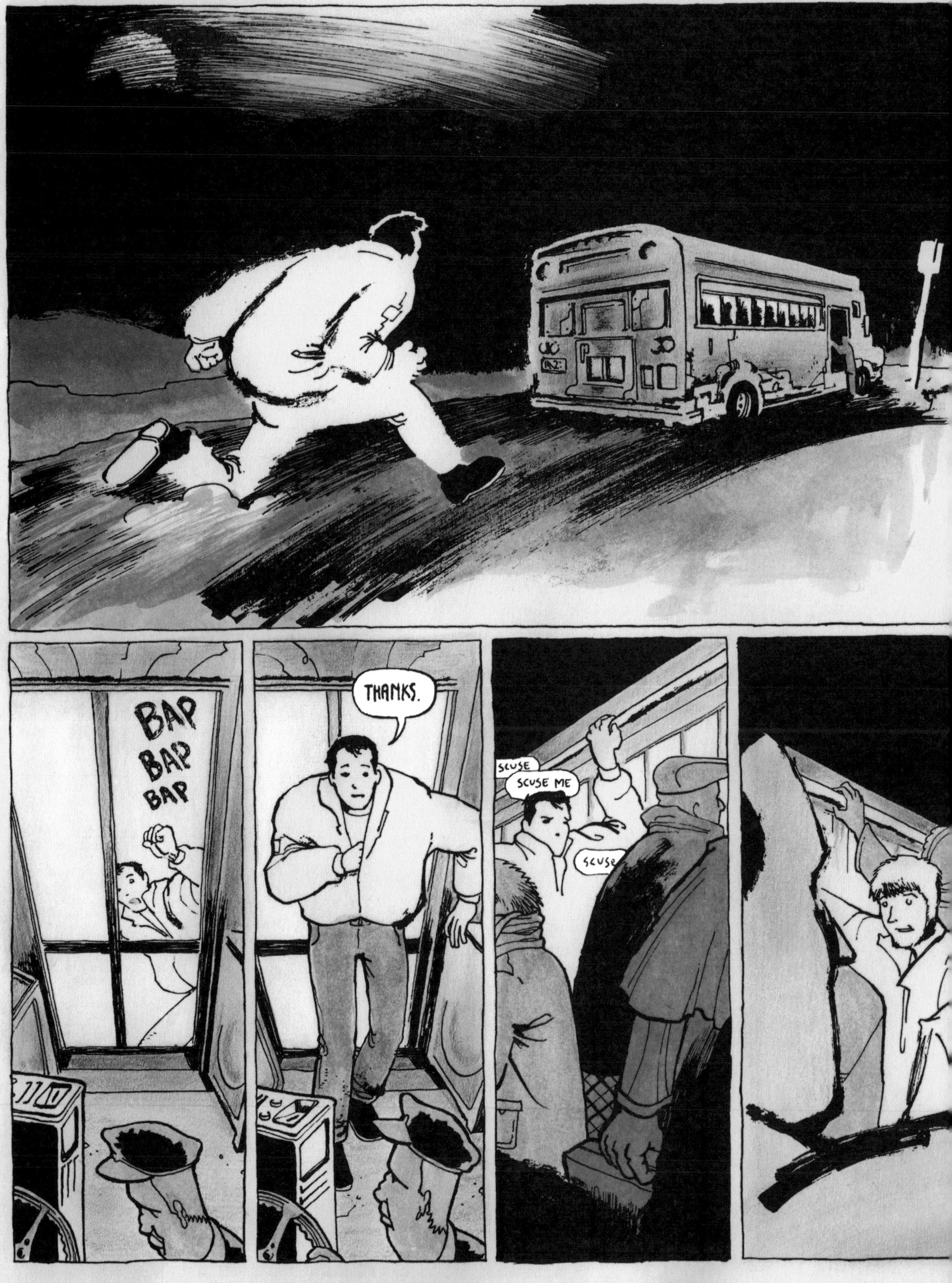
BAP
BAP
BAP
THANKS.
SCUSE
SCUSE ME
SCUSE

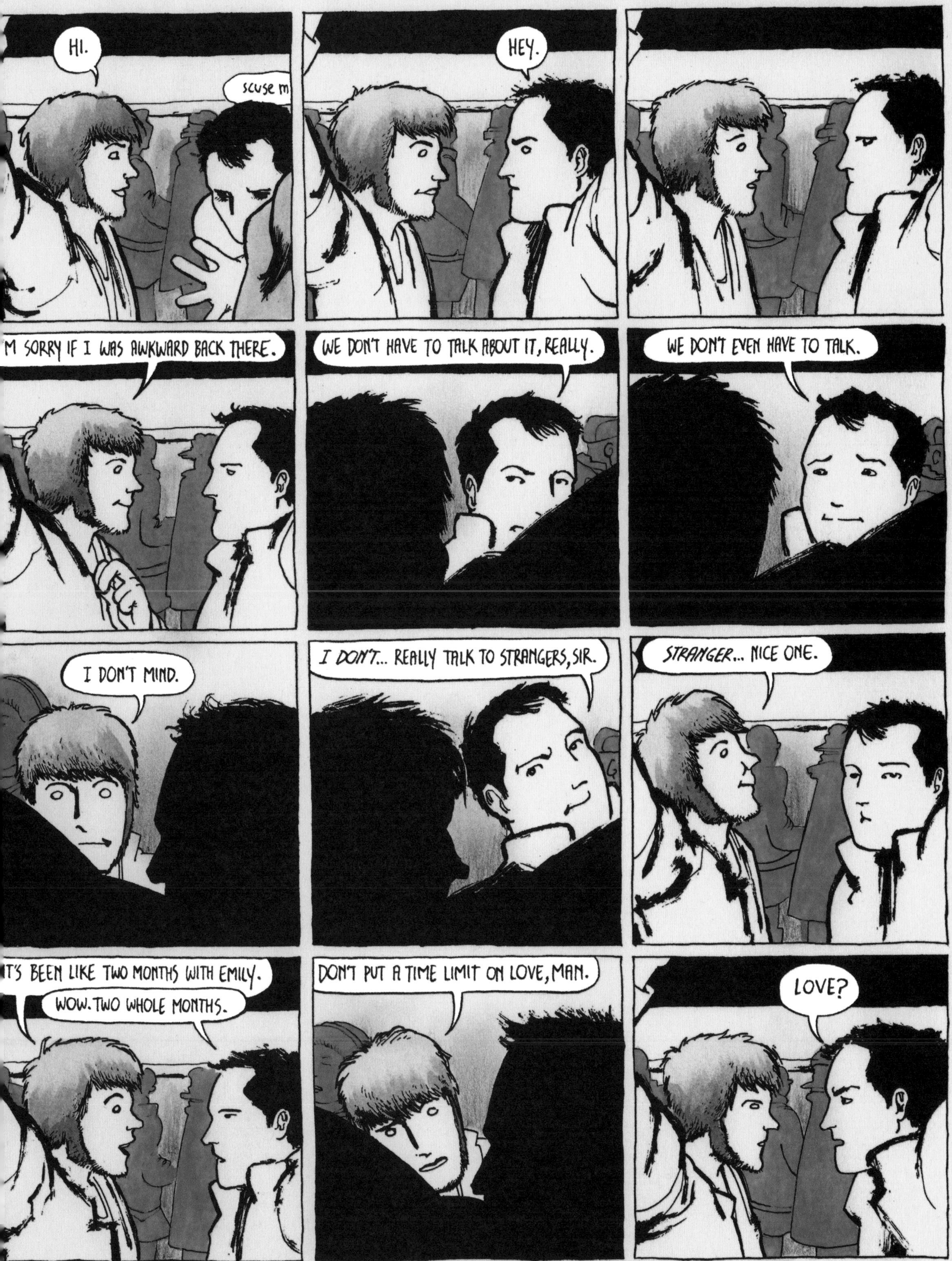
HI.
scuse m
HEY.
M SORRY IF I WAS AWKWARD BACK THERE.
WE DON'T HAVE TO TALK ABOUT IT, REALLY.
WE DON'T EVEN HAVE TO TALK.
I DON'T MIND.
I DON'T... REALLY TALK TO STRANGERS, SIR.
STRANGER... NICE ONE.
T'S BEEN LIKE TWO MONTHS WITH EMILY.
WOW. TWO WHOLE MONTHS.
DON'T PUT A TIME LIMIT ON LOVE, MAN.
LOVE?

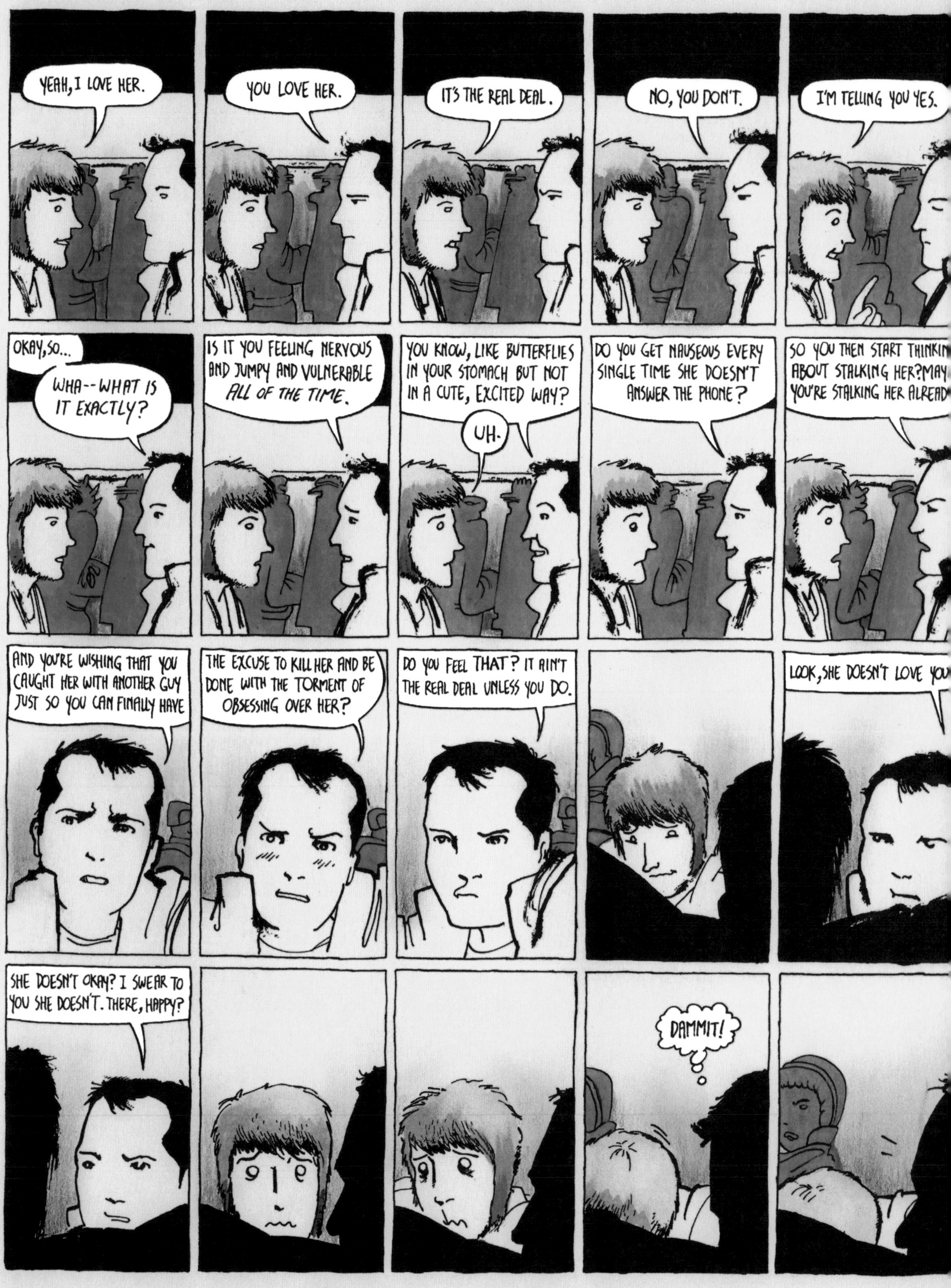
YEAH, I LOVE HER.
YOU LOVE HER.
IT'S THE REAL DEAL.
NO, YOU DON'T.
I'M TELLING YOU YES.
OKAY, SO...
WHA--WHAT IS IT EXACTLY?
IS IT YOU FEELING NERVOUS AND JUMPY AND VULNERABLE ALL OF THE TIME.
YOU KNOW, LIKE BUTTERFLIES IN YOUR STOMACH BUT NOT IN A CUTE, EXCITED WAY?
UH.
DO YOU GET NAUSEOUS EVERY SINGLE TIME SHE DOESN'T ANSWER THE PHONE?
SO YOU THEN START THINKIN ABOUT STALKING HER? MAY YOU'RE STALKING HER ALREAD
AND YOU'RE WISHING THAT YOU CAUGHT HER WITH ANOTHER GUY JUST SO YOU CAN FINALLY HAVE
THE EXCUSE TO KILL HER AND BE DONE WITH THE TORMENT OF OBSESSING OVER HER?
DO YOU FEEL THAT? IT AIN'T THE REAL DEAL UNLESS YOU DO.
LOOK, SHE DOESN'T LOVE YOU
SHE DOESN'T OKAY? I SWEAR TO YOU SHE DOESN'T. THERE, HAPPY?
DAMMIT!

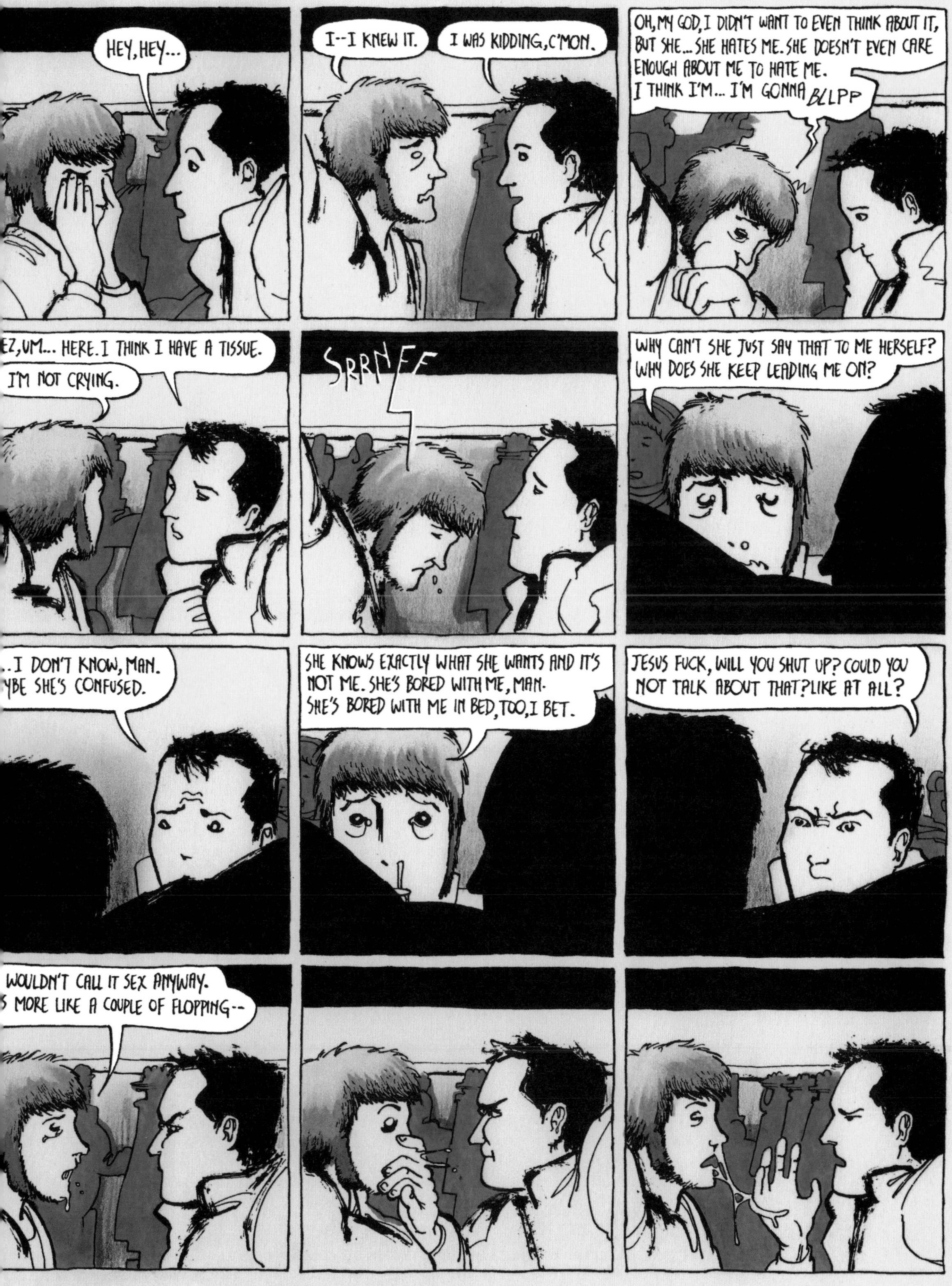
HEY, HEY...
I--I KNEW IT.
I WAS KIDDING, C'MON.
OH, MY GOD, I DIDN'T WANT TO EVEN THINK ABOUT IT, BUT SHE... SHE HATES ME. SHE DOESN'T EVEN CARE ENOUGH ABOUT ME TO HATE ME.
I THINK I'M... I'M GONNA BLLPP
EZ, UM... HERE. I THINK I HAVE A TISSUE.
I'M NOT CRYING.
SRRNFF
WHY CAN'T SHE JUST SAY THAT TO ME HERSELF? WHY DOES SHE KEEP LEADING ME ON?
..I DON'T KNOW, MAN. YBE SHE'S CONFUSED.
SHE KNOWS EXACTLY WHAT SHE WANTS AND IT'S NOT ME. SHE'S BORED WITH ME, MAN. SHE'S BORED WITH ME IN BED, TOO, I BET.
JESUS FUCK, WILL YOU SHUT UP? COULD YOU NOT TALK ABOUT THAT? LIKE AT ALL?
WOULDN'T CALL IT SEX ANYWAY. S MORE LIKE A COUPLE OF FLOPPING--

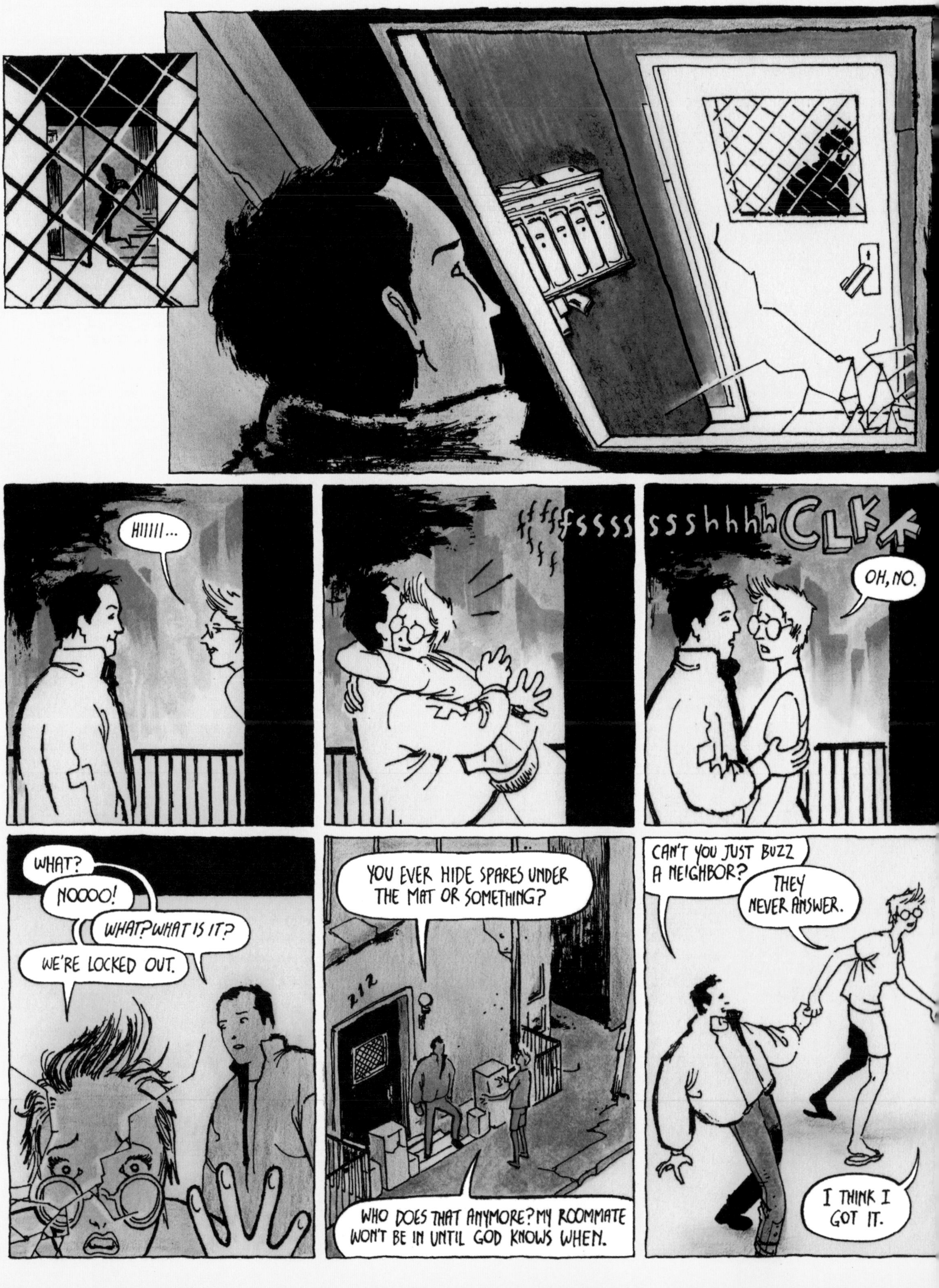
HIIIII...
ffffffssssssssshhhhhCLK
OH, NO.
WHAT?
NOOOO!
WHAT? WHAT IS IT?
WE'RE LOCKED OUT.
YOU EVER HIDE SPARES UNDER THE MAT OR SOMETHING?
212
WHO DOES THAT ANYMORE? MY ROOMMATE WON'T BE IN UNTIL GOD KNOWS WHEN.
CAN'T YOU JUST BUZZ A NEIGHBOR?
THEY NEVER ANSWER.
I THINK I GOT IT.

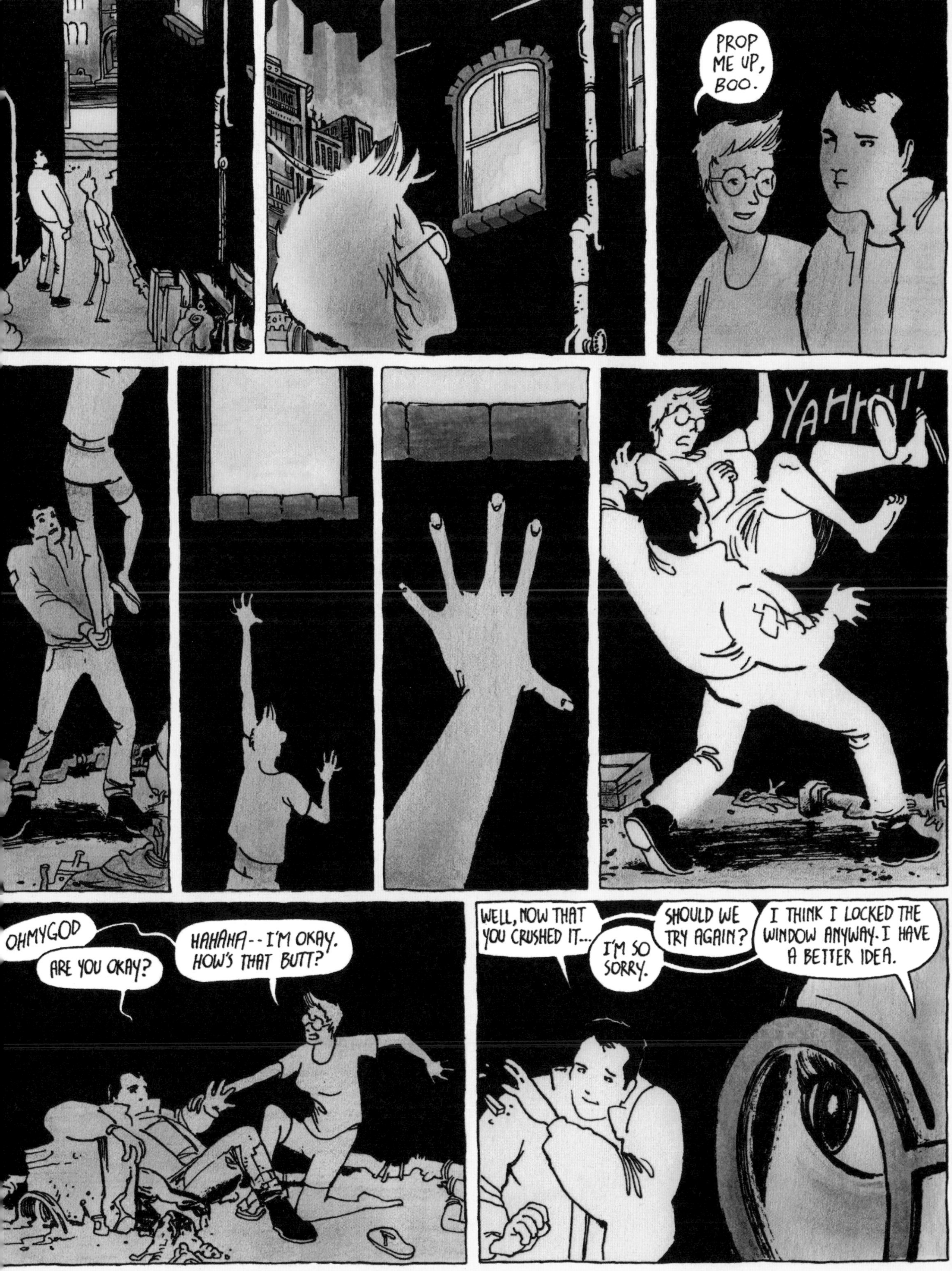
PROP ME UP, BOO.
YAHH!!
OHMYGOD
ARE YOU OKAY?
HAHAHA--I'M OKAY. HOW'S THAT BUTT?
WELL, NOW THAT YOU CRUSHED IT...
I'M SO SORRY.
SHOULD WE TRY AGAIN?
I THINK I LOCKED THE WINDOW ANYWAY. I HAVE A BETTER IDEA.

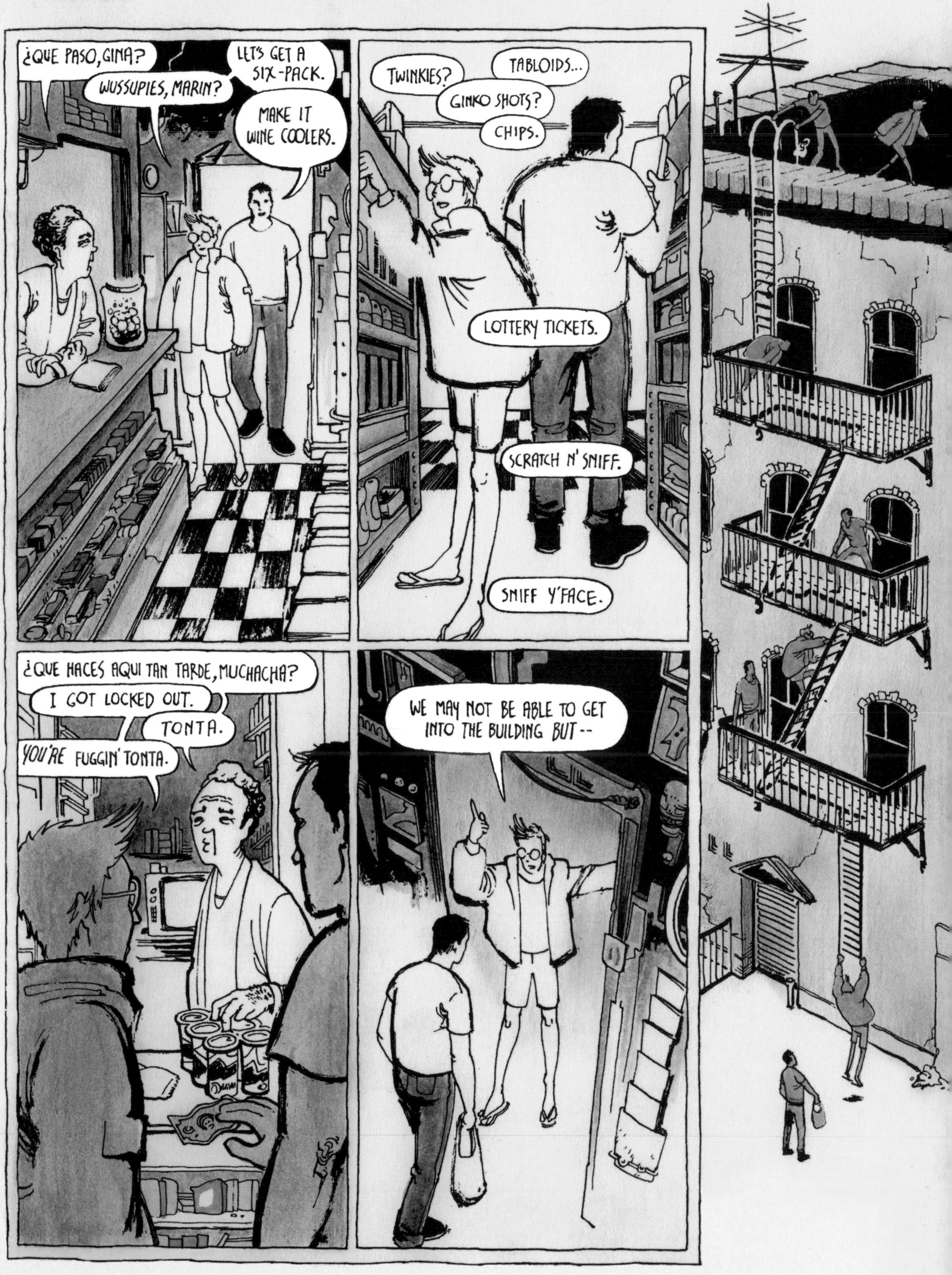
¿QUE PASO, GINA?
WUSSUPIES, MARIN?
LET'S GET A SIX-PACK.
MAKE IT WINE COOLERS.
TWINKIES?
TABLOIDS...
GINKO SHOTS?
CHIPS.
LOTTERY TICKETS.
SCRATCH N' SNIFF.
SNIFF Y'FACE.
¿QUE HACES AQUI TAN TARDE, MUCHACHA?
I GOT LOCKED OUT.
TONTA.
YOU'RE FUGGIN' TONTA.
WE MAY NOT BE ABLE TO GET INTO THE BUILDING BUT --

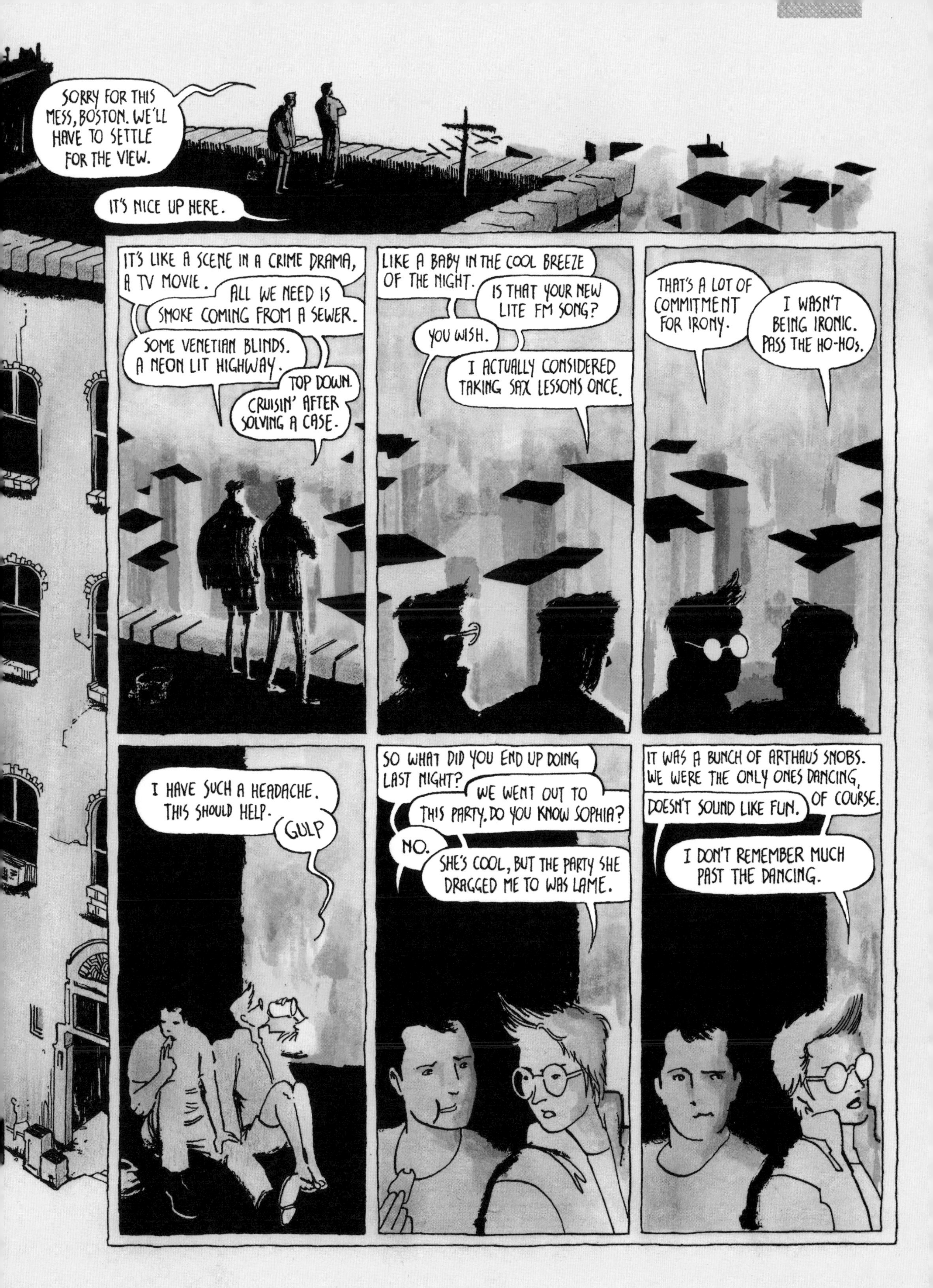
SORRY FOR THIS MESS, BOSTON. WE'LL HAVE TO SETTLE FOR THE VIEW.
IT'S NICE UP HERE.
IT'S LIKE A SCENE IN A CRIME DRAMA, A TV MOVIE.
ALL WE NEED IS SMOKE COMING FROM A SEWER.
SOME VENETIAN BLINDS. A NEON LIT HIGHWAY.
TOP DOWN. CRUISIN' AFTER SOLVING A CASE.
LIKE A BABY IN THE COOL BREEZE OF THE NIGHT.
IS THAT YOUR NEW LITE FM SONG?
YOU WISH.
I ACTUALLY CONSIDERED TAKING SAX LESSONS ONCE.
THAT'S A LOT OF COMMITMENT FOR IRONY.
I WASN'T BEING IRONIC. PASS THE HO-HOs.
I HAVE SUCH A HEADACHE. THIS SHOULD HELP.
GULP
SO WHAT DID YOU END UP DOING LAST NIGHT?
WE WENT OUT TO THIS PARTY. DO YOU KNOW SOPHIA?
NO.
SHE'S COOL, BUT THE PARTY SHE DRAGGED ME TO WAS LAME.
IT WAS A BUNCH OF ARTHAUS SNOBS. WE WERE THE ONLY ONES DANCING, OF COURSE.
DOESN'T SOUND LIKE FUN.
I DON'T REMEMBER MUCH PAST THE DANCING.

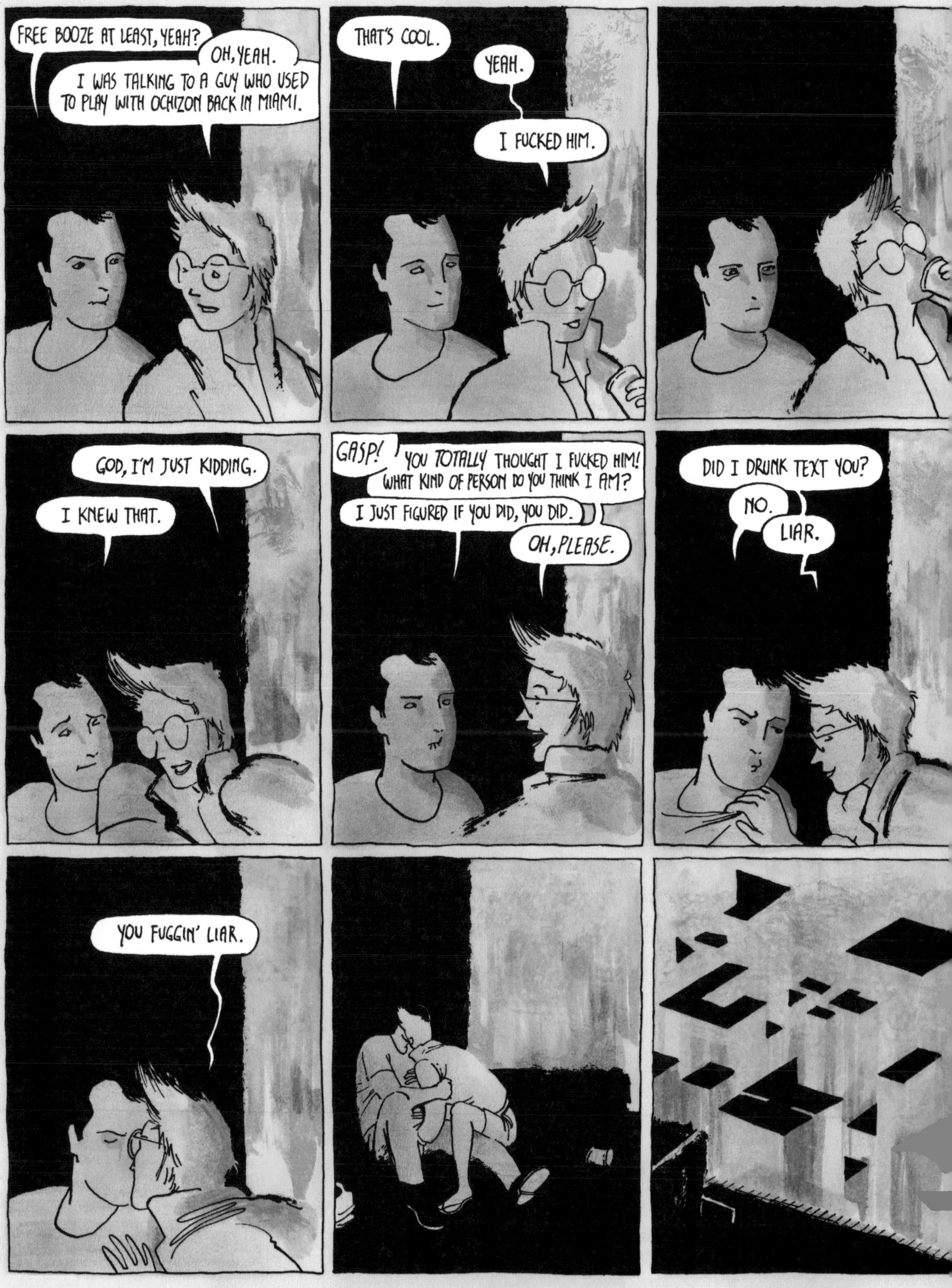
FREE BOOZE AT LEAST, YEAH?
OH, YEAH.
I WAS TALKING TO A GUY WHO USED TO PLAY WITH OCHIZON BACK IN MIAMI.
THAT'S COOL.
YEAH.
I FUCKED HIM.
GOD, I'M JUST KIDDING.
I KNEW THAT.
GASP!
YOU TOTALLY THOUGHT I FUCKED HIM! WHAT KIND OF PERSON DO YOU THINK I AM?
I JUST FIGURED IF YOU DID, YOU DID.
OH, PLEASE.
DID I DRUNK TEXT YOU?
NO.
LIAR.
YOU FUGGIN' LIAR.

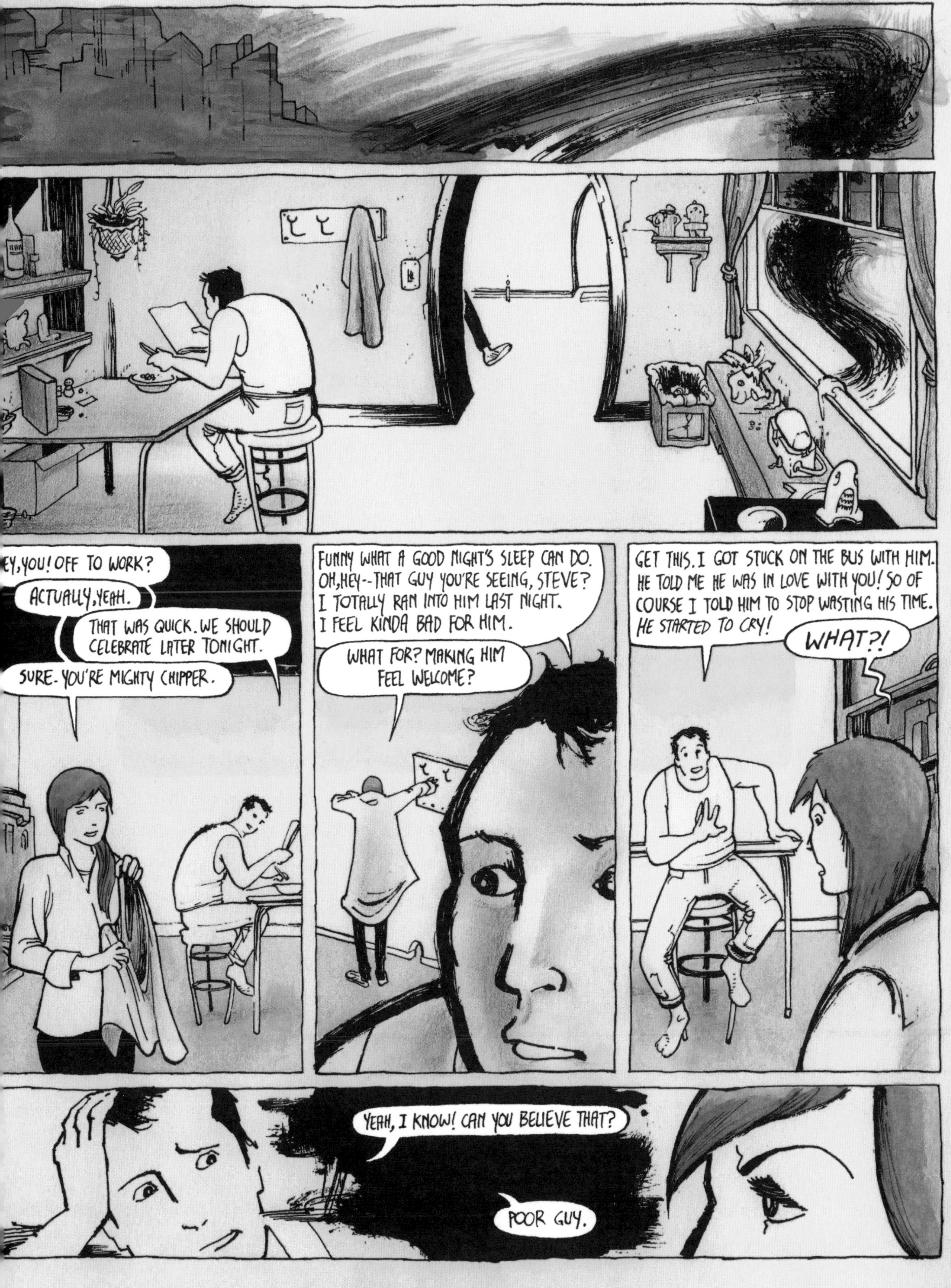
EY, YOU! OFF TO WORK?
ACTUALLY, YEAH.
THAT WAS QUICK. WE SHOULD CELEBRATE LATER TONIGHT.
SURE. YOU'RE MIGHTY CHIPPER.
FUNNY WHAT A GOOD NIGHT'S SLEEP CAN DO. OH, HEY--THAT GUY YOU'RE SEEING, STEVE? I TOTALLY RAN INTO HIM LAST NIGHT. I FEEL KINDA BAD FOR HIM.
WHAT FOR? MAKING HIM FEEL WELCOME?
GET THIS. I GOT STUCK ON THE BUS WITH HIM. HE TOLD ME HE WAS IN LOVE WITH YOU! SO OF COURSE I TOLD HIM TO STOP WASTING HIS TIME. HE STARTED TO CRY!
WHAT?!
YEAH, I KNOW! CAN YOU BELIEVE THAT?
POOR GUY.

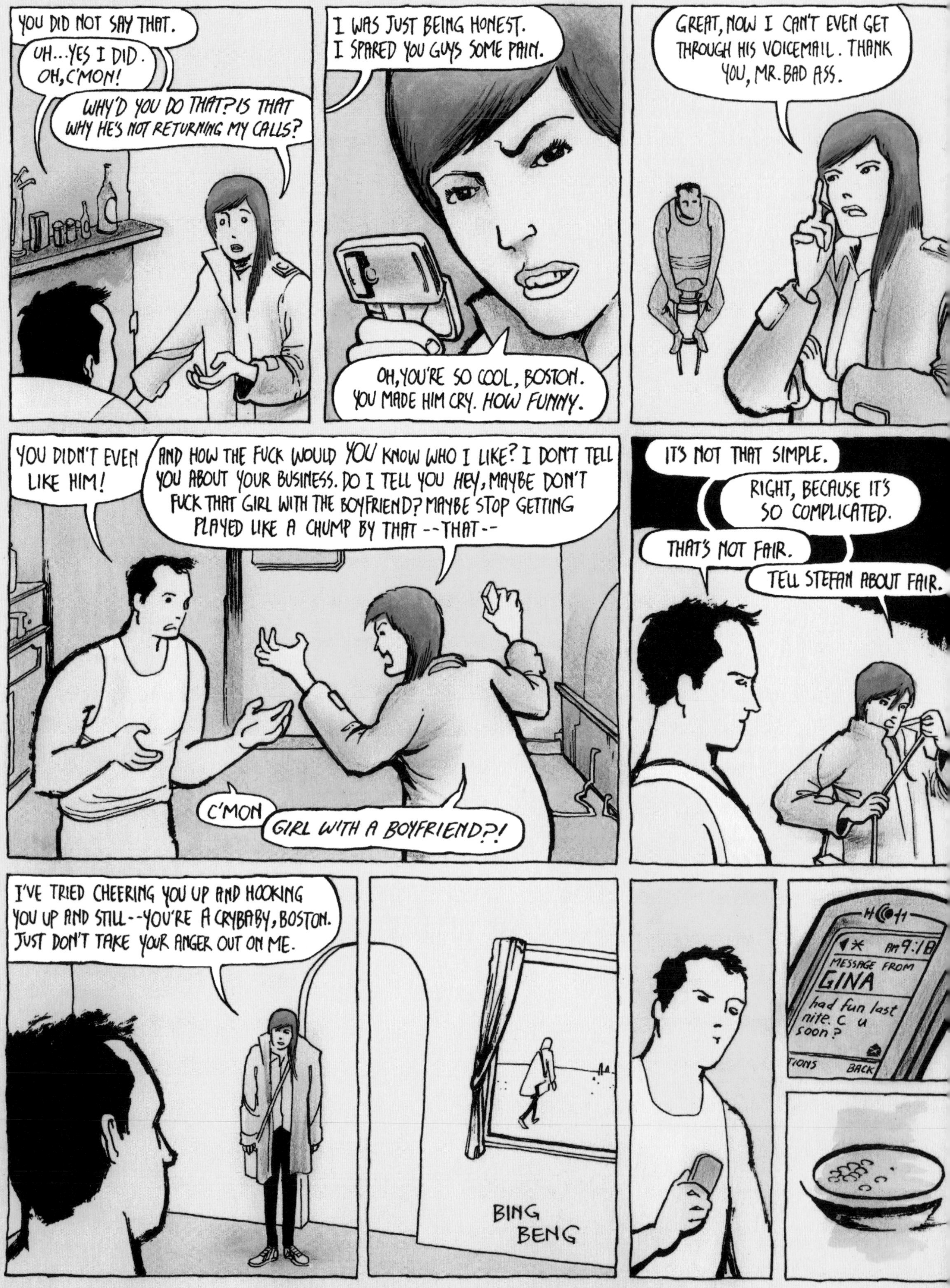
YOU DID NOT SAY THAT.
UH...YES I DID. OH, C'MON!
WHY'D YOU DO THAT? IS THAT WHY HE'S NOT RETURNING MY CALLS?
I WAS JUST BEING HONEST. I SPARED YOU GUYS SOME PAIN.
OH, YOU'RE SO COOL, BOSTON. YOU MADE HIM CRY. HOW FUNNY.
GREAT, NOW I CAN'T EVEN GET THROUGH HIS VOICEMAIL. THANK YOU, MR. BAD ASS.
YOU DIDN'T EVEN LIKE HIM!
AND HOW THE FUCK WOULD YOU KNOW WHO I LIKE? I DON'T TELL YOU ABOUT YOUR BUSINESS. DO I TELL YOU HEY, MAYBE DON'T FUCK THAT GIRL WITH THE BOYFRIEND? MAYBE STOP GETTING PLAYED LIKE A CHUMP BY THAT --THAT--
C'MON
GIRL WITH A BOYFRIEND?!
IT'S NOT THAT SIMPLE.
RIGHT, BECAUSE IT'S SO COMPLICATED.
THAT'S NOT FAIR.
TELL STEFAN ABOUT FAIR.
I'VE TRIED CHEERING YOU UP AND HOOKING YOU UP AND STILL--YOU'RE A CRYBABY, BOSTON. JUST DON'T TAKE YOUR ANGER OUT ON ME.
BING
BENG
AM 9:18
MESSAGE FROM
GINA
had fun last nite. C u soon?
TIONS
BACK

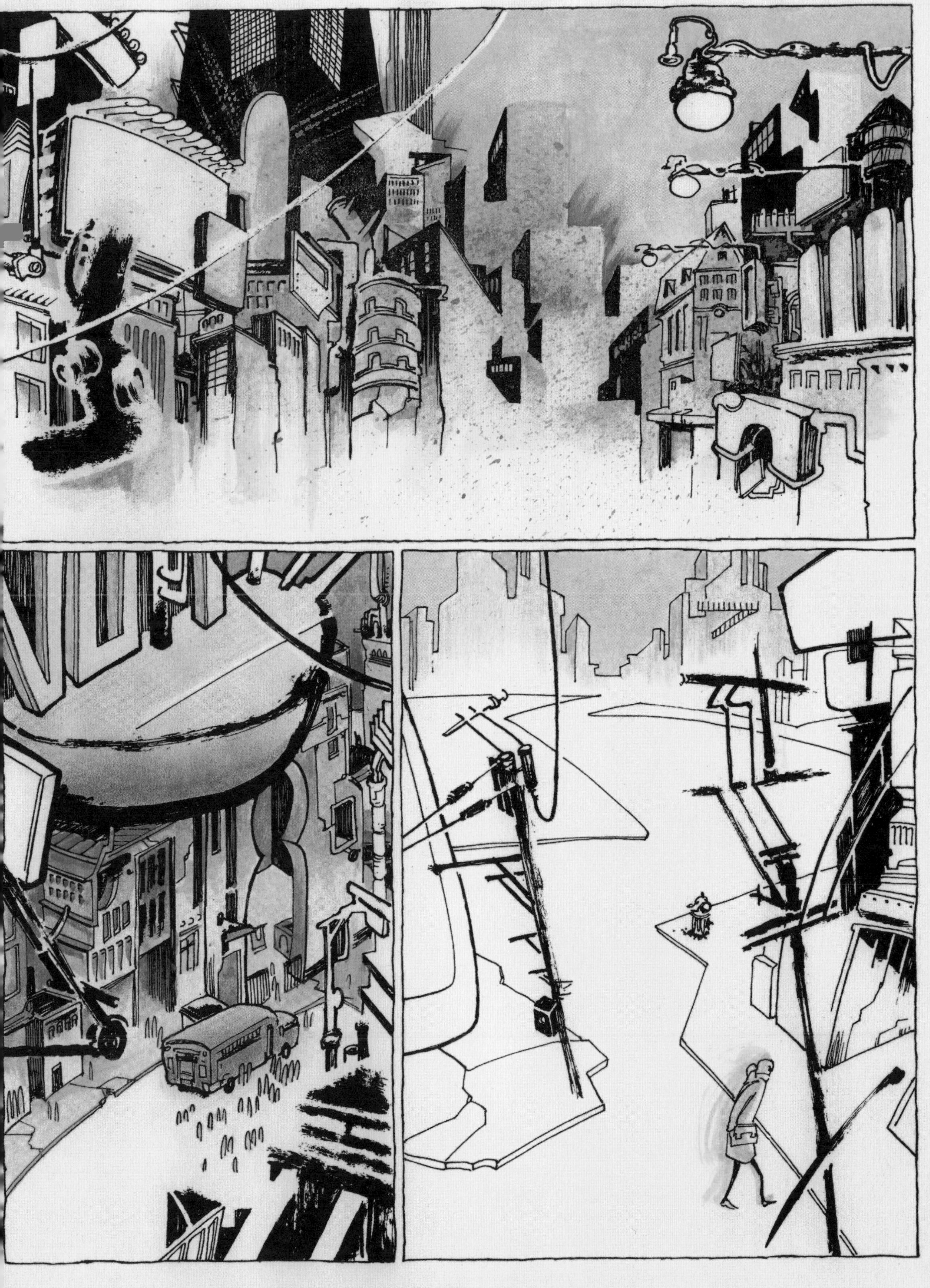

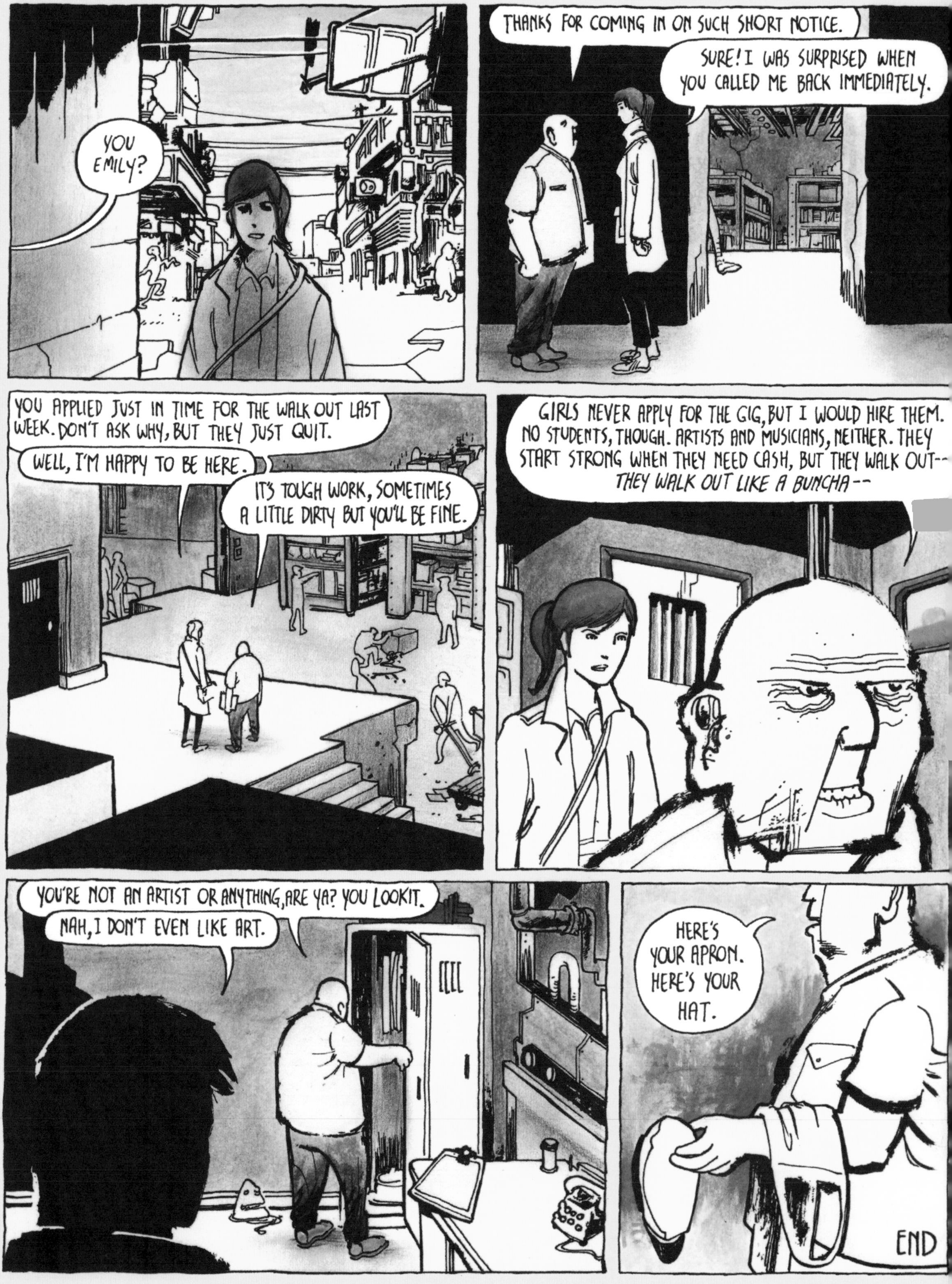
YOU EMILY?
THANKS FOR COMING IN ON SUCH SHORT NOTICE.
SURE! I WAS SURPRISED WHEN YOU CALLED ME BACK IMMEDIATELY.
YOU APPLIED JUST IN TIME FOR THE WALK OUT LAST WEEK. DON'T ASK WHY, BUT THEY JUST QUIT.
WELL, I'M HAPPY TO BE HERE.
IT'S TOUGH WORK, SOMETIMES A LITTLE DIRTY BUT YOU'LL BE FINE.
GIRLS NEVER APPLY FOR THE GIG, BUT I WOULD HIRE THEM. NO STUDENTS, THOUGH. ARTISTS AND MUSICIANS, NEITHER. THEY START STRONG WHEN THEY NEED CASH, BUT THEY WALK OUT-- THEY WALK OUT LIKE A BUNCHA--
YOU'RE NOT AN ARTIST OR ANYTHING, ARE YA? YOU LOOKIT.
NAH, I DON'T EVEN LIKE ART.
HERE'S YOUR APRON. HERE'S YOUR HAT.
END

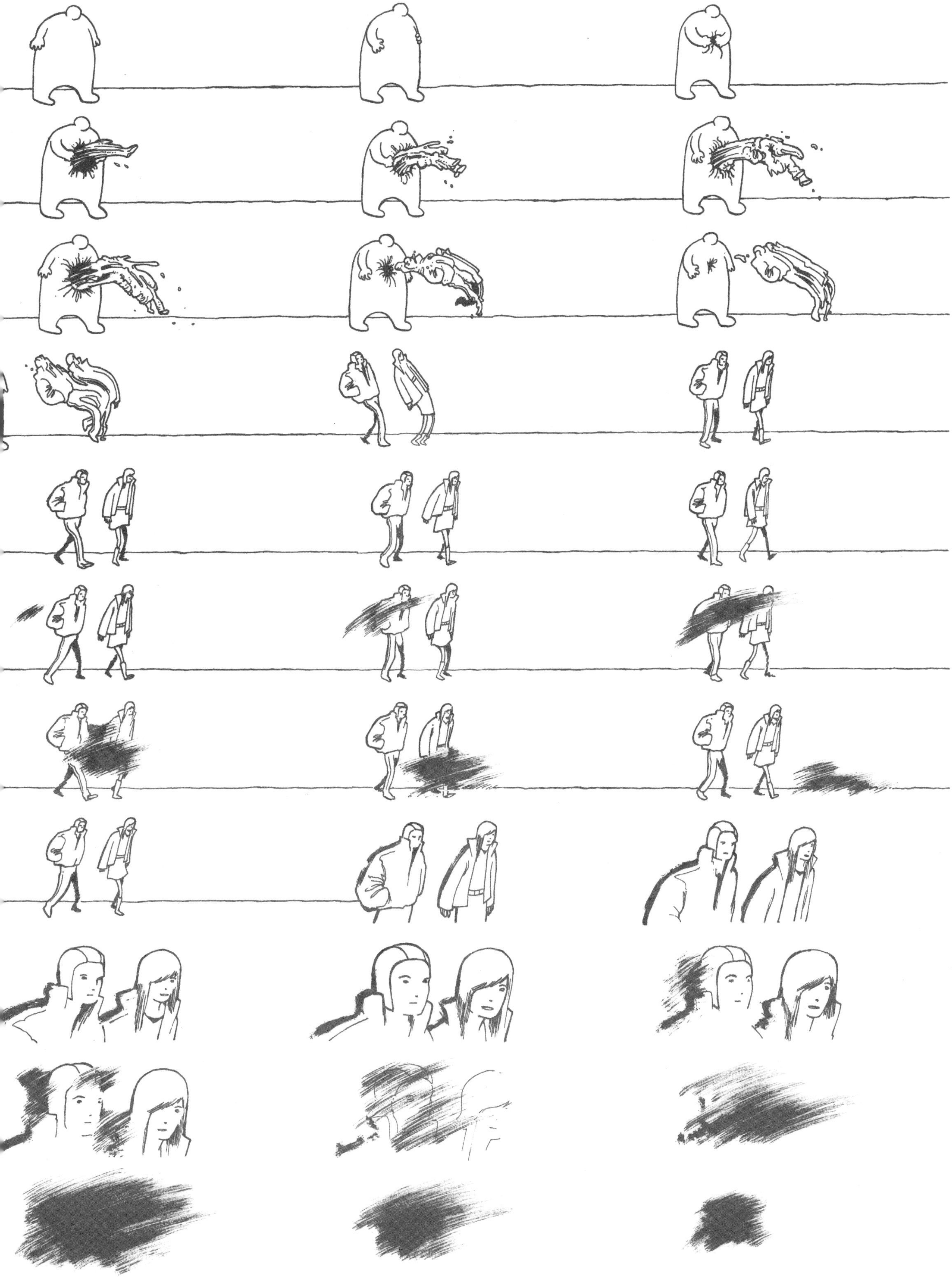

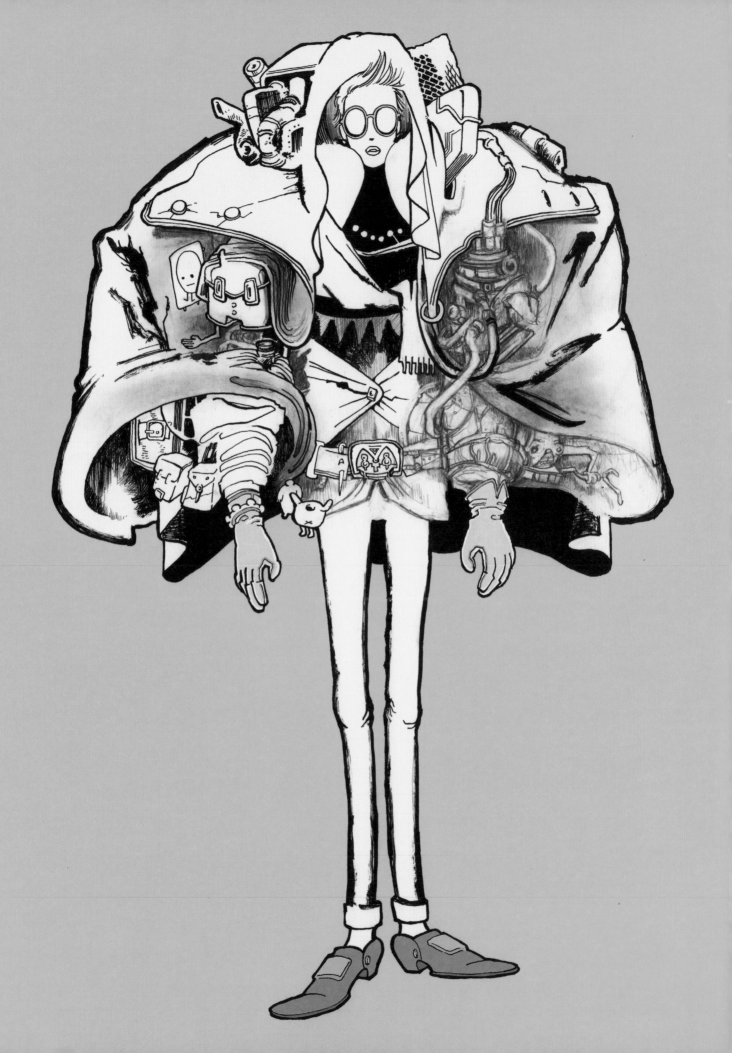

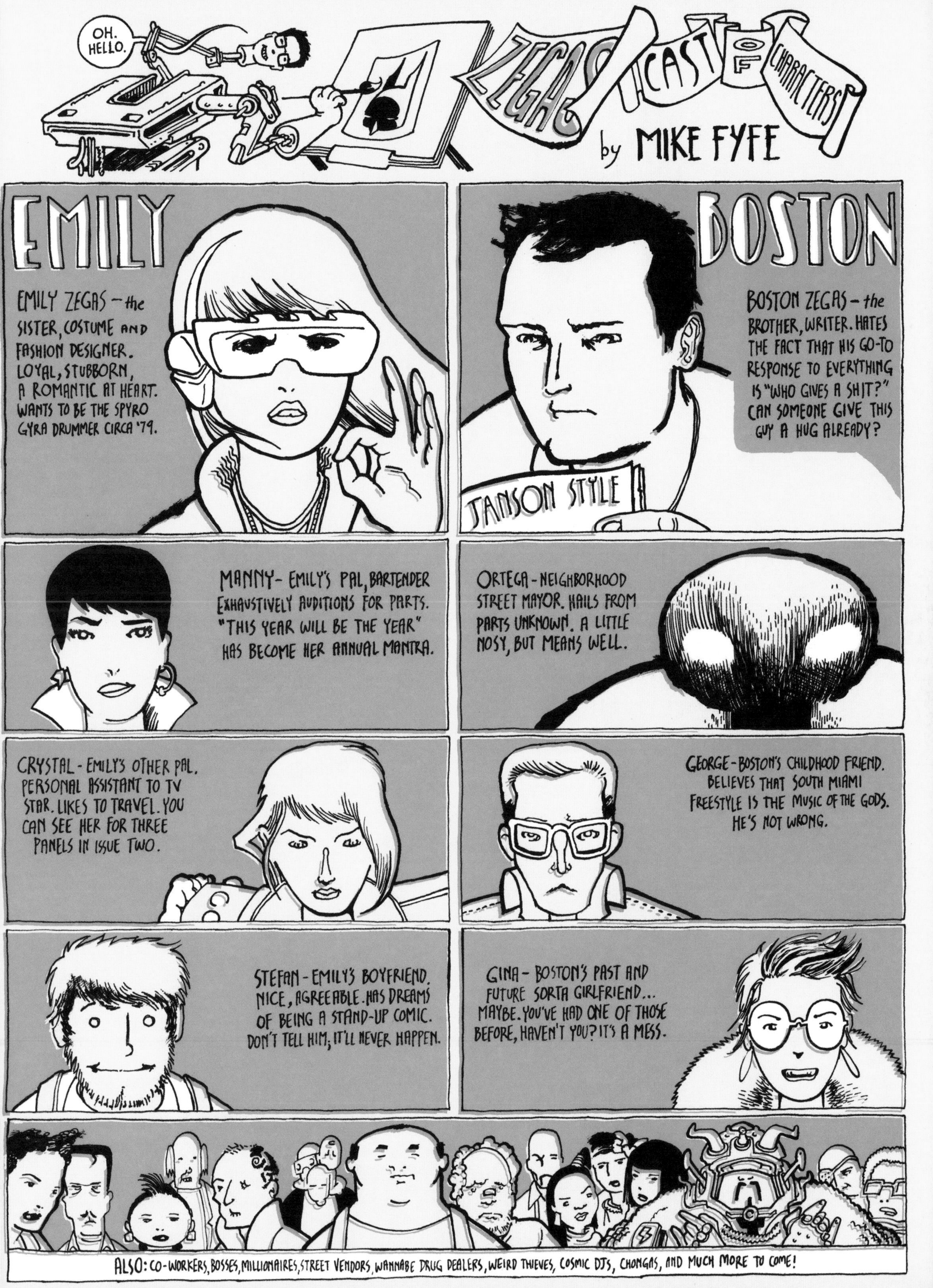

OH. HELLO.
ZEGAS CAST OF CHARACTERS
by MIKE FYFE
EMILY
EMILY ZEGAS – the SISTER, COSTUME AND FASHION DESIGNER. LOYAL, STUBBORN, A ROMANTIC AT HEART. WANTS TO BE THE SPYRO GYRA DRUMMER CIRCA '79.
BOSTON
BOSTON ZEGAS – the BROTHER, WRITER. HATES THE FACT THAT HIS GO-TO RESPONSE TO EVERYTHING IS "WHO GIVES A SHIT?" CAN SOMEONE GIVE THIS GUY A HUG ALREADY?
JANSON STYLE
MANNY – EMILY'S PAL, BARTENDER EXHAUSTIVELY AUDITIONS FOR PARTS. "THIS YEAR WILL BE THE YEAR" HAS BECOME HER ANNUAL MANTRA.
ORTEGA – NEIGHBORHOOD STREET MAYOR. HAILS FROM PARTS UNKNOWN. A LITTLE NOSY, BUT MEANS WELL.
CRYSTAL – EMILY'S OTHER PAL. PERSONAL ASSISTANT TO TV STAR. LIKES TO TRAVEL. YOU CAN SEE HER FOR THREE PANELS IN ISSUE TWO.
GEORGE – BOSTON'S CHILDHOOD FRIEND. BELIEVES THAT SOUTH MIAMI FREESTYLE IS THE MUSIC OF THE GODS. HE'S NOT WRONG.
STEFAN – EMILY'S BOYFRIEND. NICE, AGREEABLE. HAS DREAMS OF BEING A STAND-UP COMIC. DON'T TELL HIM; IT'LL NEVER HAPPEN.
GINA – BOSTON'S PAST AND FUTURE SORTA GIRLFRIEND... MAYBE. YOU'VE HAD ONE OF THOSE BEFORE, HAVEN'T YOU? IT'S A MESS.
ALSO: CO-WORKERS, BOSSES, MILLIONAIRES, STREET VENDORS, WANNABE DRUG DEALERS, WEIRD THIEVES, COSMIC DJS, CHONGAS, AND MUCH MORE TO COME!

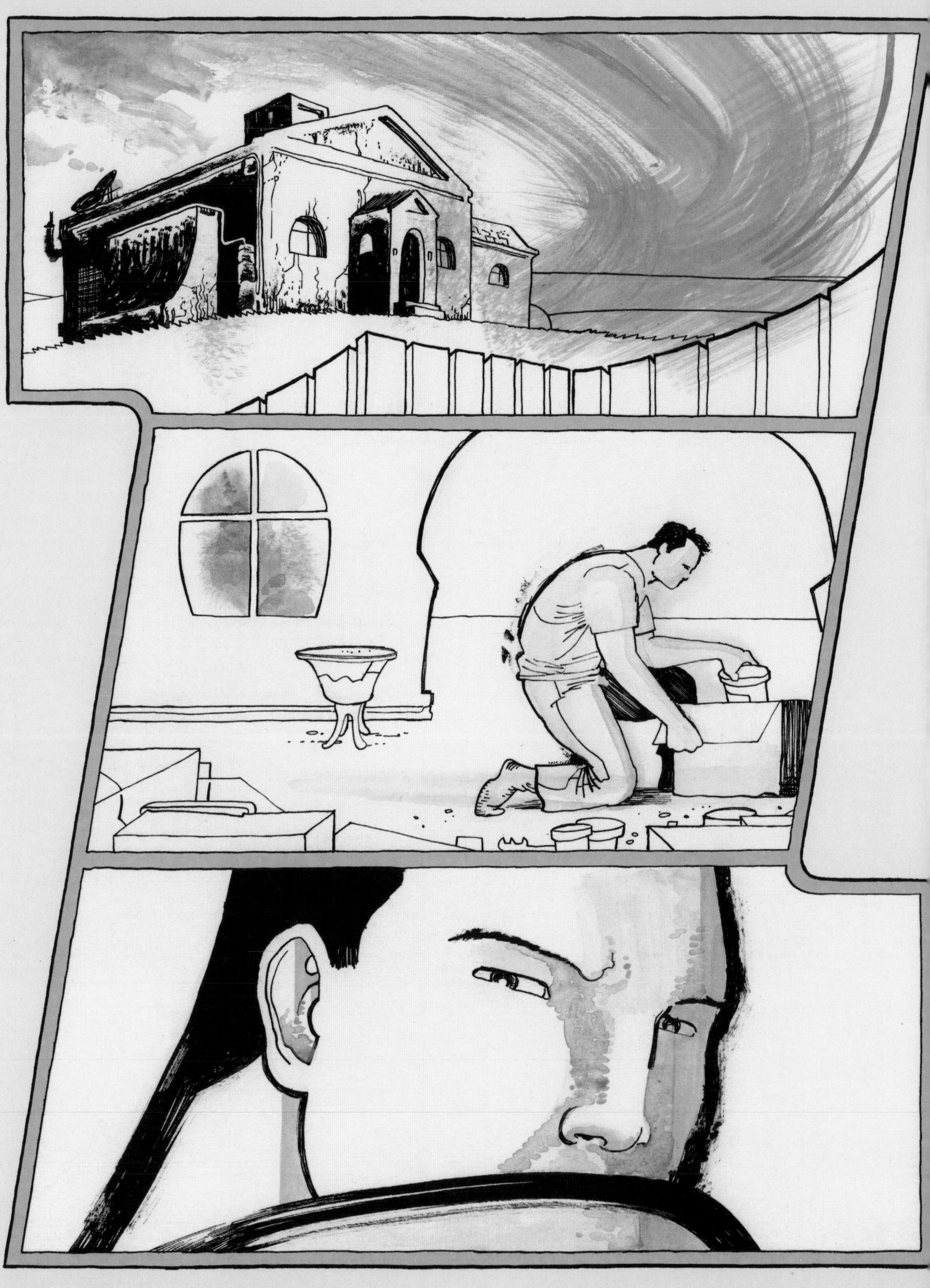

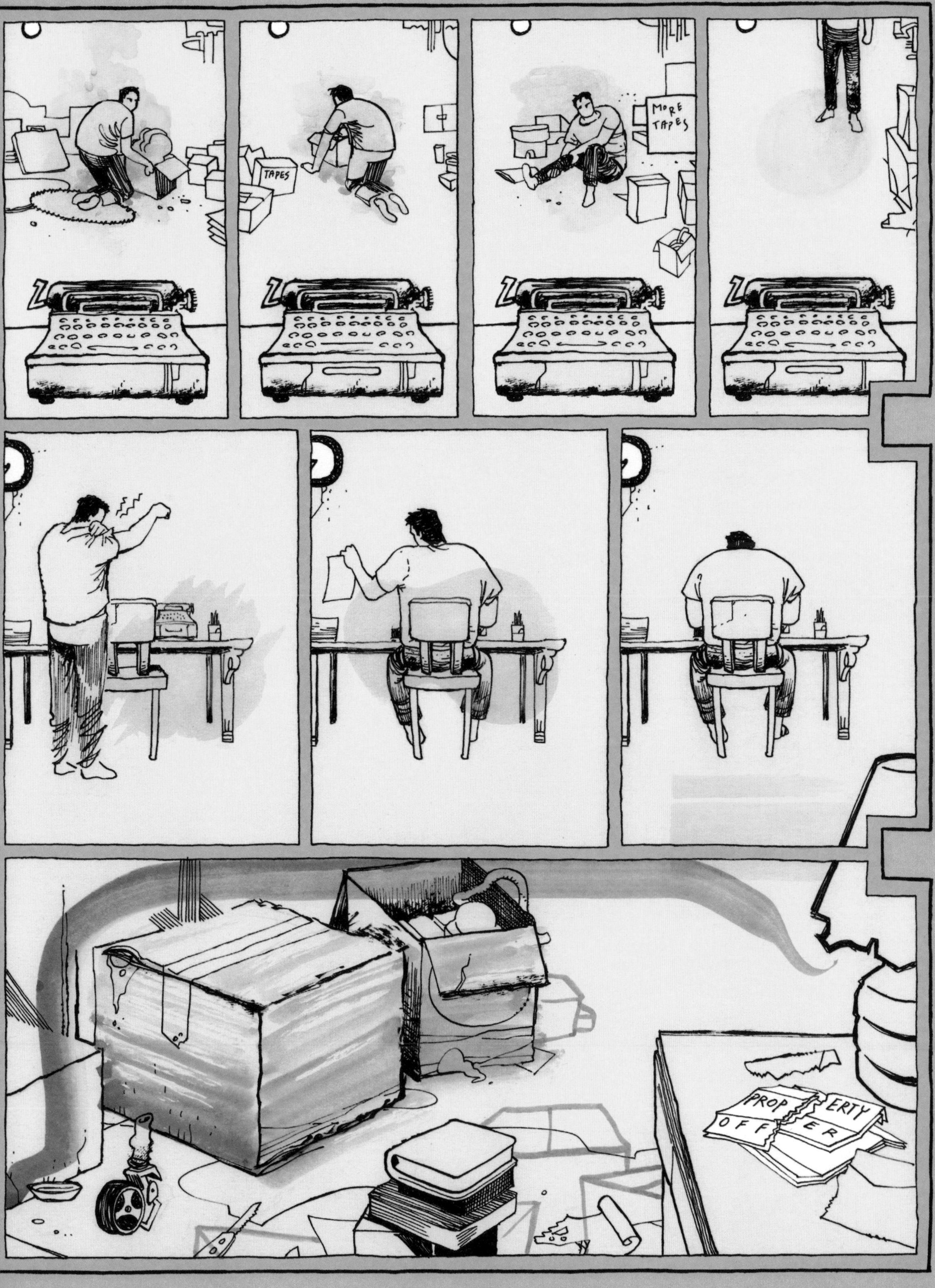
TAPES
MORE TAPES
PROP ERTY
OFF ER

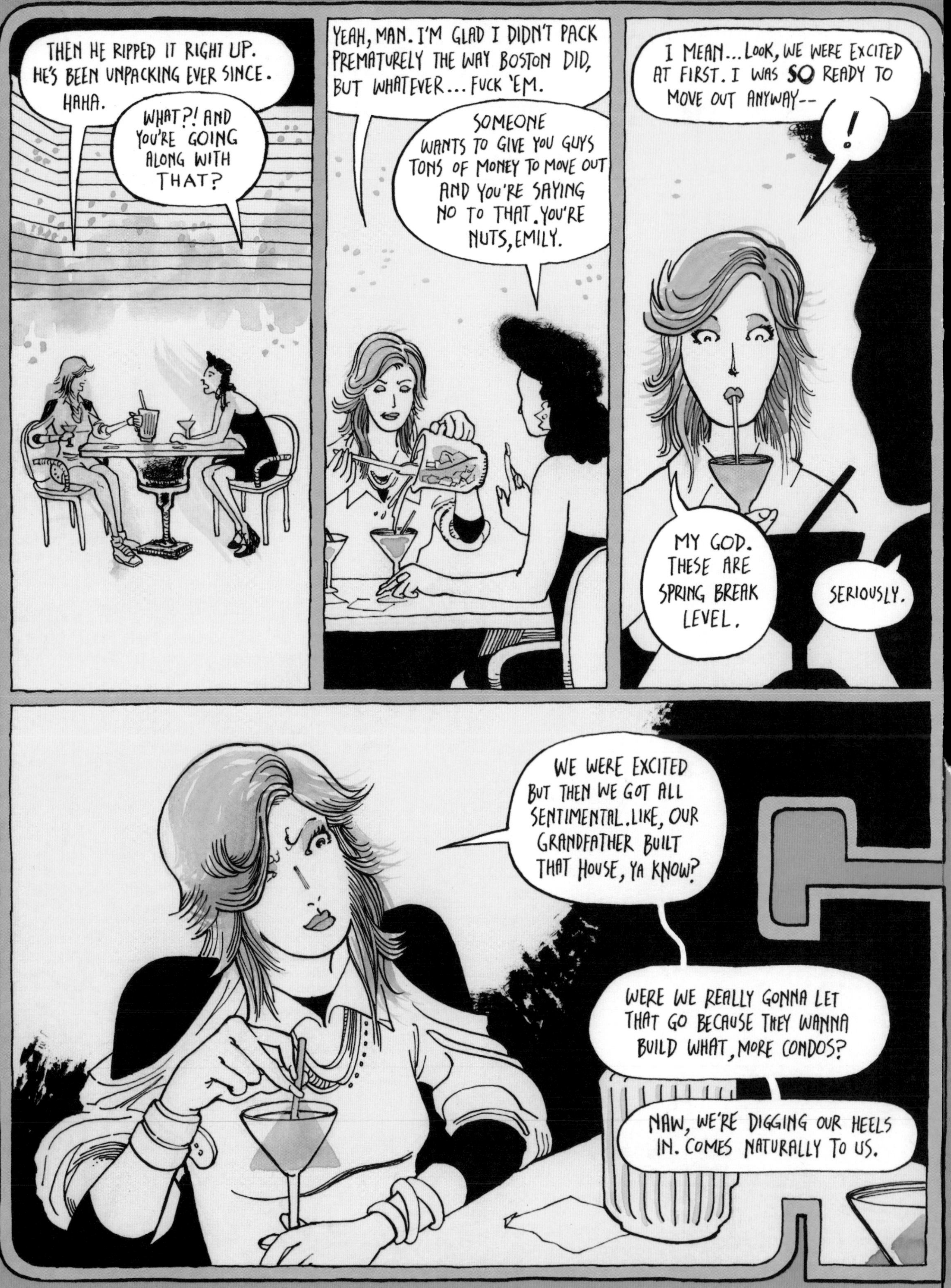

THEN HE RIPPED IT RIGHT UP. HE'S BEEN UNPACKING EVER SINCE. HAHA.
WHAT?! AND YOU'RE GOING ALONG WITH THAT?
YEAH, MAN. I'M GLAD I DIDN'T PACK PREMATURELY THE WAY BOSTON DID, BUT WHATEVER... FUCK 'EM.
SOMEONE WANTS TO GIVE YOU GUYS TONS OF MONEY TO MOVE OUT AND YOU'RE SAYING NO TO THAT. YOU'RE NUTS, EMILY.
I MEAN... LOOK, WE WERE EXCITED AT FIRST. I WAS SO READY TO MOVE OUT ANYWAY--
!
MY GOD. THESE ARE SPRING BREAK LEVEL.
SERIOUSLY.
WE WERE EXCITED BUT THEN WE GOT ALL SENTIMENTAL. LIKE, OUR GRANDFATHER BUILT THAT HOUSE, YA KNOW?
WERE WE REALLY GONNA LET THAT GO BECAUSE THEY WANNA BUILD WHAT, MORE CONDOS?
NAW, WE'RE DIGGING OUR HEELS IN. COMES NATURALLY TO US.

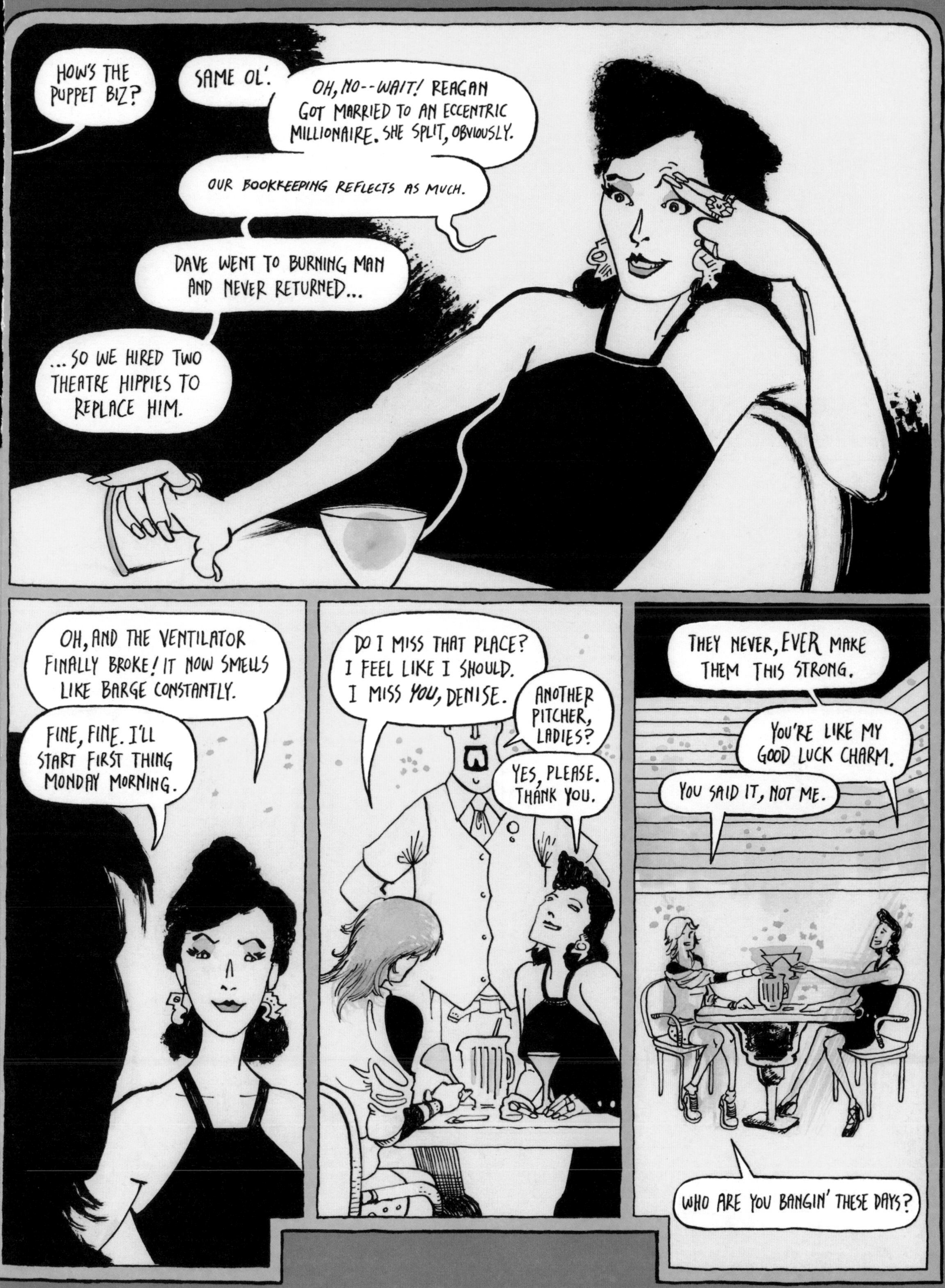
HOW'S THE PUPPET BIZ?
SAME OL'.
OH, NO--WAIT! REAGAN GOT MARRIED TO AN ECCENTRIC MILLIONAIRE. SHE SPLIT, OBVIOUSLY.
OUR BOOKKEEPING REFLECTS AS MUCH.
DAVE WENT TO BURNING MAN AND NEVER RETURNED...
...SO WE HIRED TWO THEATRE HIPPIES TO REPLACE HIM.
OH, AND THE VENTILATOR FINALLY BROKE! IT NOW SMELLS LIKE BARGE CONSTANTLY.
FINE, FINE. I'LL START FIRST THING MONDAY MORNING.
DO I MISS THAT PLACE? I FEEL LIKE I SHOULD. I MISS YOU, DENISE.
ANOTHER PITCHER, LADIES?
YES, PLEASE. THANK YOU.
THEY NEVER, EVER MAKE THEM THIS STRONG.
YOU'RE LIKE MY GOOD LUCK CHARM.
YOU SAID IT, NOT ME.
WHO ARE YOU BANGIN' THESE DAYS?

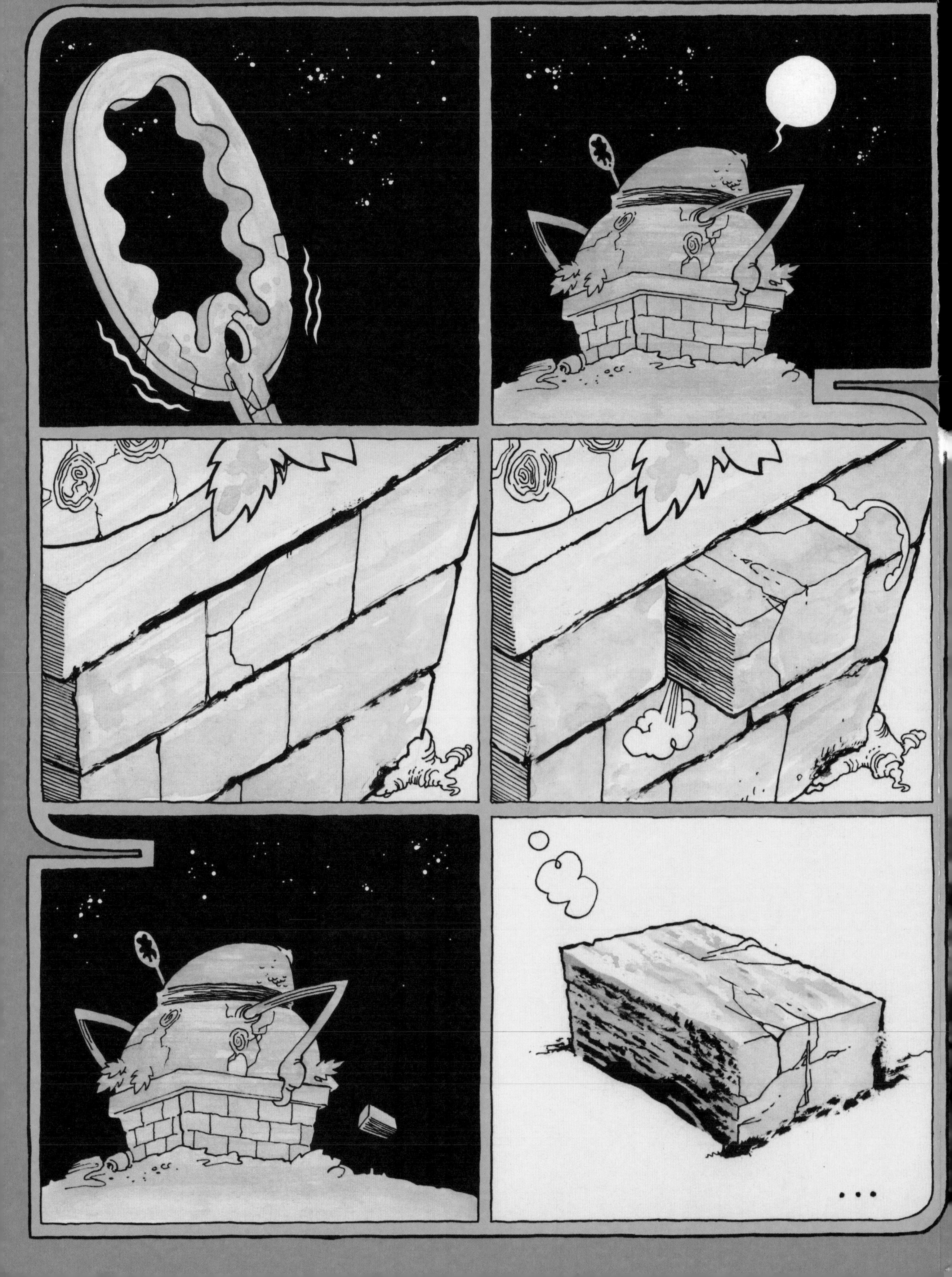